As SEEN on TV

# AS SEEN on TV

## MEREDITH SCHORR

FOREVER

New York  Boston

Forever
Hachette Book Group
1290 Avenue of the Americas, New York, NY 10104
read-forever.com
twitter.com/readforeverpub

First Edition: June 2022

Forever is an imprint of Grand Central Publishing. The Forever name and logo are trademarks of Hachette Book Group, Inc.

The publisher is not responsible for websites (or their content) that are not owned by the publisher.

The Hachette Speakers Bureau provides a wide range of authors for speaking events. To find out more, go to www.hachettespeakersbureau.com or call (866) 376-6591.

Library of Congress Cataloging-in-Publication Data

Names: Schorr, Meredith, author.
Title: As seen on TV / Meredith Schorr.
Description: First edition. | New York : Forever, 2022.
Identifiers: LCCN 2021053700 | ISBN 9781538754764 (trade paperback) | ISBN 9781538754733 (ebook)
Subjects: LCGFT: Novels.
Classification: LCC PS3619.C4543 A9 2022 | DDC 813/.6--dc23/eng/20211105
LC record available at https://lccn.loc.gov/2021053700

ISBNs: 9781538754764 (trade paperback), 9781538754733 (ebook)

Printed in the United States of America

LSC-C

Printing 1, 2022

*To my family, for always encouraging my vivid imagination, even when it dreamed up movie star sunglasses, a squeaky voice, and Mickey Mouse.*

# as SEEN on TV

# Chapter One

The TV screen zoomed in on the face of a young Jennifer Hudson a moment after Carrie Bradshaw had asked why she moved to New York City.

"To fall in love."

I groaned, even though I'd known the line was coming. "Mistake number one, Louise from St. Louis. But you'll find out soon enough."

From her spot on the couch, my mom looked over her shoulder with wide eyes. "You're home early. How was it?"

I hung the denim jacket I hadn't needed in the hallway closet. Mother Nature, in loud and clear opposition to the unofficial end of summer, had shown us who was boss with record-breaking ninety-degree temperatures, days after Labor Day. "My date stood me up. Maybe he fell off his Citi Bike and twisted his ankle, or perhaps he liquefied in the sun. Don't know. Don't care." I hadn't expected a first date with a guy I'd met on Hinge to lead to marriage, a committed relationship, or even a second date—at twenty-five years old, I'd been dating in New York City long enough to know better—but was showing up too much to ask?

Mom raised her glass of wine. "There's an open bottle on the kitchen counter. You look like you need it."

After pouring a glass of rosé, I sat beside her on our deep-blue velvet sofa in the apartment where we'd lived since I was four. I kicked off my sandals and wiggled my toes. "It's hilarious how tourists paint this city as the romance capital of America when it is the worst. The *worst*." I pointed at the screen. "Even Louise had to go back to her hometown to snag her man."

Mom wiped a smudge from the glass surface of the coffee table. "I'm not sure I like how hard you're being on our fair Manhattan, Squirt."

I made a face. I'd asked her to stop calling me that when I reached puberty and decided it was disgusting, but my complaining had the opposite effect and sealed the nickname into eternal status.

"All of your big moments happened here," she continued. "You learned to read and ride a bike. You became a woman. And I mean that in all of the important ways—you got your period, you lost your virginity, you had your bat mitzvah."

"Not in that order."

She huffed. "I should hope not. I'll report myself to child services if you were already sexually active when you stood on the bimah at East End Temple and sang 'Adon Olam' to a room of tweens from PS 19."

I snuggled into my mom's side and took comfort in her familiar scent of Estée Lauder Beautiful. "No need to call ACS."

"Relief. The blow-offs and false starts are all part of the adventure, Adi."

My bad luck with men went as far back as sophomore year of high school, when I'd been catfished by a pimply thirteen-year-old pretending to be his hot eighteen-year-old cousin. I wanted off the ride.

I muted the TV. We'd both seen the first *Sex and the City* movie at least five times.

"How are you not jaded after all these years?" I asked. Mom had been mostly single since my dad died when I was three. She insisted she didn't want to remarry, but I knew she sought something more reliable from a male companion than what she was getting on OkCupid and Plenty of Fish.

We'd always been close, but now that we were both single city girls, we had more in common than ever. Even our dating pool overlapped sometimes, despite our twenty-three-year age difference. Twentysomething men flocked to my seasoned but very well-maintained forty-eight-year-old mother as often as middle-aged men messaged me. It should have been weird, but it wasn't. To clarify, men my age wanting to bang my mom was weird. Swapping dating stories with her was not.

"Getting ghosted is nothing. Try losing your soulmate in a car crash at twenty-six." Her cringe matched mine. "Never mind. Don't try that." She kissed the top of my head and pulled back. "Um, Adi. I hate to break it to you but—"

I shot up. "I smell. I know. I only had time for a five-minute shower after spin class to make it to the date that wasn't. And it's crazy humid."

"You don't smell. But you did have a Jolly Rancher stuck in your hair."

"I had..." I touched my scalp. "What?"

She waved the hard candy in front of me—it was green apple—and stood to throw it out.

"*Eww!* Probably from some sticky child on the subway." I

shuddered and ran my fingers through my hair. What would I find next, a Reese's Peanut Butter Cup? "I'm done with this day. DONE."

Mom returned to the couch and gave me an apologetic grin. "Sorry, Squirt," she said, patting my leg.

"Tomorrow will be better." I closed my eyes and breathed in positivity like I always urged in my cycling classes—inhale love, exhale stress. I'd have a good night's sleep and start fresh in the morning.

*Ping.*

I opened my eyes, pulled my phone from my purse, and checked my Gmail. A second later, I wished I hadn't.

Hi Adina,

Thanks for reaching out! Unfortunately, I didn't get that WOW vibe over this pitch. I agree your role as a part-time barista could add a personal touch to a piece on a latte art competition, but the timing is off. Readers won't care about a summer event in the fall. Feel free to nudge me about this after the New Year. In the meantime, please keep pitching. I'm a fan!

Derek

My shoulders dropped in disappointment. Derek was the editor of *Tea*, a weekly online pop-culture magazine where I'd interned while studying for my bachelor's degree in journalism during college. It was mostly office work (coffee runs and filing), but I was also responsible for proofreading the editorial calendar and was sometimes allowed to tag along with writers out on a story. A full-time position hadn't been available after graduation, and I quickly discovered that the chances of landing my dream job as a journalist for the entertainment, media, or lifestyle sections of the *New York Times* or *New York Post* without any prior publishing credits—or even with them—were about the same as a sixth grader's.

"What is it?"

I gulped my wine. "Another oh-so-encouraging pass from DerDick." She knew all about his particular brand of charm. He passed on all my freelance proposals, always concluding his rejections with a complimentary sentence about my writing skills and eagerly inviting me to keep pitching. But I was certain our history and my access to his direct email account was a gift that would eventually give as long as I kept at it. In fact, when he'd hired me to write *Tea*'s list column for a month, to cover for a staff writer on medical leave, I scored my first four professional bylines: "Ten books to read between seasons of *Stranger Things*"; "Five vegan recipes that have meat lovers screaming, 'Yaaas!'"; "Twenty shopping trends Gen Z is bringing back"; and "Five best pet monitoring apps." These credentials strengthened my portfolio, and updating my website and social media afterward had filled me with pride. My faith in Derek wasn't entirely without justification, but it was wearing thin.

Mom mumbled, "Shit," then frowned. "I'm sorry. Keep pitching. Persistence and patience, right?"

"I guess." She was repeating what I'd always told her about trying to make a living as a lifestyle journalist. But it was getting harder to persist.

Hustling two jobs teaching spin classes and working the counter at a coffee shop while cold-pitching publications like *Tea*—not to mention the almost daily scouring of freelance sites like FlexJobs and ProBlogger for writing gigs—was exhausting. The competition in the city was merciless. When Sinatra said if you can make it in New York, you could make it anywhere, maybe he was really encouraging us to aim lower.

"I wonder sometimes…" I brought my wineglass to my mouth and emptied the contents.

"Am I supposed to complete the sentence? Are we playing that game now?"

I returned the glass to the table and looked at her. "New York City can be a lonely place. Sometimes I think we'd have been better off staying in Indiana."

Mom scrunched her face, the faint wrinkles in her forehead becoming more pronounced. "How so?"

"Less competition for jobs, for one." I could write lifestyle and entertainment features for the local paper—like the *Stars Hollow Gazette* from *Gilmore Girls*. I'd binge-watched the series on Netflix and loved it. Mother and daughter living in a storybook town, surrounded by eccentric neighbors? Yes, please.

"Not necessarily. With fewer people come fewer opportunities."

I chewed my lip. "True." I was fairly certain the *Stars Hollow Gazette* had a staff of five. "But I'll bet the residents are friendlier and not as attached to their phones." Although I was too young to remember the small town where I was born, I pictured bright blue skies, green grass, and trees—a lot of trees. I envisioned a town square buzzing with activity. I imagined being greeted by everyone who crossed our path like they knew us. Where neighbors weren't just people who happened to live on the same street but people we could trust, who watched out for us like family.

"Doubtful. Small-town life is so dull. I'm sure everyone is glued to TMZ and MTV News all day."

I mock-glared at her. "Do you have an answer for everything?"

She raised an eyebrow. "Try me."

"Dating is probably less complicated. With a smaller population, word would get around about guys who stood up their dates or went MIA after a month. Who would take the risk of being labeled a flake?" A dating pool where men sought more from a connection than their own gratification or just passing the time, and where dick pics weren't a thing, sounded heavenly.

"For one thing, love and sex are never simple. And for another, our pickings would be so slim, we'd run out of available men. You'd never have that problem here."

"You met Dad in a small town!" They'd been high school sweethearts. "I'm not sure having unlimited options is a good thing." I'd venture the single life in small towns was more about romantic walks and drinking cocoa than getting drunk and laid. Sex was great, but I'd bet it was even better in a relationship based on friendship, mutual respect, *and* attraction.

"Trust me, I'm your mother." She stood and stretched her arms above her head, and it was like staring at a reflection of my future self. We shared the same light skin with a natural blush and faint dusting of freckles, and the same naturally wavy auburn hair, except the tips of mine were dyed hot pink and she had highlights to cover the gray. At five-foot-three, she was shorter than me by one inch, and we were both small-boned with almost nonexistent boobs. The only feature we didn't have in common was our eye color. Hers were baby blue, and mine were a combination of brown and green with flecks of gold. I got those from my dad. "Moving you out of Nappanee twenty-one years ago was the best decision I ever made."

After my dad died, she hadn't wanted to be a burden on her folks, so when her well-connected best friend from college (my honorary Aunt Heather) found her a rent-stabilized apartment in Manhattan and a job with health insurance and a 401(k) at her father's medical practice, she packed her bags and toddler and headed east. She was now a certified physician assistant and a proud New Yorker. "You can go anywhere in the world and recognize good pizza and bagels. The tap water here is amazing! And what about the ethnic and cultural diversity? You can't find the same mix of world influences in small-town America." She leaned down and tapped my nose. "Trust me," she repeated. "You have no idea how lucky you are."

She was correct. I didn't. But I couldn't find the words to express my increasing wanderlust for an environment so different from the one where I'd spent most of my life. Mom would say I watched too many Hallmark movies and romanticized small-town life. She wouldn't be wrong.

My best friend Kate and I had a two-person book club where we read romance novels by Susan Elizabeth Phillips, Brenda Jackson, and Kristan Higgins, to name a few, set in quaint towns. And what began in high school as a once-a-year movie marathon in our pajamas branched into a yearlong tradition of monthly movie dates during Hallmark's Winterfest, Countdown to Valentine's Day, Spring Fling, June Weddings, Christmas in July, Summer Nights, Fall Harvest, and finally Countdown to Christmas.

After returning our empty glasses to the kitchen, Mom stood before me. "Heading to bed. You?"

"I'm going to stay out here for a bit. Not tired. Sweet dreams, Mom."

"You too, Squirt. You working tomorrow?"

"Not until noon." I had a shift at the café the next day. Living with my mom allowed me to save money, since she generously paid all the rent while I handled smaller expenses like utilities, internet, and our various streaming services. But I needed to stand on my own eventually.

I was trying to save, but it was slow going since spin instructors and coffee baristas didn't exactly make a livable wage. I supplemented my income with freelance writing assignments. The experience was good for building my portfolio, but I worked best with external accountability. My dream was to secure a full-time journalist job, writing uplifting and engaging lifestyle stories, not submitting proposals to create dry content about household appliances. Additionally, many of the best freelance writing sites charged fees, took a portion of your earnings, or both. It was often counterproductive. Until I could catch my big break, I was grateful for rent-free living and a mother with whom I got along famously and who was in no rush to kick me out. This placed me at the back of the pack in terms of evolving into a full-fledged adult, but my time would come. Eventually.

Now, alone on the couch with sole custody of the remote, I switched the channel to a *Million Dollar Listing New York* marathon on Bravo. It would be easy to use the show as an escape in the same way I watched Hallmark movies—to engulf myself in a world so foreign to my own and play "what if." But it wouldn't serve my career or further my goal of financial independence. Instead, I kept the show on in the background while I checked my regular sites for new freelance-writing job postings. Monitoring these platforms took more time than I typically had, so my goal of submitting daily often dwindled to weekly. But you had to move fast, because open slots were snatched up quick.

On the ProBlogger site, I skipped over a listing for a freelance wedding blogger. A passion for weddings was the top requirement, and based on my experience tonight, I hadn't even mastered the art of the first date. Instead, I kept scrolling until I found a posting by a small business seeking a writer/researcher for a coffee brand. They specifically sought someone with related experience, like a barista. *Bingo.* I submitted the online application, attaching my writing samples, closed down my computer, and gave *Million Dollar Listing* my full attention. I'd earned it.

I figured I'd watch an episode or two before turning in, but the effects of the day wore me down, and I found myself dozing off on the couch still wearing my dress and in full makeup. "Never go to sleep in your makeup!" *Okay, Mom!* She hadn't actually said this—tonight anyway—but it was one of the many lessons she'd ingrained in me growing up: the gospel of Valerie Gellar.

I reluctantly stood to wash my face. It would give me the requisite second wind to finish the episode. The prematurely silver-haired real estate agent Ryan was featured prominently in this one, and I had a little crush. But more than his twinkly gray-blue eyes, it was what his assistant said next that made me forget all about the damaging effects of wearing makeup overnight.

"Please explain to me what Andrew Hanes sees in the

reclusive town of Pleasant Hollow. Didn't he make his billions developing real estate in New York and LA?"

I fell back onto the couch and racked my brain for why this dialogue on a reality show struck a familiar chord. I'd never heard of Andrew Hanes or been to Pleasant Hollow. Yet I was riveted. I leaned forward as if it would help me hear better.

On the screen, Ryan propped his elbows on the granite kitchen island in the apartment he was showing that day—in one of Andrew Hanes's newest buildings in SoHo. "He follows the money and sees an untapped opportunity in an underdeveloped community. He says the area has been lost in time, completely disregarded for the gem it is." Ryan went on to explain how Hanes, the real estate mogul who had made much of his money investing in new property in Tribeca during the early aughts, hoped that by building a condo complex in Pleasant Hollow with its own shopping center, restaurant, and gym on the lobby level, he could capitalize on families searching for the luxuries of suburbia with the convenience of being close to New York City. With real estate prices driving people north of Westchester and Rockland Counties, the location of Pleasant Hollow in nearby Orange County was ideal.

His assistant smirked. "Are you sure you're not mistaking Hanes's plans with the plot of a Hallmark movie?"

My mouth dropped open and I smacked my forehead. No wonder the conversation sounded so familiar. I'd watched the same exact storyline play out on TV a hundred times. I laughed all the way to the bathroom. *Good luck, Mr. Hanes.* These sorts of business endeavors never worked out for the greedy real estate mogul in the movies.

I changed my mind about watching more television and went

right to bed after a quick shower to wash any remnants of hard candy out of my hair. But I had a restless sleep. I dreamed about walking along Main Street in a sleepy town as snow fell steadily from a star-filled sky. It must have been December, because all the storefronts were decorated with garlands and blinking Christmas lights. My nose wasn't red and running, my hair was smooth and silky, and although I was barely bundled up, I didn't feel the cold. The handsome, unmarried mayor asked me to do the honors of lighting the Christmas tree at the annual tree-lighting ceremony, even though I was Jewish.

From the podium, I was poised to press the button, when I jolted awake. My thoughts immediately flew to Andrew Hanes and whether he had ever followed through on his plans for Pleasant Hollow. It weighed on me as if I had a vested interest, and I needed to know. It was a little before five a.m. when I tiptoed out of my bedroom to avoid waking my mom, brewed a Dunkin' Donuts French Vanilla K-Cup, and powered up my laptop.

My first stop was Google. The *Million Dollar Listing* episode was probably filmed several months in advance, which meant if Andrew Hanes had moved forward with his investment in the town, it would come up among the initial results in a search of his name. The first link was: "Real Estate Tycoon Andrew Hanes to Invest Millions in Remote Upstate New York Town of Pleasant Hollow." *Score!* I fist-pumped the air. The article described how Pleasant Hollow, a hamlet with a population of just under two thousand, had been almost completely over-shadowed by the higher-profile and larger neighboring towns of Middletown, Newburgh, Monroe, and Goshen for decades until Hanes announced his interest.

I took a sip of my coffee and kept reading. According to the piece, Hanes had already purchased a large plot of unoccupied land in the town and was currently finalizing architectural and engineering plans for a combination condo/rental complex he was calling "The Hollows." From there, I went to the Wikipedia page for Pleasant Hollow, then clicked on all the reference links at the bottom. Based on the pictures online, it looked exactly like what one would expect from a small town. The majority of the businesses—a hardware store, nail salon, bookstore, diner, etc.—were located along Main Street, and there was a town square and a park that ran along the Hudson River. Pleasant Hollow's biggest claim to fame was a ballerina who was born and raised there, and a statue in the park had been erected in her honor. A brewery run by two brothers overlooked the river, and a pizza place housing a forty-year-old brick oven from Italy was the culinary spotlight. A pearl of an idea forming in my brain, I took screenshots of all the photos and saved them in a new folder on my computer.

Two hours later, after unearthing everything I could about Pleasant Hollow without enlisting the help of a shady character with access to the dark web, I veered my attention to Andrew Hanes. I tracked his professional history, saving articles about his previous ventures—Pleasant Hollow being his first in a small town—into the newly created file.

Finally, I aimed my research at Hallmark movies featuring quaint towns under attack by a big-city developer. In the last few years, movies like *Love Struck Café*, *Under the Autumn Moon*, *Christmas in Love*, and *The Story of Us* had premiered with viewership numbers between two and four million each.

My intense concentration drowned out the clunky sound

Mom's boots made as she walked through the living room from her bedroom to the kitchen and back again while she got ready for work. I shooed away her attempts at conversation with apologetic gestures toward my laptop. By the time she bent down to kiss me goodbye on her way out, I had to pee so bad it hurt. But I had an idea for my next story—my big, career-making breakout story.

# Chapter Two

The Heart of TV in your own backyard.

Close your eyes and picture a quaint small town. I'll bet your visual includes a main street lined with family-owned shops and a town square with a park running through it. The locals are happy, perhaps a little set in their ways and quirky, but loyal and devoted to the town, its people, and its traditions. Now imagine this hidden gem threatened by the arrival of a wealthy and powerful businessperson, an outsider bent on wiping out everything that makes it unique.

It sounds like the plot of a Hallmark movie, doesn't it? That's because it is. It's also a real-life story playing out sixty miles north of New York City. The town is Pleasant Hollow. The intruder is city-based real estate tycoon Andrew Hanes.

From my uncomfortable wicker chair in the café during my break later that afternoon, for the umpteenth time, I read the next paragraph, in which I'd presented my idea to do a feature on the charming and picturesque town of Pleasant Hollow, its residents, and their reaction to Andrew Hanes and the construction of The Hollows.

Was Derek reading it right now? He'd only commission me to write it if he saw, like I had, the allure of the feature. I'd stressed the massive appeal to the pop-culture-obsessed readers of *Tea*. Who could resist the story of a real small town living out a TV plotline?

Then I'd done the unthinkable. I'd granted him a forty-eight-hour exclusive, threatening to cast a wider net if I didn't hear from him by then. Whether the confidence had come from lack of sleep, overcaffeination, or actual belief in the strength of the story was anyone's guess, but I was too anxious to chance the standard wait time of between one hour and three months to hear back. The article also had an element of urgency to it, given the increased interest in Hallmark movies during the channel's Countdown to Christmas season. I'd mentioned this specifically to cut off another rejection by DerDick based on "bad timing" if we waited until after the New Year.

But what if he thought the idea was stupid? I could picture him at his desk, the only person in the open-concept offices of *Tea* with a door, albeit a glass one. He'd have his legs kicked up in front of him, arms clasped behind his head, shoulders and torso shaking with mirth over a story inspired by the Hallmark Channel.

I gazed out the window, wishing I could switch places with the little blond girl walking past, holding hands with both her mom and dad. It was a memory I didn't have. I swallowed down the lump in my throat. Then I glanced at my phone again. Five hours down, forty-three to go. *Hurry up, Derek.*

I stood with a sigh. I had eight minutes left of my break, but working was preferable to idle time when my mind was able to conjure up images of Derek laughing at my idea before returning a sugary-sweet yet condescending rejection. Why did I bother? I observed my coworkers scrubbing tables, restocking the prepackaged salads and sandwiches on the shelves, and taking orders for iced coffees and chai lattes. Was this my destiny? The month I had worked at *Tea* creating content and helping to put out a publication was the best time of my professional life. Would I ever have that again?

My phone vibrated, announcing an incoming call, and I froze, then grasped the edge of the table for support. I sat back down and answered before registering who it might be. "Hello?"

"Adina!"

Derek. My pulse jumped to my throat, and my belly fluttered with nerves. He'd always emailed his passes, never called. It had to *mean* something. "This is she." He didn't need to know that I knew who it was.

"It's Derek from *Tea*, responding to your pitch. About Pleasant Hollow. It has potential. With a few conditions."

Another thing about Derek: He almost never talked in sentences more than five words long. But he thought my story had potential!

"What conditions?" I squeezed my knee to keep it from wobbling.

"You go to Pleasant Hollow. Stay there. No phone interviews. I want legitimacy."

"I wouldn't have it any other way." If writing the story was an orgasm, a trip to a quaint small town to write it was a multiple.

"On your dime. No reimbursements. Claim it as a tax deduction. Not my business. Fee on delivery."

"Of course." I said it matter-of-factly as if I had stacks of hundred-dollar bills bursting out of a crammed safe-deposit box in a bank cellar somewhere. I had no such thing. I didn't even have excess quarters in an old-fashioned piggy bank. But I'd worry about that later. First things first. "What's your fee?"

"Twenty-five cents a word."

*Lowball offer.* Even if I didn't know the going rate for this type of article was anywhere between fifty cents and two dollars a word, I knew DerDick. "Is that your final bid?"

"It is."

I would accept it if I had to, and it took a will of concrete not to shout, "I'm in!" It was a yes after so many nos. But it was worth more than a quarter per word. *I* was worth more. And for once, I had the power to ask for it. Derek wanted this story. Otherwise he wouldn't have called me, and so fast.

"Let me think about it. Given the out-of-pocket expenses, twenty-five cents a word might not make it worth my while. A few other editors are on deck." My body shook like a tree in a hurricane at my bluff. Thank God this wasn't a video call.

"I'll double it. Fifty cents a word. It's a story. Not an epic novel. Remember that."

I gasped. It had worked. "You've got a deal," I said calmly, while gripping the bottom of my chair with my free hand to keep my butt planted firmly in place. I ached to do a victory dance, but I'd worked too hard at appearing poised and collected to break character now.

"You've got fire in your belly, Gellar. Usually, I can't get my writers to go north of 125th Street for a story, much less upstate New York!" He cackled.

Now wasn't the time to confess that leaving the city was part of the appeal. He might renege on the agreed-upon fee, claiming the story was just an impetus for a much-needed break from the city that never slept. I could practically hear him say, *Technically, I'm doing* you *a favor.* I took a calming breath. "When do you want it?"

"How's three weeks?"

I blinked. Things were moving faster than I'd anticipated. Then again, I hadn't anticipated *anything* beyond Derek wanting the story. This time the day before, I was cautiously optimistic about a first date. It felt less like twenty-four hours and more like twenty-four years. "That's...um...soon." I rolled my eyes. Bye-bye, confident lion. Hello, skittish mouse.

"It should coincide with peak holiday movie season." He paused. "Unless you're not up for it."

My body went rigid. "Three weeks is fine." How would I get there? Where would I stay? "Totally doable."

"A staff position is opening in the New Year. Impress me, and it can be yours."

I heard his words like an all-caps text message: A FULL-TIME STAFF POSITION. I wanted it. Oh, I wanted it bad. "Prepare to be impressed."

# Chapter Three

Your Uber will be here in five minutes!" Mom yelled from the kitchen a week later.

"Finally!" What sucked about packing the night before a trip was having nothing to do but wait in the minutes before departure. My phone, e-reader, and laptop were already tucked away in my backpack, and I didn't want to risk losing the charge in case there was traffic on the Thruway. Who knew if the bus had outlets? With zero distractions, I'd spent the last half hour pacing the wood floor from one wall of the living room across the Bohemian area rug in the center to the window overlooking the park—known to the residents of our multi-building complex as "the Oval"—and back.

But the wait was almost over. Just in time for the nerves to kick in. Was I really doing this?

I shielded my eyes against the sun shining through the window. "Did you ever return my sunglasses?"

Mom had borrowed them to run an errand weeks ago. I hadn't said anything because I'd "borrowed" the fuzzy purple hoodie now packed in my suitcase.

"Oops. Sorry! They're on my desk. But hurry!"

"Relax!" It wasn't going to take four minutes to grab my sunglasses. Still, I jogged the fifty feet to her room, finding the oversized white heart-shaped sunglasses where she said they'd be.

Having what I came for, I turned on my heel to leave the room, when a document caught my eye. It had the letterhead of our apartment's management company. Without thinking, I read it. My heart rate quickened with each word.

When the apartment complex was first built in the mid-twentieth century, it was meant to provide affordable housing for war veterans and had remained rent-stabilized for decades. After it was sold to a real estate conglomerate in recent years, the majority of the apartments were rented at current market rates. Until now, we'd escaped the rent hikes. It seemed our luck had run out. According to this letter, we'd be losing our rent-stabilized status with our next lease, because we no longer met the economic qualifications, and upgrades to the common areas had increased the value of the unit. We could either sign a new lease for market price or vacate.

A cold sweat crept up my neck. There was no way my mom could (or should) handle the increase on her own. She made decent money, but rent already ate up most of what she brought home.

I sat on the edge of her queen-size bed and buried my head in my hands. When I'd expressed anxiety over the financial investment staying in Pleasant Hollow for a week would entail, she offered to pay half. She then dragged me into her bedroom and pointed at my framed first publishing credit in *Jack and Jill* magazine, a publication geared toward children I'd discovered at my pediatrician's office. Her eyes lit up when she recalled how thrilled I'd been at ten years old when my story about the kid-led booths at our neighborhood's farmers' market had won the reader content competition. She insisted that if the Pleasant Hollow story led to a full-time job where I'd be that happy on a daily basis, it would be worth every cent. I'd searched for the strength to turn her down and mean it, but it didn't come.

And the whole time, she'd been hiding a major spike in our rent. My mom had been supporting me my whole life. One could argue it was her job as my mother, but when was it time to say enough was enough? If not at the age of twenty-five, then when? Derek had said I had a fire in my belly, but in terms of making a real living as a journalist, it was more of a low simmer because of the comfortable nest Mom provided. I'd taken advantage of her "mom-ness" for too long. It was time to grow up.

"Adi!"

I dropped my hands to my sides. "Coming."

I stood with renewed determination to write the shit out of this story and snag that full-time staff position at *Tea*. Then I would insist on chipping in on the increased rent so we could stay in our beloved home. Or I could move out—on my own or with a roommate—so my mother could find an affordable one-bedroom apartment and live by herself for the first time in her adult life.

# Chapter Four

When the ShortLine bus arrived at the terminal in Newburgh—the closest stop to Pleasant Hollow—I tried to contain my excitement while waiting for my Uber. I shivered in my military jacket, unsure whether it was due to an actual drop in temperature or anxiety about my impending adventure.

According to Google, it was a twelve-minute drive to Pleasant Hollow, and I spent the entire time gawking out the window like I'd never been outside of the city. This was dopey, considering I'd been born in a town with an even smaller population. And although my maternal grandparents no longer lived in Indiana, having retired to Boca Raton, Florida, their community wasn't exactly urban.

But there was something different about upstate New York. I could smell it in the air—the fragrance was minty like a forest in the winter. At first, there wasn't much to see aside from other cars on the road, but once we passed the black-and-white sign welcoming us to Pleasant Hollow, homes and businesses lined the streets.

As we zipped down Main Street, I fidgeted in my seat with my nose practically touching the smudged glass window. My skin tingled in anticipation of entering all the shops. I wasn't sure what I'd need at Mel's Hardware Store, but who couldn't use a new wrench or pliers? And lactose intolerance wouldn't stop me from indulging in a serving of dairy-free ice cream or sorbet at Lickety Splits Ice Cream Shoppe.

The driver pulled up to the curb in front of a big white colonial-style house. "Pleasant Hollow Bed and Breakfast," he said, announcing our arrival. These were the first words he'd said to me, despite my attempt to engage him in conversation when I first stepped inside the car. Very un-small-town-like, but maybe he wasn't a local.

After I thanked him for the ride and added his 20 percent tip on the app (in case I forgot later in all of my excitement), I snapped a photo of the building's exterior and wheeled my suitcase to the entrance.

This was it.

I opened the shiny black door to the B&B, stepped inside, and marveled at my surroundings. Beyond the small foyer was a common room with rhubarb-red walls and an Oriental rug partially covering a gleaming brown wood floor. Set in a circle around a cherry oak table were a dark-red velvet couch and matching recliner, a floral-printed armchair, and a wooden rocking chair. I took a moment to visualize guests drinking hot cocoa or wine by the fireplace in the evenings as the sun set. The open-space concept allowed me to see into a white-tile kitchen with matching cabinets and an island with four round stools set side by side.

I turned in a circle and called out, "Hello? Anyone here?" Without a front desk to check in or another human in sight, it was the only way to make myself known.

"Can I help you?"

My head swung up toward a white-painted staircase, where a sixtysomething woman with bleached blond hair wearing a pink-and-purple argyle sweater and mom jeans (the nineties-era version) eyed me suspiciously.

I waved awkwardly. "I have a reservation under Adina Gellar."

"Check-in isn't until four."

I glanced at my phone. It was only 2:30. Temporarily ignoring the text from my mom asking if I'd arrived safely, I gave the woman my full attention. "My bus got in early, and I had the car take me straight here. I'm so excited to be in Pleasant Hollow." I smiled. I'd forgive her gruff tone. I must have caught her off guard, but surely she'd warm up.

Crickets. We stood in uncomfortable silence. I shifted my feet. "I guess I can explore. Can I … um … leave my stuff here?"

She pursed her pink-painted lips. "Fine." Following her one-word assent with a huff, she descended the stairs and pointed at a grandfather clock in the corner of the room. "Your bag will be safe there. What did you say your name was?"

"Adina Gellar. I'm booked for a week, but I might need to extend my stay, assuming there's availability." *Read: You will probably make more money off me than most of your other guests. Be nice!* Not that the level of hospitality bestowed upon a guest should be measured by the length of their stay.

She nodded curtly. "Your room will be ready at four. You can wait with your bags until then if you'd like."

"Thanks?" I cursed the question mark in my tone. I hadn't expected the innkeeper to engulf me in a hug, dangle a fresh-out-of-the-oven sugar cookie in my face, and pry into my life story and relationship status—okay, maybe a little bit—but this was bizarre. While I was still contemplating the complete lack of cordiality, she marched back upstairs, leaving me alone. I muttered, "Why, thank you. I hope I enjoy my stay as well." I raised and dropped my arms to my sides. "Let it go, Adina. She's probably having a bad day."

"No. She's pretty much always like this."

I jolted and took a step back, belatedly noticing another human being in the common room. Sitting at the far end was a guy around my age. A cute guy. A *very* cute guy who'd witnessed me talking to myself. *Great.*

He stood. "Welcome to Pleasant Hollow."

*Very cute indeed.* His wavy, mid-length (for a guy) dark locks were brushed back in a casual windswept fashion, but I suspected they'd been worked with pomade to appear that way, and he had a short boxed beard. He was tall with a chest and shoulders I could tell were broad and capable, even through the black Henley he wore paired with well-fitted jeans. And he wasn't wearing a ring. Maybe he was the token single guy in town—the son or nephew of Ms. Grouchy.

"Thanks. I'm Adina." In case he hadn't heard me the first two times I said it.

"Finn Adams. First time in Pleasant Hollow?"

"Is it that obvious?" I joked.

He grinned, exposing straight white teeth. "Business or pleasure?"

"Business first, pleasure second," I said, relieved at his interest in my visit. I'd need more people like him and fewer like the unfriendly Uber driver and innkeeper if I was going to get my story. "I'm starving. Any recommendations for where I can get something to eat around here while I wait for my room?" I didn't plan to go full throttle on work until the morning, but if I happened to meet a chatty waiter, I'd run with it.

"There aren't too many choices, but your best bet is probably Pinkie's Diner." He pointed out a window covered with multi-colored plaid drapes. "It's two blocks down on your right."

My heart warmed at the name as I pictured a fifties-style diner like Pop's Chock'lit Shoppe from *Riverdale*. "It sounds amazing! I hope they have homemade cherry pie!" My feet left the ground in a slight hop.

"Do you always get so excited about diners and..." He coughed. "Pie?"

At the amusement reflected in his face, I felt like an ass. "Of course not. It's just..." I shrugged. "I'm living the whole city-girl-in-a-small-town fantasy."

"What kind of fantasy are we talking?" He quirked a dark eyebrow in a sexy, panty-melting way.

"Not that kind of fantasy. Obviously." The Hallmark movies Kate and I watched wouldn't even qualify for a PG rating with their closed-mouth kisses and separate rooms until marriage.

"Obviously." He smiled.

A moment passed. My thighs clenched with R-rated desire. *Check yourself.* I cleared my throat. "Right. I'd better get going. Pie awaits."

"Well, I hope Pinkie's lives up to your 'not that kind of fantasy' fantasy," he teased, using air quotes.

"I'm here on a story for an online pop-culture magazine," I blurted. "Life in Pleasant Hollow is intriguing to me after living in Manhattan for more than twenty years."

He tilted his head slightly. "What are you writing a story about?"

"The development plans for the new condominium complex in town." I purposely left out the Hallmark movie angle. He was hot, and I'd already embarrassed myself enough. "Can I get a rain check on this conversation, actually? I'm hoping to interview some locals to get their thoughts." A potential source wasn't *required* to ooze sex appeal, but as the journalist, I wouldn't complain.

Finn's lips formed an O. "Locals?"

I nodded. "Very little has been shared about the town's reaction to the new development."

He scrutinized me for a moment as if debating. Finally, he said, "I'd be happy to talk to you later."

I beamed at him. "Fantastic!"

One side of his mouth lifted in a half smile. "Who do you work for, Adina?"

"Myself." I winked. "For now." With a wave goodbye, I was on my way.

# Chapter Five

My phone rang on the way to the diner—Kate. Wait until I told my best friend about my meet-cute in the lobby. She'd die.

After I'd brought her up-to-date, she squealed. "Dead. I'm *dead*! This is so exciting. You're totally channeling a Hallmark heroine!"

I winced, turned the phone off speaker, and whispered "I'm sorry" to the passing pedestrian on Main Street.

The middle-aged man glared, then continued walking. *How rude.* Was this Pleasant Hollow or New York City? I swallowed down the urge to shout, "I said I was sorry!" and focused on Kate. "If you mean 'woman leaves big city for small town in search of career-making story and a permanent journalist gig,' then yes."

I paused my walk to sit on a wooden bench in front of Miller's General Store. I'd already gotten off on the wrong foot with one local by having a private conversation in public. Best not to risk doing it again, especially since the townspeople were critical to my story.

"And falls in love with small-town man," Kate added.

I laughed. "Stop it. I'm not here to meet someone." But Kate knew me too well. Friends for twenty years, we took our first no-adults subway ride together at eleven, sat through our mothers' embarrassing co-sex-talk at twelve, and snuck into our first bar in tandem at sixteen. These and other joint milestones bonded us for life. She was the Lane to my Rory.

"So does Finn look anything like Andrew Walker or Wes Brown?"

"He's hot, but no." Finn favored neither of our two favorite Hallmark movie actors, but he was more than worthy leading-man material. "I'm pretty sure Andrew and Wes are busy on a movie set in Canada or something." Most Hallmark movies were filmed near Vancouver. "Anyway, you're being silly."

"I'm jealous, but I can't really complain. At least Diego doesn't resemble the movie version of the workaholic boring city boyfriend." She chuckled.

"You mean the one with bad hair the heroine trades in for the hot, flannel-wearing, Christmas-loving dude? Not at all. Diego *is* a workaholic city boyfriend, but he's not boring, he doesn't have bad hair, and most importantly, you love him." Kate had met her boyfriend a year earlier when they kept bumping into each other at the Starbucks by their offices in the morning before work. Coincidentally, their law firms were located in the same building in Midtown. It was a real-life meet-cute. Kate and Diego were the rare success story. When you heard the urban legend about "the friend of a friend" who actually met someone great in Manhattan, fell in love, and lived happily ever after— or at least for now—it was probably Kate.

"All I'm saying is Pleasant Hollow would be the perfect place to meet the anti-Leo."

My stomach roiled at the mention of my most recent boyfriend—except he never really was. There'd been no forward momentum in the eleven months we were together. I was always passing along his excuses for not meeting my friends and family, convincing myself it was normal we'd never spent an entire weekend or holiday together.

When I finally asked why he didn't want to spend New Year's Eve with his girlfriend, he ogled me like I was balmy before saying, "Girlfriend? I thought we were just hanging out." And that was that—no more Leo.

It was par for the course. Since my first date at fifteen, I'd been ghosted, benched, breadcrumbed, love-bombed, kitten-fished, and roached. I'd seen it all. One could place the blame on me—I sought out unavailable men—except the only thing they had in common was a residence within the five boroughs of New York City.

"You might be right, but if we're staying true to form, the one unattached straight guy in Pleasant Hollow will be a single father. I'm too young to be a stepmom," I joked. I *did* want kids, but not for many years—first I'd need to move out of my mom's house. My throat constricted at the reminder that a move might happen sooner than I'd planned if we couldn't afford to pay the rent.

"Not even a precocious little plot moppet whose birth mom died tragically?"

I could tell she regretted her words by her sharp intake of breath. After a brief moment of silence to honor the early demise of my own father, I said, "It happens sometimes. My mom could have totally starred in a real-life-inspired second-chance romance if we'd stayed in Indiana. But she moved here and had one lousy boyfriend after another." Everything she'd done had been for me—to give me a better life.

"I bet you could find a man for Valerie in Pleasant Hollow too," she whispered, as if testing the waters. "Maybe he'll look like Gregory Harrison. He's a hottie."

"He's too old for my mother by two decades. Maybe Cameron Mathison."

Kate laughed. "That's the spirit."

I told her about my less-than-warm welcome at the B&B.

"Maybe she was unfriendly on purpose," Kate said. "You know, like waitstaff at restaurants who are snarky as part of an act to entertain diners."

"I'd have preferred a cup of hot cocoa with marshmallows, but anything is possible." I stared off into the distance, hoping to spy a farmer's market or craft fair. It was a Sunday afternoon. There had to be a community gathering of some sort, right?

"Either way, who cares about the innkeeper? Focus on the hottie from the lobby."

I continued to insist that advancing my career was my only purpose for the trip, but we both knew I was full of it. It was only September, so my dream of lighting the Christmas tree wouldn't come true, but maybe they'd have some sort of fall festival activities like apple picking or pumpkin carving. And maybe I'd meet a decent guy who wouldn't stand me up. Perhaps Finn Adams, who hopefully didn't have children yet. It was probably a silly fantasy, but this trip could change everything.

I promised to keep Kate constantly posted, and we ended the call. As I walked the half a block to Pinkie's, I daydreamed about my future encounters in Pleasant Hollow. Except when I pictured the townspeople, every male under the age of thirty-five was chiseled and fit but lacked a sexy edge (aside from Finn Adams, who was perfectly edgy), every man older than sixty resembled Santa Claus, and every young woman reminded me of an actress from a favorite childhood television program. Naturally, I blamed Kate's insistence that I was about to live out a Hallmark romcom.

# Chapter Six

From the outside, Pinkie's Diner looked like any other stock restaurant in a suburban town. I had psyched myself up for a classic railcar exterior or at least a retro stainless-steel façade. But no.

Not to be deterred, I snapped a few pictures and stepped inside. News of a stranger in a small town tended to spread like wildfire in books and movies. I expected that a customer no one had ever seen before would cause a stir. I figured the other diners would glance my way and wonder out loud who I was. Then they'd usher me inside. "Come in. Come in. Have a seat," they would say, before collectively pouncing on me to quench their thirst for answers. Best-case scenario, I'd be greeted at the door and offered a slice of pie—a new recipe—on the house.

None of this happened. The patrons of the half-filled diner sipped their Sprites and Diet Cokes and ate their sandwiches while conversing with their tablemates or typing on their phones, entirely unmoved by my presence.

Unsure whether I should wait to be seated, I read the advertisements tacked to a corkboard on the wall. Maybe I'd get lucky and find something about a town meeting to discuss the development plans. A handyman had left his business card. Someone was selling his guitar. Another person was plugging piano lessons. A babysitter was searching for ... *bzzzz*.

I slapped the insect on my palm. "Get *off*!" Silence filled the room, and all eyes turned to me. Oh, *now* they noticed me. "Pesky mosquito! I came here to eat, not be eaten." Recognizing the unintentional sexual innuendo, my chuckle got stuck in my throat. Not the first impression I was going for. "I didn't mean ..."

All heads returned to their own plates before I finished my sentence. I shrugged. Chances were the double meaning had sailed right over the heads of these wholesome townspeople anyway. Deciding this was definitely a seat-yourself establishment, I made my way to the counter. It was more conducive to making friends than getting a table, which might suggest I wanted to be left alone or, worse, was stuck up.

Disappointingly, the person behind the counter wasn't dressed in fifties gear, nor did she resemble a cute, white-haired grandmother type like in the small-screen movies or a grumpy hottie à la Luke Danes on *Gilmore Girls*. Doreen—she wore a charm name necklace—was a nondescript white woman of indiscernible, not-old-but-not-young age with large brown eyes and dark brown, wavy hair that fell just above her shoulders. She handed me a menu and placed a glass of water in front of me. "What can I get for you?"

"What do you recommend?" I sniffed the air, hoping for the aroma of something sweet baking in the oven, but got french fries instead.

Doreen removed the pencil from behind her ear. "It depends on what you're in the mood for. We serve breakfast all day, as well as burgers, grilled cheese, club sandwiches. The usual diner fare."

I leaned forward. "How's your pie? Is it homemade?" There were pastries in a glass display on the counter, but they looked stale and unappetizing.

Doreen pursed her lips. "Sorry. We don't have a bakery on the premises. We order it from the Stop & Shop over in Newburgh. I think there might be a slice of cheesecake left if you're interested."

My mouth opened and closed. No bakery on the premises? Pie from a chain grocery store? What kind of cozy town was this?

"The burgers are pretty good. We have beef, turkey, and veggie. The onion rings are decent too."

"An order of onion rings would be great. And a coffee, please. Thanks." I was still reeling from the "no bakery on premises" comment. Mentioning Pinkie's "famous" homemade pie with an accompanying picture would have made for a cute detail for the story, but it wasn't a big deal. I opened my notebook and wrote: *Doreen: friendly local waitress, held pencil behind her ear and made dining suggestions.*

Doreen poured my coffee and stepped to the other side of the counter to help another customer. I glanced over my shoulder, hoping to catch someone's eye or maybe overhear a conversation about the new condos.

The minutes ticked by, my onion rings were served, and I got nothing...except annoyed with myself. A good reporter did not wait for the story to come to her. She sought it out. She asked the right questions. It was basic Journalism 101. I hadn't come all this way to eavesdrop and hope to strike gold by chance.

"Have you lived in Pleasant Hollow long, Doreen?" I asked

when she swung by to refill my coffee. Expressing interest in a potential source, using proper names, was the first step to gaining trust.

"Coming on fifteen years."

"What would you say are the top five hot spots in town?"

She scrutinized me with wide eyes. "Hot spots? In Pleasant Hollow?" She laughed, her head dipping back to expose her nostrils. "Where are you from…um…what did you say your name was?"

*Interest at last.* "I didn't, but it's Adina. I'm from Manhattan…staying at the B&B."

*Ask me why I'm here. Invite me to a festival. Volunteer to hook me up with the town's most eligible bachelor.* A vision of Finn Adams danced through my mind, and my body flushed with warmth. I gripped my coffee cup expectantly, but instead of follow-up questions, an awkward lull filled the air.

"I'm a journalist here on a story about the fancy new condos going up in town," I finally said. "The Hollows. Do you have any thoughts on it?" I dipped an onion ring in a mixture of mayonnaise and ketchup.

She tipped her head. "What sort of thoughts?"

"Do you think it will affect business in the diner?"

"Hopefully it'll bring in more! More people, more mouths to feed."

Hmm. Not what I was expecting. "I read that the developer, Andrew Hanes, plans to add on-site amenities to enable one-stop shopping. Like a coffee shop. Are you worried about the competition?" It wasn't my job to lead a source toward a particular emotion but to ask the right questions to open a dialogue.

Doreen shrugged.

She wasn't taking the bait. Was she really this calm about the major changes to Pleasant Hollow, or was she holding back because I was a stranger—a journalist, no less? "Is this your diner?" I asked.

She snorted. "No. I'm just a waitress."

That's what I thought. Surely, not everyone in town was this impassive. Talking to business owners was one of the first items on my agenda. They'd have stronger opinions regarding the addition of an upscale condominium complex, since they had more at stake. If it affected their own bottom line, they'd care. Then again, even in the movies, opinions weren't 100 percent unanimous. There were always one or two people who hoped to be bought out for early retirement or an excuse to move away.

"What's the nightlife like around here?" It was midafternoon and we were in a diner, which wasn't the best setting to share gossip. A bar might be better. Alcohol made people blurt out their true emotions.

Doreen laughed again. "Nonexistent. Only place open past nine is Brothers Brewery. I guess it would qualify as a 'hot spot,' though."

"I'll check it out and report back!" I smiled wide. "Thanks, Doreen!"

"Okay then, Evita." She slapped a bill in front of me. "No rush."

"Adina." But she'd already walked away. My grin slid from my cheeks. I'd come to the diner for a slice of homemade pie, to find sources for my story, and, if I was being honest, to make friends. I was leaving with none of the above. Then again, I had aimed to give myself a day to relax and settle in. It was still the weekend. By that mindset, I was no worse off than I'd have been if I simply checked in and read in my room as intended. Beginning now, I would stick to the original plan, which was to get a good night's sleep and start fresh in the morning. I paid my bill, waved to whoever was watching (no one), and made my way back to the B&B.

# Chapter Seven

"Everything is fine," I told my mom on the phone.

It was mostly the truth. I'd arrived at my destination safely and didn't fear for my well-being. Since Mom didn't share Kate's and my fascination with small towns, there was no point in telling her I was so far underwhelmed by the hospitality.

When I'd returned from the diner, Mom Jeans, whose name I learned was Lorraine, checked me into Room E without further delay. She was microscopically friendlier to me, but I suspected it was because she was scanning my credit card for hundreds of dollars, not because she had an overwhelming interest in my life or thought I'd be perfect for her son/nephew.

"What are you doing tonight?" Mom asked.

"This," I said, as if she could see me stretched out on top of the electric-blue comforter on the bed like a snow angel.

Located on the second floor toward the back of the inn, Room E—"the Garden" or "Seaside" would have been a more charming name—had a queen-size bed and a small raised sitting area with a settee that overlooked the backyard garden. Various shades of bright blue and green tones gave the room a soothing seaside feel. It was nice enough, but too sterile to feel homey. The bare walls didn't help. Paintings, maybe even local art, would elevate the appeal. Just the same, I'd snapped a few pictures before messing up the bed and tossing items out of my suitcase.

"I'll watch some TV or read. I want to get an early start tomorrow. Make the most of my time here." *And the money you gave me when you should have saved it for a rainy day, given the imminent rent hike.*

"Sounds like a plan. I'm so proud of you, Squirt."

"Are you really? Or are you just saying that because you're my mother?" It was on the tip of my tongue to confess what I'd seen in her room, but she must have had her reasons for keeping me in the dark. I'd give her the courtesy of telling me on her own terms, in her own time. At least this was what I told myself to avoid raising the subject until I had a solid solution.

"I really am! After a shitty day of being stood up by a date and getting a rejection on a pitch, you corralled a gem of a new story from an episode of *Million Dollar Listing*. In the middle of the night! And you plugged it to the very same editor who passed on the first one. It takes chutzpah."

"And a pinch of batty." I bit my lip. Mom frowned upon self-deprecation and always called me out when she suspected I was fishing for compliments.

"It shows passion."

My eyes welled up at the realization it wasn't an act. She genuinely believed in me. I wouldn't let her down. My story would be impressive AF. Derek would beg me to join the staff at *Tea*.

We ended the call, and I turned on the television. The selection was decent but didn't include premium channels like HBO

Max or Showtime. I supposed most people staying at an inn had things to do outside the room. Unless they were on a romantic vacation and spent all their time boning. This didn't describe me. I glanced at the time on the clock on the nightstand. It wasn't even six—too early to go to bed, and I was too restless to spend the next several hours reading or watching basic TV. I wasn't hungry, but I could use a beer. The phone call with my mom had given me more incentive to get some answers. Maybe I'd get them at Brothers Brewery.

As I approached my destination using the directions gruffly provided by Lorraine—who was unwrapping premade pastries for the next morning's continental breakfast (did anyone bake in this town?)—the wind picked up and affirmed my last-minute decision to add a scarf to my outfit. The white accessory decorated with pink roses in bloom had been a Christmas gift from a woman in one of my spin classes, an independent designer.

The increased briskness in the air wasn't surprising, given the bar's proximity to the river. Set apart from other occupied land by several acres on both sides, Brothers Brewery was located inside an oversized log cabin, like something you'd see in *When Calls the Heart* on the Hallmark Channel, or *Virgin River*. The correct name would be Brothers' Brewery, but I assumed no one in the family was a grammarian. Several overturned tables, which I guessed had been used for outdoor seating when it had been warmer, leaned against the side exterior of the building. I took some pictures, laughing to myself at the contrast from the city, where no business owner would leave anything outside unless having it stolen was the goal.

I envisioned a rustic interior with communal tables where all the townspeople came to celebrate proposals and promotions; cry over divorces, infidelities, and other setbacks; commiserate over the daily stresses of life; and generally be there for each other in good times and bad. My mouth watered in anticipation of quality, locally brewed beer with hints of apricot, blueberry, or honey.

I pressed my ear to the door and heard nothing. But for a YOU'RE THIRSTY, WE'RE OPEN sign in the window, I'd have thought it was closed. It was probably just a quiet day, being a Sunday night and all. Either that or the solid wood foundation kept sound from seeping outside. There was only one way to find out. I ran a hand through my hair, let out a deep exhale, and entered.

My eyes immediately narrowed into a squint. It was dark, like there was no electricity, and no one had bothered to light a candle or a kerosene lamp. Instead of the scent of spicy hops or malty grains, my nostrils filled with dust.

"Achoo." The sound echoed off the walls, making it seem like I'd sneezed twice.

"God bless you."

"Thank you," I said, struggling to locate the source of the blesser. As my eyes acclimated to the dark, I spotted Finn, the hot guy from the B&B, sitting at a long bar in the back of the room. He'd swiveled his stool to face me. I waved.

"You didn't waste time finding the bar." He chuckled and patted the empty spot next to him.

"That's how I roll." I hopped onto the stool and skimmed the place, now that I could see better.

A few spots away, a man was either meditating or fast asleep, his torso slumped over the bar. *Depressing.* Two women at a small table clinked their mugs and burst out laughing. *That's more like it.* Otherwise the place was empty, aside from a young guy with long hair rinsing pilsner glasses in soap suds behind the bar and another young guy with even longer hair counting money a few feet away from him. "Are these the famous brothers?" I asked out loud.

"Actually, they're cousins," Finn said. "Their grandfathers were the original brothers and left the brewery to their sons, who left it to their sons—these guys."

"Fun. I love a place with history." I removed my notebook from my bag and scrawled, *Brothers. A family affair now run by two cousins.*

"Lots of history in New York City, right?" Finn motioned to Cousin Number Two, who'd looked up from his stack of bills.

"Can I get you something?" His deep voice was a contrast to his youthful attire of cargo shorts and a T-shirt.

"Do you have a menu?"

"We have Brothers light or Brothers dark."

I blinked. Those were my only choices—light or dark? "Do you have a pale ale or a wheat beer?"

He brushed a hair from his eye. "Just light or dark."

I shrugged. "I guess I'll take a light."

Finn coughed into his hand.

"A dark. I'll have a dark."

Finn muttered, "Wise choice."

I shook my head. How would I describe this place in my story? *Brothers turns the brewery world on its head with only two varieties of beer on the menu.* It could work. I groaned inwardly. It wouldn't work. "There's a bar in the city with only a light and dark beer, but it also has a ton of history and this whole ambience thing going for it, to make up for the lack of variety and pathetic menu of Saltines and mustard." Atmosphere of any sort was decidedly missing from this place, unless "dark and dusty with a two-item menu" counted as ambience.

"McSorley's?"

My head whipped back. "Yes! You know of it?"

"It's kind of famous."

"True." I took a sip from the glass Cousin Number One had placed in front of me and puckered my lips. It wasn't the best beer I'd ever had, but it wasn't the worst either. It was just kind of there.

"What do you think?"

I hesitated. Would Finn be insulted on behalf of the town if I told him how unimpressed I was? "It's a beer."

"Indeed it is. Cheers." He clinked his almost-empty glass of dark against mine. "How was your pie?" His lips quirked with amusement.

I rolled my eyes. "I'm guessing you knew about the no-bakery-on-premises deal, huh? Does this town have something against sweets? A diabetes epidemic or something?"

He laughed. "Not that I know of. You were so excited. I couldn't bear to squash your dream."

"Well, now I'm dreaming of a different sort of pie. The Oven is on my itinerary for dinner tomorrow, for delicious, knock-off-my-socks pizza." The decision was made right then and there, but why not?

"You surprise me."

I took another sip of beer and placed the glass in front of me. "How so?"

"You're all fired up about eating at the Oven in the boondocks when New York City is home of the best pizza in the country. And I will go to the mattresses with any Chicagoan over the title."

I shared his opinion. Deep-dish pizza was disgusting. "You've had it? New York pizza?"

He lifted his eyebrows. "Once or twice."

I cringed. Of course he had. Pleasant Hollow was less than two hours from the city, not in Siberia.

He raised a hand to Cousin Number One. "I'll close out."

*So soon?* I was hit with a pang of unexpected disappointment.

He pointed at me. "Her next one is on me."

"That's not necessary, but thank you. I wish guys in the city were as generous."

He grinned. "You're probably just hanging out in the wrong places."

"Perhaps." *Not a chance.* "You're out of here, then?"

"Early-morning meeting." He stood and removed some bills from his wallet.

"What do you do?" If he said he was the town mayor or veterinarian, I would fall off my stool.

As he slid his arms into the sleeves of his leather jacket, the bottom of his sweater rose to expose a hint of his flat lower abs and a trail of sexy hair leading downward.

I gulped and quickly averted my eyes.

"How about we save that for our next encounter?"

I lifted my chin and smiled up at him. "Sounds like a plan."

Another brush with Finn Adams worked for me. It was fair to say he topped my list of favorite things in Pleasant Hollow. Currently, the list was otherwise blank, but that would change in time.

I'd have left when Finn did if Cousin Number One hadn't promptly put a fresh new beer in front of me. At least the service was good. I took a photo, figuring it would look more inviting with the right filter, then drank the first half while eavesdropping on the cousins' conversation. I quickly discovered they were addicted to *Minecraft* and were avoiding their fathers' pleas to bring more variety back to the menu. Apparently, the original owners' passion for beer making had not been passed on to their grandsons, who, from what I'd gauged, were in it for the free beer in exchange for the least amount of labor. It was too bad, because a motivated chef or mixologist could do something special with this space.

I realized with an instinctual loyalty to the underdog that Andrew Hanes might be thinking the same thing and probably had connections to the right people to make it happen. I debated asking the cousins if they were afraid the developer would extend his interest in Pleasant Hollow beyond the construction of a condominium and put Brothers out of business, but decided against it.

One of my professors at Hofstra had compared getting sources to open up to courting a new love interest. The first couple of dates were to get to know each other and establish trust. You wouldn't go in for sex until at least the third date. Obviously, he'd never dated in the modern world, but I'd use the analogy to bide my time in digging the cousins for dirt. It was only my first visit to the establishment. Next time I entered the dusty darkness of Brothers Brewery, I'd be a familiar face. A regular.

Not making progress on my story didn't mean the trip had to be a complete waste of time, though. Smaller victories were up for grabs. The consumption of a beer and a half served to lower my social inhibitions. The two women at the table continued to laugh together. With alcohol-induced courage, I jumped off my stool and joined them.

"Hi there. I couldn't help but notice how much fun you were having, so I thought I'd come by and say hello. I'm new in town." *Please don't brush me off. Please be friendly.* I tucked a hair behind my ear with my free hand.

To my delight, the women introduced themselves and invited me to pull up a chair.

"What brings you here to Pleasant Hollow?" asked Jennifer, a pretty Asian woman with long, wavy black hair and brown eyes.

"I'm writing a story about the town," I said, disposing of my plan to "bide my time." When asked a question, I had this pesky habit of answering truthfully. "Do you both live here?"

Jennifer nodded. "Born and raised."

"What do you love most about Pleasant Hollow?"

"I'm drawing a blank," she deadpanned.

Her friend Monica's cherubic fair cheeks brightened. "The new hot tub in our apartment."

"Yes." Jennifer agreed. "We couldn't move now even if we wanted to. Not before paying it off." She scoffed. "I bet all the fancy-schmancy apartments being built will come with Jacuzzi tubs."

I couldn't have asked for a better segue. "Since you mentioned it, how do you feel about The Hollows? The townspeople's reaction weighs heavily in my story."

Monica beamed. "We'll finally have a gym in town. I hope it's an Equinox. They'll probably charge nonresidents a premium for membership, but it's worth it for no more early-morning drives to Newburgh."

Jennifer snorted. "Gym? Lifting this beer glass is about all the exercise I want. I'm excited about the fresh new meat in town. Do you know how hard it is to be a fortysomething lesbian in a town of less than two thousand?" She pointed at Monica. "The two of us have an agreement. If we're still single by the time we're fifty, we're hooking up. We tried it a decade ago and there was nothing there, but in seven years, we're diving back in. *Literally.*"

I choked on my beer.

She laughed. "We shocked the newbie."

"I was caught off guard is all," I said, waving her off. "It takes more than sexual innuendo to embarrass me. I was raised on the streets of Manhattan. Well, not literally the streets." Although I might be sleeping on the corner of Twentieth Street and First Avenue in six months if we couldn't afford our rent. *Damn it! Don't go there.* "Speaking of sex, what's the dating scene like in Pleasant Hollow?"

Jennifer raised an eyebrow. "Exactly how you'd expect it to be with less than five percent of the population unattached and over the age of legal consent."

"Are there any single, straight men in town?" I asked, hoping for some scoop on one Finn Adams.

"Greg and Aaron are technically single," Monica began, motioning at Cousins One and Two, "but they're kind of married to each other. And *Minecraft.*" She slid the pitcher of beer on our table closer to her. "And making subpar beer."

"I hadn't noticed that last part." I giggled before downing my glass. "They're not my type anyway." Too misplaced-surfer-dude for me.

"Garrett's single," Monica said.

"Garrett?"

"The handyman who installed our hot tub," Jennifer said.

A single handyman. I was intrigued, especially if he was as cute as Finn. "What about Finn?"

"Who?" the women asked in unison.

"Finn Adams? He was here earlier." The hottie with the great arms and sexy happy trail.

"I didn't notice him."

I found that hard to believe, but then again, I was a straight woman whose last several dates hadn't passed my sex test: Do I think this guy will be fun in bed? Do I like him? Do I think he will respect my body? Do I feel safe? Would I be open to the possibility of it going somewhere? Will I be emotionally okay if it *doesn't* lead anywhere? If the answers to all of these were yes, I'd go to bed with someone. I'd created the test after things went sour with Leo and I feared I'd never have sex again.

"Does the town have a mayor?" I asked. Probably not Finn if they didn't recognize his name.

"We share with Newburgh," Monica said. "I bought his book of poetry. For a politician, it wasn't bad."

I pressed a finger to my lips. "Your mayor is a poet? How romantic!"

Jennifer snorted. "You'd have to ask his wife."

He was married. *Huh.* They were always single in the movies. "What's the town doctor's name?"

Monica frowned. "Do we have a town doctor?"

I sighed. I could have kept going—bookstore owner, sheriff, town lawyer—but I was tired, and the beer wasn't sitting too well. Besides, this line of questioning was getting me zero intel on Finn and no useful material for my story. It was supposed to be about an idyllic quiet town under attack by an outsider. So far, Pleasant Hollow was proving to be less than idyllic, and all the answers I was getting about the new condos suggested folks were either all for it or didn't care either way. It wouldn't do if I was going to advance my career and help my mom financially.

I thanked Jennifer and Monica for their friendliness and said I hoped to see them again, waved goodbye to Cousins One and Two—next time I'd determine which was Greg and which was Aaron—and headed back to the B&B.

It was time to recalibrate. Before I spoke to anyone else in town, I'd go to The Man himself—Andrew Hanes.

# Chapter Eight

I woke up the next morning momentarily confused about where I was and how I'd gotten there. In my twenty-five years, I could count on my fingers and toes how many times, outside of the years in college, I'd slept anywhere besides the apartment I called home. But the walls were a vibrant cobalt blue instead of the subtle pale pink of my bedroom in Manhattan, and I had to turn to the left instead of the right to see if the sun was shining outside my window.

Once my mind cleared, I vaulted out of bed ready to start the official day one of my project. First stop: the site for the new development. According to my research, it was in the earlier stages of construction. My goal was to learn what Hanes planned to do with the building from the mouth of the Big Bad Wolf himself. It would earn me quotes from Hanes for the story and legitimate intel I could pass along to the townspeople to hopefully elicit the genuine and consistent reaction I needed. I didn't have an appointment scheduled—I could only listen to Christopher Cross and Kenny Loggins while on hold with corporate for so long—but hoped Hanes would give me a few minutes of his time anyway.

After a quick shower and a modest effort on my hair and makeup, I got dressed in a pair of black jeans, a loose ribbed sweater in various shades of green, and black slip-on sneakers. I assumed the dress code at the continental breakfast was "come dressed" and was hesitant to make extra effort for store-bought muffins and coffee I had little reason to believe wouldn't be instant or left over from the day before.

To Lorraine's credit, there was a decent selection of pastries (prepackaged), and the coffee was freshly brewed and delicious. I was prepared to beguile other guests with fun facts about New York City. Folks I met while on vacation or out of town were always shocked when I told them streets in Manhattan were rarely empty even at three a.m. and it never got blindingly dark outside because of car headlights and streetlights twenty-four-seven. But I was the only person downstairs. Everyone else had either eaten much earlier or was still sleeping.

It was disappointing on one level but also a relief, because I was eager to get to work. I wolfed down my coffee, dropped a paper-towel-wrapped muffin in my purse for lunch (an attempt to conserve my limited financial resources), and took off. Everything in Pleasant Hollow was in walking distance, which worked for me since I hadn't allotted money for more car services.

The construction site, not too far from the center of town, was surrounded by a fence with sporadically placed safety signs. Aside from steel-framed walls and scaffolding, there wasn't much of a building yet. Tables, buckets, and wheelbarrows were filled with wood, cinderblocks, and other building materials. Workers in high-viz vests and steel-toe boots stood around, occasionally gazing upward or shouting at one another. The scent of fresh-cut lumber and sawdust filled the air, and I sneezed, just as I'd done upon my entry into Brothers Brewery. And like then, the sound caught someone's attention.

"Watch out!" someone yelled.

My eyes, which had involuntarily closed from sneezing, opened, and I jolted to a stop just in time to avoid crashing into sheets of plastic that, based on the BEWARE! SAFETY HAZARD! sign in plain sight, guarded off a dangerous area.

My heart raced and I took a deliberate exhale to slow it down. "Phew," I said, wiping my brow. "Thank you. I've been here less than a minute, and you've already saved my life!" Aiming to strike a balance between professional and friendly, I straightened my back and smiled. "Is one of you Andrew Hanes?" I doubted it but didn't want to assume the boss didn't get his hands dirty along with his workers.

Silence was my initial answer as the men looked at each other. Then they burst out laughing in harmony. "Did someone tell you Andrew Hanes was here?"

"No. I just assumed he'd be on-site since he owns the property." My stomach churned. What if I got it all wrong and Andrew Hanes was no longer the principal on the project? If he lost interest, he might have sold the land to another interested third party. Thanks to my degree in journalism, I was an ace researcher, but shit always happened the second you closed the book or logged off your computer. I might have blinked and missed a pivotal switch.

One of the men, a silver fox who'd probably be played by Gregory Harrison in the *Autumn in Pleasant Hollow* movie adaptation, nodded. "Andrew Hanes is definitely the man in charge."

My shoulders relaxed.

"But he's not here."

The tension returned.

"A project in upstate New York doesn't rate high enough for Hanes's in-person presence, but his project manager—we call him Mini Andrew—is in there." He gestured to a white mobile office trailer parked about two hundred feet away.

I'd have preferred an interview with Hanes himself, but I could make do with his project manager. "Great. Thank—"

"Do you have an appointment?"

I crossed my arms over my chest. "Are you his assistant?" I doubted it since his hard hat said FOREMAN.

"Not a chance," he answered with a smirk.

"His bodyguard?"

"Does he need one?"

I chuckled as he gave me a once-over in a strictly teasing and not-at-all-douchey way. "He might, but definitely not to protect him from me."

"Okay then. Go get 'im... what did you say your name was?"

Already on my way, I glanced over my shoulder. "I didn't!" I smiled at the laughter I left in my wake.

When I reached the trailer, I climbed the four steps to the entrance and paused with my knuckles inches from the door. My hands shook as I removed my ruled notebook with my interview questions from my purse. What was I so afraid of? It wasn't the first interview I'd ever conducted, and my interviewee wasn't Stacey Abrams, Joe Biden, or anyone intimidating for that matter. It wasn't even Andrew Hanes on the other side of the door. It was his lackey! My pulse slowed. I had this. I *so* had this. Before this newfound confidence slipped away, I double-checked the pen was in place within the spiral-bound spine of my notebook and knocked three times.

"Come in."

There was no backing down now. I stepped inside and nearly stumbled at the sight before me.

# Chapter Nine

"Finn?"

"Adina. What are you doing here?"

"*You're* Mini Andrew?" I said, stating the obvious while willing my knees to be still.

He chuckled. "I see you've met the construction staff."

"Why didn't you say something?"

"You didn't ask." His grin could be showcased in the *Merriam-Webster Dictionary* under the word "cocky."

I clenched my fists. "You knew I thought you were a local and deliberately played along."

A combination of shock, anger, and disappointment overcame me, even as I acknowledged I barely knew this guy. I had no right to any of these emotions.

"You met me in the lobby of the B&B," he said. "If I wasn't a guest, what did you think I was doing there?"

"I thought you were related to Lorraine, like her nephew or something." Realizing with each word how utterly ridiculous I sounded, I dropped the volume of my voice to a whisper by the end of the sentence. Still, he heard me. *Of course* he heard me.

His neck flamed red as he barked. Not laughed—*barked*. "What would ever give you that idea?"

I opened my mouth to respond, then clamped it shut. What could I say? That I'd hoped he was the hero in my embarrassing meet-cute, a handsome and friendly townie who would partner with me to save his beloved Pleasant Hollow from the threat of gentrification?

Finn was the exact opposite. Rather than being devoted to Pleasant Hollow and willing to protect it at any cost, he was the antagonist in my planned story—the enemy. My body suddenly felt heavy, and my shoulders dropped under the strain of holding them up.

"I'm staying in the B&B temporarily while overseeing this project," he said finally.

"How long do you think that will be?" In other words, how much time did the town have to march on city hall should they choose to try? *Yes, let's drive attention away from my personal humiliation and get to the matter at hand.*

"We're hoping for spring of next year. I'll be out of here long before that, though." His expression softened. "Look, I'm sorry I misled you. I couldn't resist. But as long as you're here, sit down." He gestured to the plastic folding chair I was currently death-gripping for support. "What can I do for you?"

I slid into the chair after only a brief hesitation. I—literally—couldn't afford to walk out on this interview because of a bruised ego. "Do you have a few minutes to talk about the construction?" To write a fair piece, I had to give both sides an equal opportunity to weigh in. I just needed to squelch my regret that Finn wouldn't speak on behalf of Pleasant Hollow but rather for the real estate conglomerate who wanted to reinvent it.

"Sure."

I removed my phone from my purse and placed it on the desk between us. "You mind if I record this conversation?"

His eyes widened. "Wow. You don't mess around."

*I'd love to mess around with you.* Heat seared my cheeks at my one-track mind. I sat up straight, like there was a ruler against my back. "I take my work very seriously."

"Clearly," he said, raising a brow.

"Is that a yes?" I tapped my right foot on the vinyl flooring.

His gaze dropped to my phone. "Oh, right. Sure, go ahead."

I opened my notebook and leaned forward, anxious to get started. *Finally.*

Across from me, Finn smirked.

I groaned. "Please wipe the smug look off your face. You got me. Good on you!"

"I didn't say anything." His eyes widened with feigned and mocking innocence.

I rolled mine. "Not with words, anyway. Can we please get down to business?" I didn't wait for his response before turning on the recorder app on my phone and asking my first question.

To his credit, Finn was generous and thorough with his answers. I learned that once completed, the lobby of the twenty-five-floor luxury complex would house a coffee shop, fitness center, restaurant/bar, pharmacy, dry cleaning and laundry valet, and bank. Access to the stores inside the building would be open to the entire town and general public, but owners and tenants of the condo/rental complex would have priority or receive special discounts in some cases. My mind wandered to my new friend Monica. She wouldn't have to travel to Newburgh for her early-morning gym fix anymore. And Jennifer would have a new watering hole to meet available, single women.

"How does Mr. Hanes expect to fill such a big building? Isn't it a huge financial risk to think he can grow the town's population by more than fifty percent with one complex?"

"*Mr. Hanes* didn't make his money because he was afraid of risks. He also didn't earn his impressive reputation taking stupid ones. We did surveys and polls to gauge the average suburban dweller's interest in living in a place like The Hollows. All evidence supports the development." He leaned back in his chair with his hands clasped behind his head.

*Fair enough.* With effort, I tore my eyes away from his triceps, which were straining against his dark gray Henley. "I read that you hope to attract young couples and singles who work in Manhattan but can't afford the cost of living in Westchester, Rockland, or Long Island. My door-to-door commute here from the city was almost two hours, and I had to take an Uber from Newburgh because of the limited direct bus access to Pleasant Hollow. How do you expect folks to do that every day—twice? And will the benefit be worth the inconvenience?" *I'll see your risk assessment and raise you transportation inconvenience.*

Finn clicked his pen, once, twice, three times. "We think so." *Click.* "We understand the current commute to and from Port Authority isn't ideal. So, for those willing to make the longish trip in exchange for living in a luxury apartment set in a more remote area, we're partnering with the ShortLine bus." *Click.* "The partnership includes a shuttle directly from the building to various access points in the city, with multiple trips every weekday morning and evening. And since the land runs parallel to a Metro-North line, my boss is in talks with the MTA about eventually building a rail station." *Click. Click.*

I glared at his pen, willing Finn to get the message without requiring me to rip the writing instrument out of his hand.

He set the pen down. *Message received.*

They were big—his hands—but not grotesquely so, with long fingers. Were they rough or soft? Before I could leap across the desk to find out, I buried my own hands under my butt. *Someone needs to get laid.* "Will there be an additional cost for this shuttle?"

"Nope," he said with a shake of his head. "It will be built into the annual maintenance fees or monthly rent, along with access to the pool on the roof and complimentary wine and cheese every weekday afternoon for all tenants."

I blinked. It sounded amazing. There had to be a catch. "How much are the units going for?"

"A one-bedroom in a place like this would cost about three quarters of a million in Manhattan. Here, prices start at two hundred fifty thousand to buy and fifteen hundred a month to rent." He paused for my reaction, looking pleased, like a kid who'd won his school district's spelling bee.

"Do you live in the city?" I asked, confirming what I already knew. What had I been smoking when I thought he was a modest, straightforward, randomly hot-as-fuck small-town man? This guy before me? He reeked of "expert of all things, knows he's sexy, gets a lot of tail, girls always swipe right" big-city dude.

"Yup. I'm subletting my place on the Upper West Side while I'm here."

"I guess you've had the pizza and been to McSorley's, then?"

I freed my hands from under my tush and slid farther down my chair.

"I've even had bagels. Oh, and there's a diner in my neighborhood that makes homemade cherry pie to die for, in case you're still craving it when you get home. Apple too." His face shone with amusement.

I desperately wished I could tell him to go fuck himself, but I'd walked right into it. He hadn't done anything wrong other than take too much pleasure in my misinformation. Still, it was time to squash my crush on Finn like a bug. A city boy in a small town was still a city boy. *Been there, done that.* Besides, I'd come to Pleasant Hollow for career advancement, not to fall in love. That meant focusing on the main story, not a possible romantic subplot.

Kate would be devastated.

# Chapter Ten

Having gotten what I needed, if not what I *wanted*, from Finn, I made a swift exit from the trailer, waving goodbye to the construction staff. But my smile wasn't nearly as genuine on the way out as it had been on the way in.

The new development sounded like a dream living arrangement. Wine and cheese happy hour? Sign me up! I was tempted to fill out an application for me and Mom. Then again, it stood to reason *I'd* be impressed by a luxury building at the reasonable prices Finn had quoted. In New York City, the words "reasonable" and "real estate" were rarely uttered in the same sentence.

It was Finn's *job* to paint the development in the best light possible. It was *my* job to report both sides of the issue with an impartial perspective. Obviously, the unhappier the locals were, the more accurate the comparison to the movies and the better for my story. I'd gotten the corporate side. Now it was the town's turn.

First up was Miller's General Store. After grabbing a black stainless-steel to-go coffee mug from the back, I stepped over to the cash register and introduced myself as a journalist writing a story about Pleasant Hollow. "Would you be willing to answer a few questions about the town?"

"I suppose so." The clerk was a lanky older white man with thinning dark hair and glasses, wearing a white lab coat. I guessed he doubled as a pharmacist, since the business next door was called Miller's Pharmacy and presumably under the same ownership.

First I asked him to confirm his name (Fred), his connection to the store (owner), how long it had been open (twenty years), and if I could quote him in the story ("Why not?"). "So, Fred, are you happy here in Pleasant Hollow?"

"Happy is relative. It's my home."

"Makes sense," I said with a nod. "Would you describe it as a small and tight-knit community?"

"Small, yes. Tight-knit?" His gray eyebrows furrowed in contemplation. "Not particularly."

This surprised me, but I didn't comment. "Are you aware a big-time real estate conglomerate is building a massive residential complex in the center of town?" *Massive* was an exaggeration, but it added effect.

"I am. Yes."

"And how do you feel about it?"

"If a billionaire wants to invest in my town, who am I to stop him?"

I frowned. "Are you worried about gentrification or over-crowding? More traffic?"

"Nah. The more gentrified the town becomes, the less money I spend on gas driving my kids to Newburgh and Middletown." He gestured to the travel mug in my hand. "Just this?"

I reeled back. *And we're done here.* "Yes." I passed him my debit card, cringing when the cash register displayed the price of $19.99, and thanked him for his time.

After receiving another lackluster response in Lickety Splits a few minutes later, I took a different slant. "With the addition of this new swooping structure, the landscape of the town will be drastically and irrevocably altered. Are you concerned the building will block the river views for a significant portion of the population?" People in New York City had strong feelings about views, especially when theirs were threatened, but posing it as a question rather than leading allowed me to remain impartial.

The woman behind the counter, who I guessed to be about my mother's age, with blond hair spilling out of a white visor, beamed at me. "I'm on the waiting list for a unit on the top floor!"

And so it went.

I visited several more storefronts, including Books on Main and Twinkly Nails, where I also made a manicure appointment for later in the week. While the responses differed—some people were in favor of the construction, others didn't care—no one was concerned Andrew Hanes would shut down their business or needlessly modernize the town with chain stores like H&M and Starbucks. There appeared to be no plans to band together to stop him, either by seeking historical status for the property or by collectively buying him out—popular solutions in the movies.

*Think, Adi, think. Hmm.* Would a story about a small town with the *opposite* reaction to real estate development than what the movies portrayed be of interest to the readers of *Tea*?

*Nice try, but no.*

I wandered to the park and plopped my butt on a black

bench to think and nibble on my muffin. In front of me was the statue of Natalie Schull, the ballet dancer and only famous person born in Pleasant Hollow. The bronze replica appeared massive in photos yet was only about twice the size of the Tony Award she'd won in the 1980s. I laughed and choked on my muffin. It was too dry, and I swallowed it down with effort. My body curled in on itself on the bench. How long until I came across something in this town that surprised me in a positive way or, better yet, didn't surprise me at all because I'd seen it on my television screen hundreds of times?

I rubbed the tension out of my eyebrows. Going door-to-door to interview the local businesspeople wasn't working. Rather than continue on the same path, it was time to pivot. But how?

And then it came to me. Wherever individuals went to vent about everything, from politics to underwhelming television finales to the asshole who stole their parking spot, was the same place they'd complain about Andrew Hanes and The Hollows. Social media. With optimism in my veins, I opened Twitter on my phone, searched #AndrewHanes, and scrolled through the results. My shoulders slumped. All the posts were about deals closing in some New York City properties; nothing about Pleasant Hollow. Searches of #PleasantHollow and #TheHollows were equally unfruitful.

On Instagram, however, my search of #PleasantHollow yielded more than a thousand posts. This was initially promising, until I saw that most of the recent posts were mine, teasing my story with pictures from my bus ride and photos I'd taken since my arrival. Several other images were clearly from other towns called Pleasant Hollow located in Georgia and Missouri.

And then I noticed an interesting trend. A large portion of the photos under the #PleasantHollow hashtag were of brides and grooms, table settings, and centerpieces. All were posted from the account of a wedding planner named Davina Lawrence. I knew it was the *right* Pleasant Hollow since her posts also included #NewYorkState and #TwinklyNails, the local nail salon.

A tingle of hope ran through me. I closed out of Instagram and opened Google, where I searched for Hallmark movies featuring wedding planners. My excitement built as the screen populated with results. *I knew it.* Wedding planning was a very popular vocation for Hallmark leading ladies. Maybe I could do character profiles of Pleasant Hollow residents with Hallmark movie jobs. Despite lacking the Andrew Hanes component on its face, the idea didn't stray far from the story I'd pitched—comparing Pleasant Hollow to a Hallmark town—and it would be a hoot for the readers of *Tea*.

After sending Davina a DM on Instagram, I focused on other popular professions and landed on Garrett, the handyman. There was always a guy in the movies "fixing" things, even if he wasn't the leading man. Monica and Jennifer had mentioned he was single, which also fit the bill. I recalled seeing his card on the bulletin board at Pinkie's and would grab it on the way to the Oven for dinner and give him a call. I'd start with Davina and Garrett, a.k.a. "wedding planner" and "handyman," respectively, and take it from there.

I might just be able to pull this story off after all.

# Chapter Eleven

The cashier called out, "One veggie slice."

I practically jogged to the front of the restaurant to claim my dinner. The Oven was a typical Main Street corner pizza joint—a brick-lined exterior with a red-and-white-striped awning and a casual interior with approximately ten small and medium-size tables covered with black-and-white gingham plastic tablecloths. My eager smile turned upside down at my first glance of the slice the teenage boy working the counter haphazardly threw on a paper plate. The mushrooms and broccoli were undercooked, as if they were thrown on top of the pie as an afterthought. Not even the best, most image-enhancing filter could make these slices Instagram worthy. "Did this pizza come from your famous Italian oven?"

Teenage Boy burst into laughter. "Oh no. That broke decades ago."

If it was possible to literally shrink from disappointment, I was now four foot eleven. I begrudgingly brought the pizza and a can of Coke back to my table. Presentation wasn't everything. Taste was more important.

I lifted the slice off the plate and took a bite just as Finn joined me. Mid-chew, I brought my hand to my mouth. The pizza was hot. The Oven scored a point for that, which earned it a total of one point, considering the crust was too thick. It rated marginally lower than the beer at Brothers—closer to the worst I'd ever had than the best. The dough was soggy, and the cheese-to-sauce ratio was off—not enough sauce. Certainly not worth the Lactaid pill I'd taken first.

Once I swallowed, I acknowledged Finn with a timid smile while trying to rein in my feelings of betrayal. Finn hadn't lied to me. But he wasn't who I thought he was, and it felt personal.

He gestured at the pizza. "What did you think?"

"It's no John's."

"Oh, you're one of those," he said, rolling his eyes to the white plaster ceiling.

"One of *whos*?" I asked, folding my arms over my chest. "People with amazing taste in pizza?"

He lifted his chin in dissent. "Arturo's is better."

"Agree to disagree. And let it be noted I disagree strongly." I smiled despite myself. It wasn't all bad having a fellow city person around. "Of all the one-pizza-joints in town, you walked into mine."

Finn's lips twitched. "It's not a coincidence. You said you were going to be here."

*Am I the reason he's here?* My belly leaped in delight for exactly one second, without the Mississippi, until I remembered Finn wasn't Pleasant Hollow's most eligible bachelor who'd been waiting for the right woman—me—to come along and complete his otherwise perfect and uncomplicated life.

"How's the story going?"

"It's getting there." I sounded surer than I felt, but *acting* confident was halfway to *being* confident. I'd get the rest of the way there once I heard back from Davina—and Garrett, who I'd called on the way over. He hadn't answered, so I left a voicemail.

"You don't seem as certain as you were in my office this morning. Or are you just tired?" He cocked his head. "Long day?"

"You can say that." I broke off a piece of my napkin, then ripped it again and again until the pieces fell onto the table like confetti. "Like most things, the story is taking unexpected twists and turns."

He nodded decisively. "I'm sure it will all work out."

"Thanks. It has to."

Finn stared me down, asking a question with his sultry brown eyes.

I bit my lip, debating how much to divulge. "My writing endeavors haven't gone so well lately," I confessed. "I work two jobs in the city, neither of which uses my degree in journalism, on top of competing for freelance gigs writing uninspired content for third parties. Brewing cappuccinos? Not my dream. Making song lists for spin classes? Fun, but not my dream. Being a regular contributor for a magazine focused on pop culture and human interest? Dream. And it's within reach now." I felt buoyant at the thought. "If I impress the editor with this story, he's promised me a staff position at the end of the year." "Promise" may have been wishful thinking, but saying it out loud made it feel real.

"You're a spin instructor? Where?"

"New York Fitness Club. You ride?"

"Sometimes. I had to give up running a while back because of Achilles tendinitis. My podiatrist suggested spin, and I liked it. Even though I'm okay to run again, I still spin a few times a month."

"Nice." The segue from my story to exercise pleased me. I preferred other topics of conversation until I knew I was absolutely onto something with my character profiles. Confirmation my real-life wedding planner and handyman were willing sources would do wonders for my confidence. My phone was annoyingly inactive.

"But back to your story."

I groaned.

Finn pretended not to notice. "Maybe I can help. My boss has plans to buy more land for additional restaurants and shops. The influx of more people will breathe new life into Pleasant Hollow. It will be great for the local economy. Can you use that?"

I leaned forward in interest. "Is this land *your boss* is interested in currently unoccupied, or will he need to buy out the existing owners?" Perhaps the Andrew Hanes angle wasn't dead yet.

"I'm not at liberty to say." He paused. "Am I imagining the venom in your tone when you say 'your boss'? He's not some villain."

I chewed my straw. "You're definitely imagining it."

He narrowed his eyes. "I'm not sure I believe you. You seem determined to paint him as the enemy. Why not focus on the positive?"

"Because then it becomes a press release. Without some kind of drama or surprise, there's no story." *Certainly not the one I pitched.* I stared at my phone willing it to ring, ping, *something*.

"Adina."

I looked up to find Finn's eyes locked on my lips.

I returned the stare, imagining what kind of kisser he was. Would he be soft or firm, practiced or sloppy? I'd bet he knew what he was doing.

"You've got something..." He touched a finger to the corner of his mouth.

"Oh." I wiped the side of my face and pretended I hadn't thought we'd been exchanging mutually lustful gazes.

He chuckled. "Wrong side." Before I knew what was happening, he leaned over the table to wipe my mouth with his thumb, his eyes teasing yet kind.

"Th-thanks," I stuttered, mesmerized as he licked the sauce from his finger. I released the breath I was holding just as an Instagram notification popped up on my phone, alerting me to a message from Davina. *Finally.* "A potential source just DMed me," I said. "I have to read it."

"Don't let me stop you." Finn motioned at his half-eaten slice. "I'll finish my delicious pizza."

I made a grossed-out face before opening the message.

Thanks for reaching out, Adina! I'd be happy to speak with you. I'm currently in Florida, but are you free tomorrow morning at 9:30 for a phone call?

I did a little dance in my seat.

9:30 is perfect. On what number can I reach you?

I didn't even have time to update Finn before Davina replied with her number. "I have an interview set up for tomorrow morning," I said, clapping my hands together.

"Who with?"

I leaned back in my chair and eyed him with feigned suspicion. "Why? You worried it's an enemy of Andrew Hanes?"

He raised a brow. "Should I be?"

*I hope so.* I wasn't quite ready to admit defeat on the Hollows angle. It was entirely possible Davina had strong, negative feelings about the development, but I was relieved the feature wouldn't rest on it. "A local wedding planner," I said, ignoring his question.

Finn's cheeks pinked with amusement. "This keeps getting more and more interesting. Where's this interview taking place? The B&B for breakfast?"

"She's currently in Florida, so we're talking on the phone. Speaking of breakfast, there was no one there this morning."

"I think we might be the only guests this week."

A vision of Finn and me in our pajamas covertly raiding the fridge in the middle of the night flickered through my mind. At least we were wearing PJs. Keeping my visions PG was a wise move. "I was going to stop by the brewery, but I think I'll save that for tomorrow. Better to go home and prepare some interview questions."

"Home?"

My face warmed. "You know what I meant. Although it must feel like home to you by now. You're so well versed in the town, I assumed you were a local."

"I remember." He returned my mock glare with a snicker. "Part of my job is to read up on the history of the town I'm helping to develop. But I soaked up a lot of esoteric knowledge just by being here, like the fact that Aaron and Greg from Brothers are actually cousins."

"How long *have* you been staying at the B&B?"

"Almost a month."

I whistled through my teeth. "Your boss has deeper pockets than mine."

"Your boss currently being you, right?"

He was good at remembering details. "Right. I'm still freelance, so the magazine isn't picking up any of my travel expenses." I doubted *Tea* would do that for full-time employees either. "My mom is helping, though. God bless her." Terrified as I was to let her down, the pieces of the puzzle were finally coming together with this new angle, and I was seriously stoked.

"You're lucky to have her support."

"I am. She's my emotional rock." With a wrinkle of my nose, I said, "My financial one too, but not for long, with any luck." Why was I revealing such personal information to a stranger? I pressed the top of my straw with two fingers. "What about you? Are you close with your parents?" Asking the questions was my comfort zone.

A shadow crossed his face. "My mom died when I was young."

My chest constricted. "Oh, I'm so sorry! My dad died when I was three." I second-guessed sharing, fearing he'd think I was making it about me.

"I'm sorry too." He broke eye contact, like our shared half-orphan status was a topic he didn't care to discuss, then stood and pointed at my plate. "Are you finished here?"

I'd left the crust, something I never did on quality pizza. I nodded. "Like I said, it's no John's." Beating him to it, I added, "Or Arturo's! Did you know the forty-year-old Italian oven broke decades ago? False advertising!"

He dumped both our plates in the trash and turned to me with a guilty expression. "I did."

"And you didn't want to crush my dreams of amazing pizza."

"Exactly." He grinned. "I'll walk back with you. I'm finished for the day too."

"No beer for you tonight?"

"Not at the brewery, at least."

Did this mean he had a stash of booze in his hotel room? I was met with a vision of the two of us sharing a bottle of wine on his bed. Except this time, there were no PJs.

During the ten-minute walk from the Oven to the B&B, we shared a comfortable silence. While glancing in the shop windows, I worked on wiping the vision of Finn sans clothes from my brain. "Everything closes so early here."

"We're not in Kansas anymore, Dorothy." He nudged me playfully. "Although we might as well be. This town is a dead zone by eight most nights."

"Doesn't the town do things?" I smiled at an older couple walking past us in the opposite direction. They shot me a dirty look in response, but at least neither stuck out their tongue. I was afraid to glance over my shoulder and be proven wrong.

Finn stopped walking. "Do *things*? Like what?"

We were at the entrance to Twinkly Nails. A lone customer had her nails under the dryer while the manicurist tossed annoyed glances at the back of her head in five-second intervals. *Someone wants to go home.* "I don't know." But I *did* know. "Like festivals and stuff. A corn maze? Apple picking? Pumpkin-carving contests? Do they even have fireworks on the Fourth of July?" *Anything to use in my story.* The stores had no Halloween decorations. Granted we were about a month out, but it seemed like it should be more decorative.

"No fireworks, but the cousins set their lawn on fire with firecrackers gone wrong."

I tugged the bottom of his jacket. "You're joking, right?"

"Unless they were lying."

"They told you?"

"They *bragged* about it like it was a worthy accomplishment." He laughed. "Anyway, I haven't heard anything about any festivals here. But I went home last Saturday for the Oktoberfest on the East River." He resumed walking and gestured for me to keep up.

"No way! I was there too. It's right near my apartment." My amazement at the smallness of our world momentarily overrode my disillusionment over the lack of local events to celebrate the autumnal season.

"I thought you looked familiar!"

My eyes bugged out. Between my mom, her best friend Heather (my honorary aunt and the person responsible for finding the apartment we were in danger of losing), Kate, and me, we'd pointed out a fair number of attractive men (and women, in Aunt Heather's case) in the crowd, but Finn had not been among them. "Really?"

"No. Not really."

I returned his playful nudge from earlier. "*Anyway*, Brothers Brewery should do something for Oktoberfest. It could boost their business." We'd arrived at the B&B and I walked through the door Finn held open for me. "Although your boss probably wouldn't like that." It was in Andrew Hanes's best interest for the brewery to be on the verge of financial collapse—easier for him to swoop in and buy them out with a lowball offer.

"My boss has bigger things to worry about than a beer festival."

We walked single file up the stairs with me in the lead. "Then you won't care if I suggest it to the cousins." If they scheduled it before I left, I could refer to it in my article.

Finn stopped outside the room next to mine. "I care so little, I'll forget about it the second I close this door. Although they might want to expand their beer selection."

I'd be damned if I conceded his point. "Have a nice night." I plucked my room key from my purse and opened the door.

"Sweet dreams, Adina. I hope your interview is everything you want it to be."

I turned to him, expecting to see an expression of sarcasm on his ridiculously handsome face to contradict his words, but all I saw was sincerity. A warm gooey feeling spread through me without my permission. I croaked out a thanks, right as he stepped inside his room and closed the door behind him.

# Chapter Twelve

*I*'d planned to call Davina from my room the next morning but changed my mind at the last minute. I had to go downstairs to fill my new to-go coffee mug anyway, and the common room was quiet and completely empty—like my own private office. The decision had nothing do with the possibility of running into Finn. *Nothing.*

Now, ten minutes into the call, my spirits climbed steadily with each word out of my source's mouth. I'd told her my story angle was Hallmark characters come to life. Davina loved their movies as much as I did, which made sense since she basically lived one. She was currently telling me how she got into the wedding-planning business.

"I started off working with caterers, which is where I earned my experience, but one of the items on my list of goals before turning thirty was to open my own shop. I accomplished it with a year to spare, and five years later, here we are!"

My cheeks hurt from the strain of smiling so hard while I jotted down notes. It was a careful dance to capture everything while maintaining legible handwriting. But the outlook for my story was blue skies for days. A turning-thirty bucket list was adorably romcom-y. "Tell me about some of the favorite couples you've worked with." I took a sip of coffee and shook out my hand.

"They're all my favorites!"

"You have to say that."

"I do." She chuckled. "I really enjoy second-chance couples. Last month, I planned a wedding for college sweethearts who'd broken up after graduation when he moved to London for a job and she stayed home. They *happened* to run into each other in Barbados while on separate vacations and fell back in love, of course. Now he works in his company's Albany office, and hopefully they'll live happily ever after."

I nodded as if she could see me. "I love it. Estranged sweethearts reuniting is a popular trope in the movies."

"There's more. It's so textbook, I'm almost embarrassed to tell you."

"Tell me!" I bounced in my chair like an overactive toddler.

"I'm married to a divorce lawyer. Our practices were in the same office building, and we hated each other at first sight. Only we really didn't. I'm pretty sure there's a Hallmark movie with the same plot."

There was. It was called *For Better or For Worse.* But I was too embarrassed to confess this knowledge to Davina and out myself as an honest-to-goodness Hallmarkie. "This is fantastic. *You* are fantastic!" I put the phone on speaker and shimmied my hips in joy, freezing at the arrival of Finn in the common room.

He was wearing a light-blue button-down shirt with the sleeves rolled up to his elbows, black jeans, steel-toe work boots, and an expression of unrestrained amusement. "Nice moves,

Shakira," he said before relaxing onto the red velvet couch with a newspaper.

My skin burned like I'd been trapped in a furnace. Embarrassing myself in front of Finn was becoming a *thing*. And why was I so charmed by him reading an actual print newspaper?

I sat back down and faced the other way, returning my focus to Davina. Finn would forget about my impromptu jig by the time the interview was over. Probably.

"Can you tell me some of the places in Pleasant Hollow where you've planned weddings?" I couldn't think of anywhere appealing, but maybe couples did small backyard receptions or obtained permits to get hitched in the park. Pictures would be great if Davina was willing to share.

"Pleasant Hollow? I've never planned a wedding there."

I blinked. "But your office is here, right?"

The air was silent aside from the crinkling of paper. *Finn.*

"Um, no. I'm a city girl like you. Only Albany, not Manhattan."

My heart went *bam, bam, bam.* "But you hashtag all your Insta posts with Pleasant Hollow."

Davina laughed. "Oh, right! My older sister Laura owns Twinkly Nails, and I try to help her with exposure as a thanks for investing in my business before we knew it would succeed. She's an amazing manicurist, and her salon is the only one within a fifty-mile radius that carries the full line of Bettie Pain nail polish. You'd be surprised how many people will travel for it. Are you there? In Pleasant Hollow?"

"Yeah." I gazed absently through the window as Fred from Miller's General Store walked by. "My story is about the town." Whispering so Finn wouldn't hear me, I added, "The

Hallmark-come-to-life angle banks on the sources being locals. I thought you were."

"Oh no. Can you still use the interview?"

I released a sad sigh. "Unfortunately, the setting of Pleasant Hollow is inherent to this particular piece, but you are fabulous, and someday I'd love to feature you." Random people who happened to have jobs common to those held in the movies lacked the cohesiveness I required and strayed too far from the story I'd pitched. "I'm so sorry for wasting your time." It was my mistake to assume she was from Pleasant Hollow based on her Instagram feed. Assume = Ass + U + Me.

"No worries. Definitely check out Twinkly Nails, and tell my sister I sent you! Good luck on the story."

"Thank you so much." We ended the call. My spirits deflated like a Mylar birthday balloon a week past its shelf life.

"How'd it go?"

I answered Finn with my eyes closed. "Great. Just great."

"You're not dancing anymore."

I bent over so my head was between my legs. He *had* to mention it. Of course he did. I was so tired. It was only 10:15 in the morning and I was ready for bed.

It occurred to me it was 10:15 and Finn wasn't at work. I sat up. "Don't you have a project to manage?"

Just once, I wanted to run into him when things were going well. Why couldn't he witness me in action as a capable journalist, not a boogying fool with pizza crumbs on her lip and a stalled story?

"I was on my way out when I saw your impersonation of JLo."

"I thought I was Shakira."

His lips quirked. "The interview didn't go well?"

"It went fabulously, until she told me she lived in Albany, not Pleasant Hollow." Except it wasn't her job to tell me. It was mine to ask.

"Shit." His expression reflected compassion but not pity. "Can you find someone else who lives here instead?"

"That's the plan." All wasn't lost. It was still a solid idea. I'd search for alternatives—people who were actually from the town—and follow up with Garrett as well.

"Why don't you come with me to the building site first? You can talk to my staff for more *impartial* intel." He flashed a lopsided smile.

"Give it a rest."

"Come," he said, tilting his head in the direction of the front door. "You might get something you can use."

"Okay." It was early, and I had nowhere else to be at the moment. "But just until my next interview." Which, as of now, meant I had all the time in the world.

# Chapter Thirteen

You're back." The silver-fox construction worker from the day before wiped his hands along his dirt-stained blue jeans and greeted me with a smile.

"Vick, meet Adina," Finn said by way of formal introduction. "She's writing a story about Pleasant Hollow for..." His voice dropped off and he looked at me apologetically. "For where?"

"It's called *Tea*." I turned to Vick to clarify. "It's a digital magazine focusing on pop culture and entertainment."

Three more workers in our vicinity, two men and one woman, all wearing white hard hats, orange vests, and steel-toe boots, stopped stacking slabs of wood and turned their attention to us.

Against a backdrop of dump trucks and excavators making *beep beep* sounds, a tall and lanky thirtysomething guy covered head-to-toe in freckles said, "For a price, I can give you dirt for an exposé. Behind the Scenes: The Hollows."

The female worker knocked twice on the side of his hard hat. "Yeah, photos of you falling ass first off the ladder yesterday would get millions of views, I'm sure."

I gasped, but my initial reaction of concern was superseded

by the laughter around me. The guy standing in front of me wasn't on crutches, wasn't wearing an orthopedic boot or even a Band-Aid, so obviously any injury resulting from his fall had been minor. But at least the nickname on his hard hat—"Clumsy Smurf"—made sense.

Finn smirked. "Don't tempt her." To me, he said, "I'll be in my trailer, but stay as long as you like. These guys don't need any excuse to take a break." The fond looks he gave his staff belied his disparaging words. "Just be careful. Steer clear of the heavy equipment and any area that's fenced off."

"Worried I'll sue you?" I joked.

"More like concerned you'll lose a limb, but that too."

"Noted." His sincerity was both touching and irritating. The former because it was sweet. The latter because "sweet and touching" made the flame of my pesky crush burn hotter, when what I needed was to extinguish it before I got carried away.

This wasn't the small-town romance of my fantasies. Finn was paying attention to me. One could even say he was *flirting*. But it didn't mean anything. I was a convenient distraction. Another visitor in town staying in the same hotel. I couldn't lose focus on the purpose of my trip. Since I wasn't writing a story for *Hustler* or a similar publication, picturing Finn naked was not the way to go.

I didn't have any questions prepared, but Vick and the three other workers—Emma, Johnny ("Clumsy Smurf"), and Dean—made conversation easy. From the moment Finn walked away, they talked and talked . . . and talked. They spoke over and around each other, and my head whipped from side to side as I struggled to catch everything. I couldn't use Johnny's devotion to the paleo diet, Emma's argument with her mother about the safety of store-bought egg salad, or the video of Dean's son's solo in the church choir in the story, but all had excellent entertainment value.

Vick, the patriarch of the quartet, raised his voice over the others. "Since Adina's too polite to ask how any of this is relevant to her story, I will."

The three of them looked adequately chagrined, but it was Johnny who stepped forward. "I can show you a blueprint of a unit if it would help."

"I'd love to see one! A two-bedroom, maybe?" The enthusiastic response was more personal than professional. My city-loving mother would never agree to move here, but it couldn't hurt to check it out.

Johnny unfolded a long piece of construction paper and laid it on top of a stack of plywood the height of my belly.

Hovering over the floor plan, I focused immediately on the square footage as noted on the bottom of the page. A two-bedroom apartment at The Hollows was 1,314 square feet, as compared to the 900 square feet of my home. The master and second bedrooms were located on opposite sides of the unit for maximum privacy, with the common living/dining area and kitchen in the center. Based on what I could see in black and white (or blue and white, in this case), it was a great setup.

"Originally, there was going to be a washer and dryer in each unit, right here," Johnny said, pointing to a space on the floor plan next to the foyer now labeled Closet.

"What happened?"

"The Hollows was meant to be affordable luxury living. Finn made the point that in-unit washers and dryers would drive prices up and make it harder to attract the intended demographic—namely, buyers who couldn't afford the same frills closer to the city."

"It was Finn's idea, huh?" My lips tugged up with a will of their own. "Is that his job? I'm not too proud to admit I have zero clue what a project manager does."

Johnny laughed. "He's in charge of keeping us within budget and on schedule, among other things."

"Where did you end up putting the washers and dryers?" In my development, there was a common laundry room on the ground floor of each of the buildings.

"Each floor has three washers and dryers each. More luxurious than hauling your clothes on the elevator, but not so fancy that it drives prices sky-high."

"Clever fellow, that Finn. What's he like as a boss?" The answer wasn't relevant to the story, but it was important to me for some reason.

"Reasonable but tough. He runs a tight ship while acknowledging we're human beings with lives outside of this site."

"Mini Andrew even lets us have snack time and pee breaks," Emma, who was digging soil a few feet away, piped in.

My head drew back quickly. "Is that rare in your line of work?"

Her cheeks dimpled. "I'm teasing. Finn's all right. He doesn't treat the job like a hierarchy, expecting us to kiss the feet of His Royal Highness." She shrugged. "I'll be sad to see him go."

I frowned. "Is he going somewhere?"

"His 'passion project' awaits," Dean said, using air quotes.

Vick joined us. "Once The Hollows is up and running, he wants to move on to one of his boss's low-income housing projects."

My eyebrows shot up. "Really?" My research hadn't disclosed any interest from Hanes in low-income housing.

"Finn volunteered for Habitat for Humanity for years and then worked for them as a paid construction manager before Andrew Hanes scooped him up."

"Color me intrigued." My cheeks warmed as I realized I'd said that out loud. To avoid making eye contact with Vick, who was studying me curiously, I bent over and pretended to be engrossed in the floor plan.

But I made a mental note to ask Finn about his experience with Habitat for Humanity later. It didn't align with the back-story I'd imagined for him, which I supposed was why clichés like "Don't judge a book by its cover" existed. It was time to move on, at least for now. More knowledge about Finn wasn't going to get me the story.

With renewed focus, I asked if any of the crew were working on other properties for Hanes in town. When all answered in the negative, I took it up a notch. "Do you know if he has any other potential investments here?"

Among a chorus of nos and shaking heads, my phone rang—an unknown number with an 845 area code. I stepped to the side. "Hello?"

A deep voice replied, "Hi. Is this Adina?"

"Yes, it is. Who am I speaking to?"

"My name's Garrett. You left me a message last night."

*The handyman.* The corners of my mouth lifted in a smile. I could now cross "follow up with Garrett" from my afternoon to-do list. "Yes. Thanks for returning my call."

"Sorry it took so long. It's been a busy couple of days between mold removal from the Gordons' shower and a leaking toilet at the Smiths' place. I've been crawling around in muck."

I recoiled. *TMI.* "Um...sorry?" Feces and fungus. Gross. Two topics I wouldn't raise in my interview. I shook away the visual before I dry-heaved.

"You said you were a journalist from the city?"

"That's correct. I'm working on a story for an online magazine about the town and The Hollows. Do you live here in Pleasant Hollow?" Monica and Jennifer had implied as much, but after what happened with Davina, I'd confirm on my own, thank you very much.

"Only my entire life. I'd love to talk to you."

I pumped my fist in the air. "Great. When are you free to meet?"

"Now would be good."

"Meet me at the B&B in ten minutes?" After he confirmed, we ended the call.

I called out a goodbye and thank-you to my new friends, then glanced fleetingly at the office trailer. I was dying to know more about Finn's experience with Habitat for Humanity and his "passion project." But my work had to come first.

# Chapter Fourteen

"Thanks for meeting with me," Garrett said, his front teeth sparkling like a teeth-whitening commercial come to life as he smiled at me.

I pulled the neck of my shirt away from my chest and let it snap back. It was balmy in the common room of the B&B. Or maybe it was Garrett. He was a snack in mustard-colored overalls, and his biceps strained against the long-sleeved white T-shirt he wore underneath. "No, thank *you*. You're doing me a favor." I was saved from giggling like a schoolgirl when my phone, which was resting on my thigh under the table, pinged with a text message.

Who would play him?

Kate didn't need to clarify. I knew she meant in the movie. When Garrett had gotten up to refill his thermos of water (I found his carrying a thermos strangely fetching), I'd texted her that I'd found *the* single guy in town and was, at this very moment, interviewing him for my story. *Finn who?* I'd described Garrett as a sexy handyman, knowing Kate would respond right away, even if she was in the middle of a deposition or whatever lawyers did all day. I'd been right.

After giving him a rundown on the story I was writing, I asked my first question. "So, tell me a little bit about yourself and what you do here in Pleasant Hollow," I said, while debating my casting choices.

"Oh, I do everything for the folks in town, from plumbing to air conditioning, flooring, heat and cooling, roofing…"

I nodded in interest while slickly texting Kate back.

Steve Lund with lighter hair.
Can't talk. BRB.

"…kitchen and bath, remodeling, minor electrical issues, carpentry…"

I blinked. "Wow. You're a busy guy." Busy and sexy. But this was work, not play. "You mentioned you've lived in Pleasant Hollow your entire life. Are your parents still here too?" Proximity to extended family was big in the movies.

"Sure are. I built their new house."

I pictured Garrett and Finn, both with bare chests, in a dueling house-building competition. Talk about a provocative movie scene. I cleared my head of the distracting image. "Both of them are still alive?"

"And well!"

"Have you ever been married?" More of a personal question, but also relevant. This was a character profile, and including Garrett's relationship status would help flesh it out. The handyperson in the movies often had a partner or ex-partner.

"Not yet. Still searching for my person to meet at the

Empire State Building at midnight." He grinned like we shared a secret.

Except I wasn't in on it.

"You know... *Sleepless in Seattle. An Affair to Remember.* Or maybe Katz's Deli." He called over to Lorraine, "I'll have what she's having," and burst out laughing.

"Oh! Movies set in New York. Got it."

"What's dating like in the city?"

"How much time have you got?"

"Are you a Kat, Sutton, or Jane?"

I chuckled. My life was nothing like *The Bold Type*. "I've never thought about it. Jane, maybe? We're both journalists."

"Yes!" He slammed his palm on the table. "You're the quintessential New York City career girl. Like Carrie Bradshaw."

"That's the dream, at least." In an attempt to steer the conversation back to him, I asked, "Do you enjoy the freedom of working for yourself?"

"Can't complain." He leaned forward. "Is your boss more Miranda Priestly or Jacqueline Carlyle?"

There was no denying the man knew his Manhattan-based TV. It was too bad this article was about Pleasant Hollow. Ignoring *his* question, I asked another of my own. "What's your favorite part of living in a small town?"

"It's... hmm." He pushed his lips together in thought. "What's *your* favorite part of living in a big city?"

I would kill for a sesame bagel with cream cheese right now, but that wasn't it. "My mom and best friend are there. Speaking of friends, who do you like to hang out with? People you went to school with, or your clients? Do you have weekly poker nights or... or...?" I chewed on a nail. What did friend groups in the small-town TV movies do for fun? "Do you go Christmas caroling every year?" I refrained from rolling my eyes at my own cheese, but every activity my mind pulled up was holiday-related.

Garrett pulled a face. "Pfft."

I waited to be disappointed but must have finally numbed to Pleasant Hollow's lack of community-organized festivities. "What about ice skating?"

"There's IceTime Sports Complex, but it's in Newburgh." His cornflower-blue eyes lit up. "Your turn. Better rink: Rockefeller Center or Bryant Park? Go!"

"Bryant Park, no question." It was where Mom and Aunt Heather taught me and Kate to skate the year it opened. We went back every season.

"Cool. Cool. Cool. Are you best friends with the women from your magazine? Let me guess, you all meet in the fashion closet and talk about sex." He ran his tongue along his lower lip.

The room got even hotter, not out of lust for Garrett, but as the memory of Finn licking his finger after wiping my mouth the night before popped into my head. *So much for "Finn who?"* "I'm freelance and work remotely." And I would stay that way if I continued to let Garrett flip the roles of this question-and-answer session. "Back to you. Any fun anecdotes you can share about being a handyman in such a small town?"

He laughed. "Folks here are boring! What's it like living in Manhattan?"

"Like living anywhere else," I said with a clenched jaw, knowing it wasn't the glamorous answer he wanted. "Just busier. And louder. And more expensive." I laughed, brushing a hair from my eye.

"I'm sure it's nothing like Pleasant Hollow." He leaned in. "Do bars stay open all night?"

"Some do. Unlike Brothers Brewery."

He grinned. "What about cab drivers? Are they as wild as they're always portrayed?"

"Maybe?" I said, raising my palms. "I don't take many cabs, because of car sharing and the subw—"

"The subway! I've seen it in the movies." His cheeks rosy, he folded his hands in interest. "Have you ever been there when someone got pushed onto the tracks?"

My mouth fell open. "No! Thank God." His only reference to the subway was in the movies? Were we in upstate New York or Bluebell, Alabama?

"What about famous people? Do you see them everywhere?" Garrett's eyes glowed.

With a lift in my tone to lighten the mood, I said, "Who's interviewing who here?"

He looked sheepish. "I'm sorry. It's just... I'm obsessed with the city."

"I hadn't noticed," I said, more amused than annoyed. "Everyone's experience is different. And, yes, I've seen famous people, but it's not like it happens every day." I took a sip from my coffee mug.

"Anna Wintour. Have you seen her?"

Lukewarm coffee dribbled out of my nose. What was happening here? Of all the celebrities in the world, this ripped man in overalls was most curious if I'd seen the editor of *Vogue*? I wiped my mouth with the back of my hand and glanced around the room for hidden cameras. This entire interview had to be a joke. Had *Tea* set me up? Had *Finn* set me up? Unless he'd followed me from the construction site and was hiding behind the grandfather clock, he was not a witness to this interview. "Why don't you find out for yourself? Road trip?"

He clenched his teeth in a grimace. "Oh no. I couldn't do that."

"Why? It's so close. I came here by bus and didn't even use a half day of travel."

"The muggings. The cockroaches. Did you ever see *Rats*?" He shook his upper half exaggeratedly. "I couldn't."

And I couldn't believe my ears. He both revered and feared Manhattan, based only on what he saw in television and movies.

*Who are you to talk?* My heart hiccupped in horror. How was Garrett making assumptions about life in the big city, using iconic movies and shows like *Sex and the City* and *The Bold Type*, any different than what I'd done with small towns?

I shrugged off the comparison. This was different. Wasn't it? I squeezed my eyes shut. This wasn't the time for self-analysis. I had a story to write. Or not write. I wiped down the table, catching my spilled coffee before it trickled onto the wood floor.

In one last-ditch effort, I asked, "How do you feel about The Hollows? Anything you're afraid will change for you personally or professionally with the influx of new people?" Latching on to his last comment, I added, "Are you afraid the crime rate will go up?"

"What's the murder rate in New York City? Is it true the stories from *SVU* are ripped from the headlines?"

I sighed. Over the next two minutes, Garrett asked if I lived near Times Square, how many times I'd been mugged, and if I'd ever gone to the Radio City Christmas Spectacular. Finally, I told him I had to bounce to FaceTime with my ex-model cousin who'd just been released from jail for drug dealing. I had no such cousin, but why not play into the fabulous yet dangerous world Garrett had conjured up for me in New York City? He ate it up. At least one of us got what they needed from this interview. I was spent, but as I clambered up the stairs to my room for a much-needed nap, I received another text from Kate.

> Call me later. I want all the
> deets. #winning.

My lower extremities took a deep dive. If having zero material for a story due in a little more than a week was winning, I hated to think what losing looked like.

# Chapter Fifteen

A few minutes later, I sat cross-legged on the bed with my laptop, notepad, and phone set out in front of me, determined to climb out of the hole I'd fallen into and come up with a workable story angle.

The character profiles of Pleasant Hollow residents with romance-movie-like careers had been a clever idea that hadn't panned out the way I'd hoped. Davina would have been perfect, aside from the significant snag of not living in Pleasant Hollow. And Garrett had been great on paper, but not so much in the flesh. My mind conjured up an image of his thick, rock-solid thighs straining against the denim of his overalls. Scratch that. He was a *fine* specimen in the flesh, but how could I use him as the poster boy for the "real-life" small-town handyman when he'd provided minimal details about his life in Pleasant Hollow? Why had I let him turn our meeting into a Q&A about New York City instead? My chest caved in embarrassment. Garrett was like me in reverse, only taller and with bigger muscles: City girl enamored with small town meets small-town guy obsessed with the big city. *That* was a story. Too bad I was too mortified to tell it. *Moving on.*

There had to be something I could utilize, though, either from my at-home research, the historical facts about the town I'd collected since arriving (most provided by Finn, of all people), and/or the multitude of pictures I'd taken, to develop a different story.

From the photos of Main Street, the park, the waterfront, and even the exteriors of Pinkie's Diner, Brothers Brewery, and the Oven (most of them filtered for optimal effect), Pleasant Hollow could easily pass for a quintessential small town. Unfortunately, it was a façade, like a movie set. The name "Hollow" was apt, given the people who resided there.

Okay, that wasn't fair. The residents of Pleasant Hollow weren't *bad* people. (Not all of them, anyway. My memory latched on to the elderly couple on the street who'd glared at me in response to my friendly smile.) But the real-life innkeeper, waitress, and handyman were nothing like their novel and movie counterparts. *Nothing*.

There was no sense of community. The townspeople mostly stayed in their own lanes. And come to think of it, I hadn't seen a single dog since I'd arrived. Cuddly and often charmingly misbehaving dogs made an appearance in the majority of books and films set in cozy small towns. I hadn't seen any kitties either. Seriously, what did Pleasant Hollow have against domestic animals (and pie)?

I could own my naivete in thinking all small towns were like the fictional Evergreen and Angel Falls. But the story I'd been contracted to write had been pitched as a Hallmark movie come to life. At this point, I'd have to use significant literary license or flat-out lie to make it work. I couldn't...*wouldn't*...do either. To add spoiled cream to my stale coffee, not a single person had expressed concern about The Hollows, which meant I was currently zero for two with both aspects of my story. What could I write about? A new condo complex going up in a not-so-special town equaled a whole lot of nothing.

Still scrolling my photos, my finger froze on a picture of the statue of Natalie Schull, the ballerina. According to Natalie's Wikipedia page, she was born here in 1961 and joined the New York City Ballet at seventeen before making the leap to Broadway and winning a Tony for her role in a revival of *Sweet Charity*. After she retired from performing at the turn of the century, she moved across the pond to teach at the Royal Ballet School, where she still resided with her British choreographer husband. Connecting with her would be difficult given the geography, and even if I reached her parents, assuming they were still alive and hadn't left Pleasant Hollow, then what?

Derek hadn't commissioned me to write about a retired ballerina/Broadway star/dance instructor who fled Pleasant Hollow at the first opportunity. Especially since, unlike her Hallmark alter ego, she didn't move back for a second chance at love with her high school sweetheart. There was nothing Hallmark about it. It was too depressing to expend more thought on, so I closed my laptop and placed it on the floor next to my bed. Then I slipped under the covers for a nap.

I jolted at the sound of my phone ringing—Derek. My scalp prickled with unease at the unexpected contact over a week before my deadline, but I had to answer. There was no way I could sleep wondering what he wanted. "Hi, Derek. How are you?" I pushed the sheet off my chest and yawned with my free hand covering my mouth.

"The movie about the mom-and-pop cookie factory in danger of being shut down by the corporate agent."

It was the longest sentence he'd ever uttered to me.

"Seen it?" he asked.

"Of course!" I winced. *Take it down a notch.* "I mean, yes, I have."

"We're watching it now. Not exactly like your story. But close."

I assumed by "we," he meant himself and his wife, and I wished the reason for his call was as easily deciphered.

"Yes. It's similar, but not identical," I said, repeating his sentiment, just with different words.

"How's small-town life? Spill it here." He laughed.

"It's going great," I lied.

"That's all you've got for me? 'It's going great'?"

"I don't want to give anything away and spoil the surprise." I ground my teeth in a grimace, then poured it on even thicker. "But the town is everything I expected it to be and more. I promise you'll be impressed."

"I believe it. The cookie movie had four million viewers. Match that with your story, and the full-time job is yours."

Four *million*? The listicles I'd published during my temporary gig at *Tea* had each garnered somewhere between five thousand and fifteen thousand views. My blood ran cold. Was he out of his mind? "I'm not sure I can—"

"Ha!" Derek's laughter reverberated through the phone line at such a high volume over the next several moments, Finn could probably hear it in his room. "Oh, Adina. Of course I don't expect your story to be read by four million people." The cackling continued.

My body begged to be relieved of the tension he'd just caused, but I was still afraid to breathe.

"Let's aim for twenty thousand unique hits. And send me your résumé with the completed article."

"Will do!" I accepted his challenge of reaching twenty thousand readers with an outward confidence that disguised how doubtful I was in my ability to stream together even four hundred words.

After we ended the call, I turned the phone on silent and crawled back under the covers into the fetal position. How did I get here? Derek had finally green-lit one of my pitches and I'd blown it. And rather than come clean, I'd full-on lied to him. *I promise you'll be impressed.* I called him Der*Dick*, but what if the problem was me, not him? Maybe he knew something I didn't—that I was a decent stand-in for a real journalist in a pinch but didn't have what it took to do it for a living.

I swatted the notion away like a fly and closed my eyes. It wasn't over until it was over. If I was lucky, my dreams would show me the way out of this mess or at least inspire me in the right direction.

I opened my eyes and stretched out in bed, then checked the time on my phone. It was past seven. I'd napped for almost three hours and missed a text from Kate, undoubtedly inquiring about Garrett.

> Please tell me you're still with the sexy handyman. How many interrupted kisses have you guys had so far?

I snorted. If I had been about to lock lips with Garrett, I'd have told the interloper, probably Lorraine, to take a hike. Speaking of Lorraine, if this were a movie, she'd show concern

I had locked myself in my room all day and knock on my door with a pot of Earl Grey tea and a plate of gingerbread cookies. But as I'd established, this wasn't a movie, and the only edible matter in my room was the coffee dregs in my to-go cup and a red-and-white-striped peppermint hard candy I'd plucked from the nail salon after my interview. I was starving. I considered my choices. Pinkie's or the Oven. The Oven or Pinkie's. While I decided, I texted Kate back.

Plot twist. To be continued.

A full explanation would require me to admit out loud how worried I was. I was still hanging by a thread of hope that a solution would magically appear, but if it didn't, I knew Kate would be there to brainstorm or give me a virtual hug. Either way, I would call her soon. She had a life too, and I wanted to hear what was new in it.

After a quick freshen-up—specifically, two swipes of deodorant and a teeth brushing—I slipped into my jacket and grabbed my phone from where I'd tossed it on the bed. On the screen was a notification of a new email I'd received from the coffee shop. The preview was enough to get the gist of the entire message. They wanted to know if I was picking up shifts for the following week. Was I? Would I need more time to finish the story? Could I afford to give up another paycheck? Should I call it quits and check out tomorrow?

I didn't know the answer to any of those questions. All I knew was I was no longer hungry...for food anyway. I needed a drink.

# Chapter Sixteen

"Where are you off to?"

I stopped at the top of the stairs and turned to face Finn, who was leaning against his open hotel room door, filling the frame completely with his broad torso and holding a glass of water.

"Brothers."

"Don't waste your time. They're not open tonight."

"What? Why?" I frowned. "Is it a holiday?"

"It's Dungeons and Dragons night." His eyes twinkled. "Which, to the cousins, is a holiday. A weekly one."

"I won't even bother to ask for more details. Anywhere else serve alcohol in this town?"

Finn pointed his elbow behind him. "Finn's Tavern is open for business if you want to join me."

My shoulders tensed. Finn's Tavern had four walls enclosing a small space, a bed, booze, and Finn. Finn and a bed. My fantasy from the night before of the two of us, naked, sharing a bottle of wine, sprang to mind. But it was the only gig in town. "Is it BYOB? Because I don't have anything."

"I have plenty more where this came from," he said, raising his glass.

I wanted what he was having, which wasn't water after all. And if I was being honest, I really enjoyed Finn's company, city boy or not. I was also dying to know about his "passion project," but I'd wait until it fit naturally into the conversation before prying. "Count me in."

He smiled and held the door open for me to walk through. His room was similar to mine, only the color scheme was a softer blue and gray, and there was an exposed brick wall behind his queen-size bed.

Focusing my attention everywhere except the bed, I stood awkwardly while he knelt over his mini-fridge.

"I have a six-pack of Heineken and small bottles of Tanqueray, Tito's, Crown Royal, and tonic water."

"Wow. That's quite a selection."

A flush crossed his cheeks. "This project drives me to drink sometimes," he said, rubbing his neck. "But I keep it to one or two."

I waved a hand. "You're over the legal drinking age. No need to justify."

He laughed. "Sorry. Been a long day." He pointed at the refrigerator. "What's your poison?"

"G&T. Thanks."

"Lime?"

Accustomed to men back home pouring Two-Buck Chuck into a Solo cup and expecting me to drop my panties, I jerked my head back at Finn's offering of fresh lime. "Yes, please." I watched him prepare my drink. I also blatantly checked out his ass. My time with Garrett had done nothing to defuse my attraction to Finn.

"For you." Finn handed me my drink and motioned to a

wooden rocking chair with a pastel-blue seat cover. He sat on the edge of his bed and raised his glass. "Cheers."

"L'chaim." I took a sip. "Mm. This is good."

"I aim to please. So, how'd it go at the construction site? My guys help at all?"

"Unfortunately not, but they're great. Tell me about your time with Habitat for Humanity." So much for easing into the topic organically, but I was a journalist. Asking questions was what I did.

Finn blinked at me. "What do you mean?"

"Your crew told me Andrew Hanes recruited you from there," I said.

"What else did they tell you?" He stood and paced the room.

Had I raised a sore subject? "Um…something about a passion project."

"Motherfucker. Do those guys know how to keep their mouths shut?"

Gin and tonic spilled from my cup as it shook in my hand. "It's my fault. I asked what you were like to work with, and they said you were pretty great. Then they said you might be leaving them to work on a low-income housing project. Was it a secret?" The last thing I wanted was to rat out his staff.

He scraped a hand up his jaw. "Sorry. It's not a secret. You just caught me off guard."

"I was surprised too. Andrew Hanes doesn't strike me as someone who cares about the less fortunate. I imagined you building billion-dollar homes for people who could afford it, not volunteering to build houses for people who can't."

Finn narrowed his eyes. "Once again, what do you have

against my boss?" He relaxed his shoulders. "Fine. Building lower-income housing comes with a government tax credit, so it's not completely altruistic." He pointed at me. "Don't look at me like that. He's not a bad guy."

I smirked. "So, tell me about the passion project."

He sat back down. "I never wanted to be involved in luxury real estate, but it was his condition I get The Hollows up and running before he'd let me do what he hired me for, which is to help develop permanently affordable housing in low-income communities."

"It's an interesting passion."

"I was homeless."

"You were...wow..." Realizing I had no idea how to respond, I clamped my mouth shut. What was the proper reply to a disclosure of this magnitude? It was so unexpected and frankly shocking. "I'm so sorry." *I'm sorry? Really?* It was just, living day-to-day not knowing where I'd find shelter for the night was a reality so foreign to my own. It was a privilege I'd taken for granted until I was today years old. My heart ached for Finn, who hadn't been as fortunate. His time with Habitat for Humanity made a lot of sense now.

He lowered his gaze. "It was a long time ago. After my mom died, my dad, older sister, and I lived in his car and from shelter to shelter for almost a year. Making sure others have a roof over their heads is important to me. It's a part of my past I don't like to talk about." His eyes met mine again with a silent plea to drop the subject.

I could take a hint. "Your boss reminds me of my editor, with his *conditions*. The full-time position can be mine only if this story does well." I stopped rocking and tapped a foot along the wood floor. "I can't really blame him. Why pay me a regular salary and health benefits if my freelance story tanks?"

"It won't tank."

"It might." I rubbed my lip. He'd confessed to being homeless, and that was huge. I could be honest too. "The apartment where I live with my mom is losing rent-stabilized status when our current lease expires. It's why I need a full-time job, stat. My mom pays all the rent herself. I never planned to live with her forever—"

"Sure you didn't."

"Ha ha." I laughed off the teasing while secretly fearing that a twenty-five-year-old woman living with her mother would be a turnoff to a man who kept fresh lime in his hotel room. "She'd never kick me out, but I hate that I can't afford to contribute more or get my own place. And I'm not sure she'd want to move anyway. We've lived there since I was four. She loves it."

"What about you? Do you love it?"

I met his eyes. "I live in a perpetual love-hate relationship with the city. It was closer to hate when I left to come here."

"You want to talk about it?"

"No." Admit to Finn I blamed the city and its residents for my failure to launch in career and love? Absolutely not.

He winked. "Gotcha. Is your building allowed to raise the rent? Is it legal?"

"I only skimmed the paperwork, but between my mom's increased income and the improvements they've made to the common areas, like the lobby and elevators, I don't think we have a basis to stop them." I shrugged. "My best friend is a lawyer. I can ask her."

"You should."

I nodded. "Anyway, it's not the same as being homeless. Please don't think I'm making the comparison. But we're in danger of losing our home, and I'm scared."

"So write this story and get the full-time position."

There was so much sincerity in his expression, it threatened to steal my breath. "You make it sound so simple."

"Why is it complicated?" Finn leaned toward me, keeping his hands on the edge of the bed.

I took a sip of my drink. The clinking noise of the ice moving around the glass was the only sound in the room. "I compared Pleasant Hollow to a Hallmark movie town in my pitch, so, well, you tell me why it's complicated."

He clucked his tongue. "No pie. No corn maze. No Oktoberfest. No warmth."

"You watch Hallmark movies too, huh?" I teased, in an attempt to lighten the mood.

"I have a sister. And I've dated one or two women in my life."

Something sharp poked at my gut at the thought of Finn with a girlfriend. "So you must know that in the movies, a city developer coming to town is always a bad thing and the locals lose their minds over it."

Finn's lips formed a circle like he was about to whistle. "This explains your antagonism toward my boss."

I squirmed. "For my story to work, he's supposed to be the enemy."

"Let me guess. No one hates him?"

"No one I could find."

Finn's eyes gleamed.

"Don't rub it in."

His mouth formed a thin line. "Do *you* think The Hollows is bad for the town?"

I thought of nightly happy hours, convenient businesses in the lobby, and direct shuttles to the city for commuters. "I plead the Fifth. I don't want to incriminate myself."

He stared me down for a beat. "Off the record."

"Off the record, this town could use some enhancements. The food sucks. The beer is...*functional* at best. And would it kill them to have a carnival? A farmers' market? Something *townie*." I was rambling. And Finn was looking at me funny. "What?"

"Adi." His eyes gleamed. "Not all small towns are like what you see on TV. And when they are, some are more like *Deliverance* than Hallmark."

"I'm well aware," I growled, even as my belly flipped at his use of my nickname. "Were you listening when I said my story rests on the comparison to Hallmark?"

He stopped laughing. "No. You're right. This is your career at stake. What are you going to do?"

"I don't know. I have to find something quaint, cozy, and community-centric about Pleasant Hollow without lying. The struggle is real."

"While you're working on it, can I make you another drink?"

Something pulled in my chest. All I'd wanted to do after this disaster of a day was drown my sorrows in mediocre beer all by myself. Sharing a drink with Finn hadn't inspired a miraculous breakthrough in my story, but it had drastically improved my mood. Hooking up with the city guy wasn't in the script, yet there wasn't a molecule inside me that didn't want to stay for another G&T and talk more. And if talking led to kissing, then... Especially since it didn't look like I'd be including The Hollows in my story, thus removing any conflict of interest.

"Adi?" Finn studied me curiously.

I nodded and held out my glass. "I'd love another drink." *And for you to keep saying my name: Adi. Adi. Adi.*

A minute later, he handed me a fresh G&T. "You asked about me, huh?"

"What?" I bent to pick up the napkin I'd dropped on the floor.

"You asked my staff what I'm like to work with. What was that about?"

I froze as heat whipped across my cheeks. "Oh, that." I straightened, fully expecting to face Finn's cocky grin. Instead, he looked almost bashful, like he'd dipped his toe in flirting and worried he'd be met with icy water. My insides turned to goo. There was nothing wrong with acting on a crush as long as I didn't expect a physical connection to lead to a happily ever after.

"It was a strictly professional question. For my story." It wasn't, and he knew it.

"I figured as much." He stared at me.

I stood.

"Going somewhere?"

"I just need to stretch." When I raised my arms over my head, my sweater rose above my belly and I hoped Finn would have the same reaction to my bare navel as I'd had to his. I watched his gaze travel from my stomach and linger there. *Yup.* I approached the bed and sat next to him. "You mentioned dating."

"What about it?"

"Do you have a girlfriend? Or anyone you're seeing regularly?" I purposely asked the question both ways since hot guys in the city tended to be creative in their definition of "girlfriend." They could sleep with the same woman every week for a year and claim it wasn't a relationship because they'd never "discussed" it. Case in point: Leo. I didn't encroach on other women's territory, even for a hookup.

"Why do you ask?" And there it was: the "I'm hot and I know it" grin I'd expected earlier. "Anyway, I'm very much available."

If he was lying, it wouldn't be the first time, but the question had been asked and answered. It was up to me to take him at his word, and I would. "You have something in your…" I brushed a finger through his hair and removed the imaginary lint, food crumb, whatever. It didn't matter since it was imaginary. "Hair." The strands felt soft and silky against my skin, with no evidence of sticky pomade or gel like I'd assumed.

"Thank you." He wove a few of his fingers through mine. "You do too."

I giggled. "Kiss me, you fool."

He leaned in. I leaned in. The air fizzed between us.

*Brriiinng! Brriiinng!*

I jumped.

Finn cursed. "I've gotta take this." He stood and walked to the opposite side of the room. "It's fine. What's up?" He threw an apologetic glance my way.

I let my back fall against the bed with a frustrated sigh. A giggle bubbled inside of me at our kiss-interruptus. It figured the one thing that came straight from the movies involved me *not* kissing a hot guy.

Kate would die. I owed her a phone call. I was a bad friend. At least my almost-kiss with Finn gave me something to tell her about besides my story fail. Did Derek check up on all his writers mid-assignment or just me?

Finn's bed was comfy. I was tempted to crawl inside for another nap. Why was I so lethargic? I'd bet it was lack of exercise. A body in motion stayed in motion. But without a gym in town, my options were limited. A run along the river would be nice—minus the running part. I wasn't a fan. What did the locals do for exercise? I doubted they all drove to Newburgh.

I sucked in a breath and sat up. Most people cited inconvenience as their excuse for not working out, and commuting by car to another town was certainly inconvenient. Which meant the residents of Pleasant Hollow were probably seriously out of shape.

Why couldn't I organize a town-wide exercise program while I was here like Zoe did in *Hart of Dixie*? It would do wonders for the town's collective health and bond them as a community. More importantly, I could use it in my piece as a bona fide example of one of the close-knit town's "community events." My brain whirred with ideas. Maybe I didn't need to stop at an exercise campaign. I'd only been half-serious when I'd mentioned it to Finn, but why not also approach the cousins about hosting Oktoberfest?

My insides tingled with excitement. This could work. With some adjustments, Pleasant Hollow could live up to its quaint, cozy, and community-centric potential. I vaulted off the bed, eager to form a solid plan, but my chest tightened at the sight of Finn on the phone. His expression was pinched, but every so often, he'd glance up at me and smile. He was adorable. It was too bad our goals were at odds. My plan to bring the town closer together could negatively impact his purposes if it united them *against* outsiders. I liked the guy…a lot…but we barely knew each other. I had to put my career before lust and deliver the story I promised. He'd understand.

On a piece of notepaper, I scribbled, *Gotta go. Have idea for story. Talk tomorrow.* I held it in front of him.

His eyes scrolled the paper and his lips formed a smile. "Good luck," he mouthed.

I whispered "Thanks" and let myself out.

# Chapter Seventeen

When I got back to my room, I called Kate to brainstorm ideas. And brainstorm we did. Kate tossed out suggestions like a champ. She was like the Energizer Bunny until I reminded her I needed to create only enough shared experiences to make for a convincing story about a Hallmark-like town.

"You *must* have some sort of baking competition. Like pie making."

"No pie!" I practically shouted into the phone.

"*Okaaay*, no pie. What about cupcakes or gingerbread houses?"

"Pleasant Hollow doesn't seem to like sweets." I peered out my window. It looked like it was going to rain.

"That's crazy talk."

"But I could ask Pinkie's Diner to sponsor something culinary, like a *MasterChef: Pleasant Hollow*." *Maybe?*

"And all the profits from the entry fee can go toward planning the Christmas parade!"

"What Christmas parade?"

"There's no Christmas parade? Is there at least a tree-lighting ceremony in the town square? Have mercy on me and lie if you have to."

"Yes, of course. There's also an ice sculpture contest and a town-wide snowball fight."

"That's more like it."

I laughed for a beat, until a negative thought popped my amused bubble. "How am I going to convince the town to do any of this? They don't know me."

Silence filled the airwaves between our phones, and then Kate yelled, "Got it!"

I braced myself for what I hoped was pure genius.

"You can take the floor at the next town hall meeting and propose the ideas."

My shoulders dropped. "I don't live here, and honestly, I'm not sure there even is a town hall in Pleasant Hollow, or any meetings for that matter." Kate still hadn't accepted this wasn't a movie town. "I'll check, though."

I heard the sound of tapping on a keyboard. "You're right. The town is too small for its own mayor, but there is a town legislator. Her name is Lorraine Jenkins."

"Did you say Lorraine?"

"Yes, why?"

"That's the name of the woman who runs the B&B."

"There you go."

I fell back on my bed. "She doesn't like me."

"Everyone likes you."

"Honestly, the only people who've been friendly to me, besides Finn—"

"Ooh, Finn! The hottie from the B&B. Do tell. Who is he? The town sheriff? Vet?"

"Not quite. He's actually not a local at all. I'll get to him later."
I stood and paced the room. "But I met two women my first
night who might agree to be the town faces for these activities."
Monica could take the lead on the exercise program. Jennifer
might be able to help me convince the cousins to host an Oktoberfest. They already had picnic benches. It would be perfect. "I'll
have to sort out the details later. Maybe I can call in favors with
friends at New York Fitness Club to come up for the day and
teach yoga or Pilates in the park before it gets way too cold."

"This all sounds great, Adi."

I bounced lightly in place. "Thank you for dropping everything to help me. Are you still at work?" Her job often required
long hours.

"I'm home. And no need to thank me. You know I live for
this stuff."

I grinned. I did know that.

"Besides, it was a great distraction."

"Distraction from what? What's going on with you?"

"Oh, nothing." She sneezed.

My Spidey senses went up; Kate had a tell when she lied.
"You sneezed."

She sighed loudly. "Adina. Sometimes a sneeze is just a
sneeze." She sneezed again.

"Is it Diego?" Until now, Kate's romantic relationship had
been blessedly free of drama.

"No. He's great."

"Work?"

"No." *Achoo.*

My pulse picked up. "What's happening at work? Tell me. I'll
get it out of you eventually. It's what I do."

"I failed the bar."

"You failed the..." I gasped. "Oh my God. I'm so sorry." Kate had been a ghost all through winter, spring, and the early part of summer while studying for her bar exam this July. She'd holed herself in her apartment most nights and weekends. "When did you get the results?" I slid to the floor by the window with my legs stretched out in front of me.

"Last week." Her voice was pained. "I haven't broken the news to my parents yet."

"Shit. Why didn't you tell me?" I pressed my hands to the floor to stand up, then changed my mind. "Never mind. It's not about me. What are you going to do? Is there anything *I* can do? Do you want me to draft a note to your mom and dad to break the news? I can spin it positively. Or write a letter of recommendation to the bar association?"

When we were little and got in trouble for one thing or another, I'd draft cute notes of apology, like "Kate and Adi are sorry we played Frisbee with your favorite plate and broke it. Here are some daffodils we pulled from the Oval." I was also in charge of specialized birthday cards naming all the reasons we loved our mommies—and in her case, daddy and little brother—and pleas to go shopping for the newest hot toy or fashion accessory.

"I'll pass when I take it again in February, but it looks bad. The partners treat me differently now, and the associates are smug."

"You're probably imagining it." Even as the words left my mouth, I knew they weren't true. Higher-ups were fickle, and peers could be competitive in any industry. *Fuck.* "I hate that I'm not there."

"You'll be home soon. Get me drunk as my last hurrah before I lock myself up again."

"Deal."

"Tell me something good. If Finn isn't a townie, who is he? Who's hotter, him or the handyman?"

"Finn. No contest." I caught her up on the latest with Finn since my initial assumption he was a local, from learning he worked for the real estate developer to our almost-kiss less than an hour ago.

"I cannot believe you had an interrupted kiss. Was it as annoying as it is on TV?"

"Worse. And now I can't yell at the characters for letting it happen. It's harder to recover from an interrupted kiss than it looks."

"Ha! I knew you'd meet someone in a small town."

"You said I'd meet a local, not another city guy. I could have just as easily met Finn on Tinder or at a bar. It doesn't count."

"Why not?"

"If history is any indication, hooking up with city-boy Finn is a one-way trip to nowhere."

"You shouldn't make assumptions. You've had bad luck, but not every guy is like Leo or the other losers you've dated. There are plenty of men in New York City who want to be in a serious relationship and just haven't met the right girl yet." She raised her voice. "You could be that girl for Finn."

"Simmer down now. I'm A-OK with a fling."

"He passed your test?"

"With flying colors." A fling between me and Finn might not qualify for romcom status, but that didn't mean it wouldn't be fun.

Kate sniffled. "Hmm, banging the Big Bad Wolf from the city is not typical leading-lady behavior. But you have my blessing."

"The Big Bad Wolf's *helper*. And let's not get ahead of ourselves. We're not at that scene yet."

"What happens next?"

I smiled. "I create warmth and kinship in this cold, dead-end town, one community-building initiative at a time."

# Chapter Eighteen

My first stop was Brothers. Of all the ideas we'd brainstormed, Kate and I agreed Oktoberfest had the most potential as a far-reaching community event. What was more festive than beer, singing, and revelry?

"And why would we do that?" The younger cousin, Aaron, draped a dishtowel over his shoulder and leaned over the bar.

"Because it'll be a fun way to get the town together," I said.

"And day drinking. Hello!" Jennifer, who I'd brought along for local support, piped in.

Fortunately, there were only three Jennifers from Pleasant Hollow on Facebook, and her public profile picture confirmed her identity since you couldn't count on running into someone on the street exactly when you needed to, even in a town as small as Pleasant Hollow. I had an entire speech prepared for our phone call, but she'd stopped me mid-sentence and said, "You had me at Oktoberfest." She agreed to help me convince the cousins to get on board. I'd been certain the young brewery owners would share her enthusiasm.

I nodded my agreement and pointed at her. "What she said. Everyone loves an excuse to drink during the day."

Aaron scrubbed down the bar. "Why do we need a formal Oktoberfest? It'll be October. We'll be open. Isn't that enough?"

I glanced around the almost-empty space. "Think of all the money you'd make. You can advertise it as a special event, maybe even bring in customers from the neighboring towns."

He stopped scrubbing and studied me as if considering.

"Cold Spring has a beer festival every summer. They charge twenty-five a head!"

He wrinkled his nose. "But we'd need to open early. So much work."

I half expected him to stamp his feet like a petulant child. *What a lazy son of a . . .* "You can ask some of the townspeople to volunteer. I'm a barista. Not quite a bartender, but I can pour beer and deliver it to tables, and I know how to use a cash register." I'd be back in the city by then but would come up for the day if it meant sealing this deal.

"I'd help too," Jennifer said. "You can pay me in free beer."

I beamed at my new friend. I *loved* her.

"What do you say?" I crossed my fingers behind my back.

Aaron glanced at his older cousin, who'd been quiet until now. "What do you think?"

Greg pulled his ponytail tighter. "We're not even German."

"It doesn't matter," I said, careful to keep my voice steady. "Not everyone who celebrates St. Patrick's Day is Irish either. It's an excuse to drink." I looked to Jennifer, hoping she'd back me up.

She shrugged. "I'm out."

I jerked my head back. "What do you mean 'you're out'?"

"We tried. They don't want to do it. Want to share a pitcher while we're here?"

My lips parted in confusion. "No!" I didn't want to drink ass beer right now. One of Finn's G&Ts would hit the spot, though. I suddenly missed him passionately, which was ridiculous, considering I'd just seen him the night before and had only known him for three days.

Jennifer glared at me.

Crap. I hadn't meant to yell at her. I backpedaled. "I mean, not right now. Thanks." What I *wanted* was to convince the cousins to sponsor a two-day event. I'd settle for one. Besides, it wasn't five o'clock *anywhere*, except maybe Asia, but I didn't have time to work out the time difference.

After Jennifer left us for a more willing drinking buddy, I yanked my phone out of my purse and searched #Oktoberfest on Instagram, hoping to show Aaron and Greg what they'd be missing out on. Pictures of attractive busty women in low-cut tops and traditional Bavarian skirts instantly filled the page. A lot of close-ups of cleavage. A guy holding a liter of beer. More cleavage shots. I scrolled faster, sensing the cousins losing interest. The images didn't really represent the laid-back party atmosphere I was going for, and I couldn't imagine anyone in Pleasant Hollow wearing those costumes. I was running out of ideas. More cleavage. Wait. *Cleavage.* I shoved my phone in Greg's face. "See?"

His mouth fell open. There might have been drool.

"You like that, huh?" *Of course you do, you pig.* "The closest Oktoberfest is in Poughkeepsie. You'd make bank."

Aaron peered over his shoulder and they continued to scroll. "Check her out!"

"How come some of them are so buttoned up and others are so..." Their eyes widened, probably from fawning over a busty woman. "Nice!"

"What the hell is that dude wearing?"

Laughing ensued.

Curious, I leaned over the bar. "It's a traditional men's costume. Lederhosen."

"Lederhosen? *Loser*-hosen is more like it." The two snort-laughed.

I pretended to join their mirth even though my eyes were desperate to roll to the ceiling. "Doesn't it look fun?"

The two continued to scroll, point, and laugh.

"Guys?"

They raised their heads. "Huh?"

"What do you say?"

They stared at me with glazed expressions.

"You in?"

They locked eyes in a private silent conversation, turned back to me, and at the same time said, "Nah."

Pounding my fist against the bar, I said, "Your loss," before plucking my phone from their hands and giving them my back. They were still laughing about loser-hosen and tits, and planning a road trip to Poughkeepsie when I reached the exit. I should have given up while I was behind. But I couldn't. Not yet. There was too much riding on this. Next stop: Pinkie's.

"The diner in my grandparents' town held a contest where the people had to come up with a new menu idea, like a grilled brie-and-honey sandwich or avocado toast with Cajun corn and tomatoes. The winner had the dish named after them." I beamed at Doreen. "It totally revived the place." To my knowledge, no such contest was ever held at the Sunshine Diner in Boca Raton, but she wouldn't take me seriously if she knew the idea came from a made-for-television movie.

"Evita. Is that your name?"

I bit my lip. "Close. It's Adina."

"I'm just the waitress here. For any contests or speed-dating, eighties nights, karaoke, or singles' events you suggest, you'd need to speak with the owner, Judie. But she's in Djibouti."

"Judie's in Djibouti? Ha!"

Doreen blinked. "Yes. She's on a snorkeling adventure."

"Do you know when Judie will be back from Djibouti?" I pressed a fist to my lips to keep from laughing in Doreen's stoic face again. Apparently only one of us saw the humor.

"Not for another three weeks. Sorry." She hustled to the other side of the counter before I could say anything further. But it didn't matter. I'd been dismissed.

With my head low, I made my way to the exit and, WHOOMP, right into Finn on his way in. I slowly backed away, but not before intentionally drawing in a deep inhale. Whatever detergent he used smelled like lavender, cedar, and deliciously clean man.

"Easy there." He placed his hands on my shoulders to keep me steady. "What's wrong?" He frowned. "Don't tell me you're still upset about the no-pie situation."

I managed a smile. He was like the sun breaking through a cloudy day. "No. I just..." I drew in a breath and released it. "My plan isn't coming together the way I hoped."

"You have a minute to sit?" He angled his head toward the counter I'd just vacated.

"Sure. But can we get a table?" I didn't want to talk in front of Doreen.

I followed him to a booth in the back and gave him the SparkNotes version. "With just a little guidance from me, I thought Pleasant Hollow could become the sort of quintessential small town portrayed in the movies and my story wouldn't be DOA." I gazed longingly at the bacon on Finn's plate. My mom's parents hadn't kept kosher in their home and neither did she. As a result, I enjoyed my share of BLTs and cheeseburgers.

"Take."

"Thanks." I plucked a piece from the top. "What do you think?" *Crunch.* The bacon was expertly cooked—well done, with just the right amount of thickness. It was too bad a bacon-frying competition was off the table.

"It sounds like a lot of work just for a story."

My muscles tensed. "It's not *just* a story. You know that."

He raised a hand. "I know. It's the story that can jump-start your career. It's just—"

"You think it's stupid, don't you?"

"Not stupid. Ambitious."

"I finally got my foot in the door after months…" Bite. *Crunch.* Swallow. "*Years* of rejections and drafting vapid content for no credit while surviving on my big dreams. Then I came up with this story and actually got a contract. I have to make it work." I *had* to. "I can't bear to start over from scratch after getting so close, especially with things up in the air with my mom's and my future living situation." My voice shook. Despite lagging behind some of my peers in terms of still living at home in my mid-twenties, it had never occurred to me that option could be taken away. It was a sentiment I didn't dare express in present company.

Finn studied me thoughtfully. "Like I said, it's ambitious. But if anyone can make it work, it's you."

I laughed. "You don't even know me!"

"True." He grinned sheepishly. "But it's the sort of encouragement the guy in the movie would offer when trying to woo the romantic lead. Isn't it?"

My knees wobbled under the table. "Are you trying to woo me, Mr. Adams?"

"Is it working?" He placed his hand over mine.

"Maybe." *Definitely.* I was over fighting it.

"To be continued." He motioned for the check. "Where are you off to next?"

"I don't know. I had high hopes for Brothers and Pinkie's and got nothing."

"Only because the cousins are clueless and Judie's in Djibouti." His lips twitched.

My belly flipped. *I like you.*

"There are at least two other businesses in this town."

"You speak the truth." I hadn't exhausted all of my and Kate's ideas *quite* yet.

"I'm pulling for you."

My knees went soft at his words. Did he mean them, or was he toying with me? I searched his face for the answer. Either he was a talented actor, or he sincerely wanted me to succeed. Once again, it was up to me to take him at his word, and I needed all the encouragement I could get.

After a less-than-five-minute walk to Lickety Splits, I was greeted by the woman I'd interviewed earlier in the week. "Can I help you?"

I opened my mouth to give my spiel but thought better of

it. Finn had been so encouraging earlier, and I wanted to pay it forward. What would be his favorite flavor of ice cream? I pulled up an image of him licking a cone and tried not to veer into erotic territory. All I knew about his culinary preferences was he liked pizza, bacon, and beer. "Do you have anything on the savory side?"

"For instance?"

"Anything bacon, pizza, or beer flavored?"

She shook her head. "Sorry. We're not quite that exotic here."

I tapped my finger to my lips in contemplation.

"What about green tea? Or rum raisin?" she suggested.

"Rum raisin!" Not exactly savory, but at least it would complete his liquor collection. "To go, please." When the woman smiled, it bolstered my confidence to get to the primary point of my visit. "So...uh...do you ever hold events here?"

"We have BOGO deals a few times a year."

"That's great, but I was thinking something more communal, like ice-cream socials or sundae-eating contests."

She pressed her lips together. "No. The space is too small."

I scanned the venue. "I don't know about that. I bet you could fit thirty or so people in here."

"Like I said, it's not something we've done." She held up the cup of ice cream. "Sprinkles?"

"No thanks." I didn't think Finn was a sprinkles type of guy. "Would you consider it, though? Maybe in the warmer weather when you could have some of the crowd spill outside?" I could picture it now. Tables crammed with people cooling off from the hot summer sun with creamy ice cream.

"We've reserved the store for kids' birthday parties, if you're interested."

"I don't have kids."

"Oh." She motioned for me to follow her to the cash register.

"But if you've held birthday parties here, why not for town gatherings? What's the difference?"

She squinted at me, her arms tight to her sides. "Do you have an event you want to hold here?"

"Not me personally. No." I fumbled with my wallet and pulled out a ten-dollar bill. "I just thought an ice-cream shop would be a great space for a town gathering. Who doesn't love ice cream?" I grimaced. Substitute "ice cream" with "day drinking," and you'd get the same speech I gave at Brothers.

"I thought you were a journalist writing a story about Pleasant Hollow." The woman's hands were now on her hips, and her eyes were shooting daggers at me.

"I am. I just thought Pleasant Hollow could benefit from more togetherness, especially with the new condos going up."

She thrust my change and a bag with Finn's ice cream into my hand. "Unless you plan to share how exactly you'd benefit by my holding these events, I think you should leave."

The hostility was unexpected. Doreen and the cousins had at least humored me before stomping on my ideas like they were the butt of a lit cigarette.

I brought a shaky hand to my forehead. "Fine. In my story, Pleasant Hollow is supposed to be the sort of town where everyone knows each other and people do things together. And no one does anything here!"

I stopped and stared down at my feet. My heart pounded like there was a marching band in my chest. When all else failed, the truth could set me free, but the truth was I sounded like I'd lost my mind. Who was I to tell her how to run her store or to tell this town how to be *better*? I had no right to manipulate Pleasant Hollow for the purposes of a story. Finn had been too kind when he said my plan was ambitious. It was absurd and desperate. Worst of all, it had failed.

When it dawned on me that the shopkeeper hadn't uttered any sort of response to my outburst, I slowly raised my head, afraid I'd be peering straight into the barrel of a shotgun. Thankfully, I was met with an expression of distaste and distrust, but no weapon. But that didn't mean she hadn't alerted the police or the town shrink when I wasn't looking. It was time to go.

"I'm sorry. Please forgive me." With that, I ran out of the store and back to the B&B.

# Chapter Nineteen

I knocked twice and waited. *Please be here.* I had my hand poised to knock again when the door opened.

Finn grinned. "Hi there." His face dropped. "What's wrong? Things didn't go well at your last stop?"

I pushed my way into his room. "I don't want to talk about it." I didn't want to talk at all.

"How can I help?"

When I turned around, he was right there in front of me. Close enough to kiss. Too close *not* to kiss.

So I did.

If he was surprised, he recovered quickly, confirming he wanted this too. My hands clutched the front of his sweater and my feet lifted off the ground when he wrapped both his arms around my waist. His beard scratched against my cheeks. His mouth was warm and wet, and I sighed into it. He slipped his hand under my sweater and rubbed my back. It felt *so* good. And exactly what I needed. I didn't want to think about my disaster of a day...disaster of a trip. And then he pulled away. "Why..." I placed small pecks on his lips. "Are you not..." I tugged on the zipper of his jeans. "Kissing me?"

I didn't know him well enough to be so bold, but the unfamiliarity made me braver. Besides, it was obvious he was into it, at least from a biological standpoint. Then I realized consent went both ways and dropped my hands. "I'm sorry. Did you not want to? I thought..." I avoided eye contact, as if my not looking at him meant he couldn't see how embarrassed I was for completely misreading the situation.

"I totally..." He stroked my cheeks and combed his fingers through my hair. "Want to kiss..." His brown eyes pierced mine. "Every part..." He nipped at my ear. "Of you."

"Oh, thank God."

He laughed.

"Did I say that out loud?"

"You did," he confirmed.

"How do you do that?" I asked before lifting my shirt over my head. Another bold move, but I was on a roll.

"Do what?" he asked, pulling my top all the way off and placing it gently on the rocking chair like it was an original Oscar de la Renta and not twenty dollars from Forever 21.

"Look at me like you've known me forever."

"It's just the way I look at you." He ran his thumb along my wrist bone, making me shiver. "Do you want me to stop?"

"Please don't stop." I placed his hand on the lace trim of my bra. "Any of it."

His eyes crinkled at the corners. "I like you, Adina."

The feeling was mutual. Pleasant Hollow had disenchanted me at every turn with one exception, and he was standing before me. Eventually, I would need to face the reality of my situation and come up with a plan, but right now I wanted to lose myself in Finn, or rather, let him lose himself inside me.

I shimmied out of my jeans. "No more talking."

I kissed him again, and our mouths and tongues explored while I frantically helped him remove his shirt. When my hands grabbed onto bare skin instead of cotton, I pulled away to take in the sight and gulped. "Wow. Just…wow." I could practically feel my eyes dilating. He had a swimmer's lean muscle tone and a smooth chest with just a line of black hair leading from his navel downward. I stroked it with my finger, like I'd been dying to do since his shirt rose up at Brothers.

"Just so you know, you said that out loud too." He cupped one of my breasts with one hand and unclipped my bra with the other until we were skin to skin.

My nipples hardened upon contact with his broad chest. I pushed him on the bed and straddled him. "No. More. Talking." Except he was still wearing pants. I unbuckled his jeans and peeled them off his legs until he wore nothing but black Calvin Klein boxer briefs. It was my favorite male underwear as long as the guy had the goods to pull it off. Finn had the goods. I climbed off him. "Flip over."

"You're sexy when you're bossy." He slapped my ass and did as told.

"You take direction well," I said to his back. I slowly pulled the fabric away from his skin, gasped, and let it snap back. *Oh yes, he had the goods.* "Just as I thought. Your ass is perfect." I climbed off him. "You can turn around now."

He swung around and regarded me with hooded eyes. "I like a woman who takes charge."

I licked my lips. The view from the front was even more impressive. I went dizzy with desire at the thought of how he would feel inside me.

Lifting his upper back off the bed, he tugged on the sides of my panties. "My turn now." He brushed his hand along the outside of the fabric...teasing.

"Those come off, you know."

He flipped me over, so he was on top. "All in good time." His face hovered over mine, and he held my arms down.

"No time like the pres—"

He kissed me before I could complete the sentence. We kissed until my lips were swollen and the rest of my body begged for attention. Then, finally, Finn scooted down the bed and spread my legs apart. My imagination with respect to how his beard would feel between my thighs couldn't compete with the real thing. His tongue. My God. I bucked against him, pleading for more. "Finn."

He applied more pressure. Somehow, he instinctively knew what I wanted before I even asked.

"Yes! Just. Like. That. Oh *Gaaad*." I was so close. I fisted the sheets and lifted my pelvis off the mattress. "Condom. Please." My body screamed for release.

"You sure?" His breath tickled my most sensitive spot. "Because I can finish."

"You can. I can't," I panted. Mouth play could get me right to the edge, but I needed more...bigger...harder...*thrusting*...to cross to the other side. "I'm sorry."

He jumped out of bed and over to his dresser. "Sorry for what? Telling me what you want?" Returning with a condom, he said, "Never be sorry for that."

"Who are you?" I put my hand up. "I know I said it out loud again."

He grinned before climbing into the bed with me. "My name is Finn Adams, and I'd like to fuck you now. Is that okay?"

"Yes, please."

He slid inside me agonizingly slowly, entering only part of the way and back again...over and over, torturously...until I was begging for more. I tightened my legs around his hips and pushed him deeper. The mattress squeaked with our movements. Soon I was panting, and we were both slick with sweat. We came together, loudly, and I hoped Finn was right about being the only guests at the B&B. Then, while the ice cream I bought him melted into liquid sugar, we did it again. We probably fucked for the duration of at least one Hallmark movie, including commercials.

And it was *way* better than okay.

# Chapter Twenty

I sighed happily—deliciously spent.

"That was nice," he said. "Thank you."

I flipped onto my side to face him. He was flat on his back with his arms over his head, and I was relieved to see from his goofy grin that he was playing with me.

"I had fun too." Performance-wise, his score was a solid A+. But I knew this wasn't a long-term thing. If I hadn't been mentally prepared to be a temporary fuck buddy, I wouldn't have knocked on his door tonight.

Except when he looked at me like *that*—he'd curled onto his side as well, so the tops of our heads were practically touching, and the expression on his face was an almost familiar fondness. There'd been no sappy after-sex cuddle or, on the opposite extreme, a cruel leap out of bed to cleanse himself of my bodily fluids or smell. But that *fondness* might be hard to give up, especially to dive back into the general dating swamp of uninterested guys who didn't give two fucks if you came or went. Pun intended on the former.

Even though we'd just met, I felt like Finn *knew* me. But it was probably the oxytocin from the sex fooling me into thinking we were closer than we were.

"Adi?"

"Huh?"

He was doing it again. The fondness thing. And calling me by my nickname like it was the most natural thing in the world. His face was so close, I could count the faint freckles on the bridge of his nose. It was impossible to picture a miniature version of this man living in a car.

"Are you in there?" He tapped lightly on my head. "I know we went at it pretty hard, but I sure hope I didn't literally bone your brains out."

I snapped out of my trance. "How did you get Andrew Hanes to recruit you? This isn't for the story. I'm curious, is all." I was dying to ask about his homeless experience—what caused it, how long it lasted—but I was a hookup, not his girlfriend. "Was it your mad woodworking skills? Your way with a tool?" I covered my mouth with my hand to hide my smile. He definitely knew how to use his tool.

Finn laughed. "Building a house is more than woodwork. There are mundane aspects like installing drywall, window frames, gutters." He cocked his head. "Cut me off at any time. The idea of house-building is sexier than the reality. I don't want to lose any points with you."

"There's zero risk of that." It was funny how my mind had wandered when Garrett spelled out all his handyman projects, yet listening to Finn talk about installing drywall got me wet like foreplay.

"Most people who volunteer do it once or twice for the experience, but few segue it into a career. Andrew was looking for guys like me...young, strong, good with tools..." He blushed.

I squeezed my thighs together under the covers. A hot guy blushing was so damn *hot*.

Finn was still talking. "...from the New York area to add to his team."

"I'm sure your muscles didn't hurt," I said, using it as an excuse to run my hands along his tight abs and pectorals.

"For sure. I'm August in the company's swimsuit calendar," he deadpanned.

I jabbed his belly button. "I will not fall for your trickery again," I said, still embarrassed he'd gotten me with his joke about looking familiar from Oktoberfest.

He grabbed my hand and kissed my pointer finger. "Enough about me. What happened after we left the diner? Obviously, something drove you to my bed. I'd like to believe it was the powerful magnitude of my sex appeal but—"

"It was!"

"Seriously. What happened?"

I sat up and pressed a pillow against my chest. "My plan." I sighed. "It was so...so..." What word was I going for? "Absurd!" Yes, absurd. "Pleasant Hollow didn't check any of my boxes on either a personal or professional level, and so what did I do? I tried to singlehandedly change it. In one day!" I made a fist and extended my index finger in a circle by my ear. "Absurd and desperate. Even worse, if I hadn't been interrogated at Lickety Splits, I might have kept going. Another idea was a fitness program. Can you imagine?" I shook my head. "You encouraged me. Were you secretly laughing?"

He made puppy-dog eyes. "Not at all. I wanted you to

succeed as much for me as for you. I have to temporarily live in this town, remember? I even planned to enter the sandwich contest at Pinkie's."

I propped myself up on my elbow. "Do tell."

"Nope," he said, zipping his lips. "Not until Judie returns from Djibouti, in case they change their minds."

I grinned at our shared sense of humor. *Take that, Doreen.* Then reality caught up with me once again. "It's time to face the hard fact."

Finn squinted at me. "Which is?"

"If I want a story to match my pitch, 'The Heart of TV in Your Own Backyard,' I'll need to find another town, one that also has the benefit of a greedy city person barging in on their territory."

He grabbed my knee under the covers. "Wait. Am I supposed to be the greedy city person in this scenario?"

"Yes. And you were a major failure in the role." We shared a smile.

"What are you going to do?"

I covered his hand with mine. "I'll figure it out later. Maybe you can pound some creative mojo into me?"

He winked. "It's a dirty job, but someone's gotta do it."

# Chapter Twenty-One

*I* spent the night with Finn and tried to ignore the twinge of guilt for wasting over a hundred dollars on a hotel room I didn't sleep in. Now he was at work, and it was time to face reality.

First thing Thursday morning, I called Twinkly Nails to cancel my appointment. It was a luxury I couldn't afford, and the return on investment wasn't worth it. They'd laugh in my face at a suggestion for a town manicure-a-thon. Hadn't I already made a big enough fool of myself?

I sat on the bed with my laptop sprawled across my thighs and scrolled through my private Twitter list of magazine editors, hoping for inspiration. I read through *Tea*'s latest columns. One of the staff writers had done a piece comparing the most popular dating podcasts. One professed to give men guidance on how to succeed in dating, whatever that meant. Dying to know how the host defined "success" and what kind of advice he handed out to lead men toward it, I searched for it on my podcast app and clicked Get to listen later. Then I tossed the phone across the bed.

*Enough is enough.* No more procrastinating.

My story wasn't going to write itself, but I couldn't write the one I'd pitched. What *could* I write? I tapped my socked feet on the comforter, watching my laptop bounce up and down. I needed a shower. Sometimes I got my best ideas as hot water cascaded down my back.

A half hour later, I was as fresh as a summer breeze and no more inspired. I walked circles around my hotel room, wishing I could snap my fingers and turn it into a coffee shop. Nothing spurred my creative juices like a coffee shop. Since there wasn't one in Pleasant Hollow—yet—I did the next best thing (or the thing after that). I grabbed my to-go cup and my computer and walked downstairs to the common room.

There was no low hum of coffee roasters or yacht rock playing softly in the background, the aroma of breakfast was decidedly missing, and there were no other patrons to acknowledge awkwardly before actively avoiding eye contact. But the coffee and soy milk were free, and the clock was ticking on my deadline. It would take a gargantuan effort to push aside memories of Finn moving inside me, whispering how good I felt, but I had to focus. I'd use the incentive of doing it again...and again...to propel me forward.

Trying to compare Pleasant Hollow to a Hallmark movie town was like trying to make salt taste like sugar. Maybe that was it...

I sat up straighter in my chair. If I couldn't write an article comparing the *similarities* between Pleasant Hollow and the cozy small towns as seen on TV, why not write one highlighting the *differences*? Using those parameters, I had more than enough material. I stretched my arms over my head, rolled my shoulders, and got to work.

What you'd find in a Hallmark movie: A maternal innkeeper who smells like fresh-baked bread, invites you to tea, serves you crumpets, and lovingly meddles in your business.

What you get in Pleasant Hollow: Told it's too early to check in and reluctant directions to the town watering hole.

What you'd find in a Hallmark movie: Overwhelming participation in a slew of community events, from Christmas parades to harvest festivals to Easter egg hunts.

What you get in Pleasant Hollow: Infantile business owners who put more effort into playing tabletop games than making money, much less sponsoring events focused on uniting the community.

What you'd find in a Hallmark movie: A march on the town square protesting the construction of a twenty-five-floor condominium complex.

What you get in Pleasant Hollow: An underdeveloped town sorely in need of the likes of Andrew Hanes and the improvements he'll bring.

And from there, the words just flowed.

"How's it going?"

Mid-review of my first draft, I lifted my butt off the seat in pleasant surprise. I grinned at Finn. "I did it. I wrote the story."

He sat down across from me and gestured toward my laptop. "May I?"

"Sure." With his boss, and him by association, no longer the villain of the article, I had nothing to hide. I shifted my computer toward him. "It still needs tightening."

I was proud of it, but critical feedback could only make it better. As long as he didn't say it was complete and utter crap. I twisted my hands. "Let me know if you find any typos!"

Without looking up, he said, "No interruptions."

I mumbled an apology and excused myself to the downstairs half-bath to avoid trying to read into every movement of Finn's face while he read. *He blinked. What does it mean? He scratched his ear. What does it meeeeeean?*

When I got back, Finn was on the phone. I sat down and bored a virtual hole in his head with my eyes until he finally ended his call.

"Well?" I assumed he was finished reading, since the article was under five hundred words, and seriously, how long could it take?

"Well, what?" His blank expression gave away nothing.

"Finn."

"Adina."

I clenched my thighs at his teasing eyes. The fondness would be my ruin. "What did you think?"

He grinned. "I think you slayed it."

"Really?"

"I especially liked your change of heart regarding my boss."

"Yeah, yeah, yeah." I rolled my eyes. "It's not what I promised Derek, but I'm crossing everything he'll take it."

"You've got nothing to lose."

He was wrong. I had everything to lose. But I had no other choice unless I was prepared to either create a false reality where the town and the circumstances surrounding The Hollows matched the story I'd pitched or give up without even trying. Neither of those was an option. The income from the article itself would be nominal, since Derek was paying by the word, but it was the catalyst for securing a full-time job with *Tea*.

Finn tapped his head. "You wanna hang out?"

It hit me like an earthquake that once I sent this story to Derek, my business in Pleasant Hollow was completed. I would say goodbye to the town. And to Finn. I pushed aside the mounting gloom and smiled at him. "Let me finish this and I'll be right up."

# Chapter Twenty-Two

With my story signed, sealed, and delivered to Derek, I had nothing to do the next day but wait to hear back from him. My room at the B&B was paid through the weekend and nonrefundable. Based on my calculations, the money I'd spent on the inn was more than what I could make if I was lucky enough to snag a last-minute rotation working at the café or teaching a spin class back in the city this weekend. It was more economically feasible to stick around until Sunday than go home early. I called my mom to let her know.

"Break it to me gently, Squirt. You've fallen in love with Pleasant Hollow and are abandoning New York City to live there."

I paced the room. "Not quite. It's...um...not what I expected."

There was silence before she said, "But you got your story?"

"I got *a* story, yes."

"That's all that matters."

"Let's hope." I wet my dry lips. "I'll let you get back to work. Happy Friday!" We exchanged "I love you"s and ended the call. Then I sat on the bed and texted Kate.

> I slept with Finn. Twice.

Her response came so quick, I missed the dancing bubbles.

> !!! How was it?

I responded with the fire emoji. Five of them.

> Yaaas! Do you like him?

I typed the B in "Because duh" but paused with my finger on the phone. Finn was pretty perfect—smart, kind, funny, charming, *hot*. But I had to keep it real.

> Best. Fling. Ever.

Most guys didn't pass my sex test, so it wasn't like Finn had scads of competition, but I knew great sex when I had it.

> Look at you living your best life.

> I'm giving it my all! Any updates on your end?

I crossed and uncrossed my legs while I waited for her to respond. Kate had been near the top of our class at Eleanor Roosevelt High and had received a 165 on her LSAT. The possibility of her failing the bar had never even crossed my mind.

Crawling my way out of denial against my best judgment. It's nice in here.

I laughed and told her I'd write more or call her later. Since I'd painfully established the town had nothing going on—not even an uninspired hot chocolate cart in the park—I accepted Finn's offer to join him at the construction site later that day while he finished out the workweek. It was lunchtime, and he ordered food for his crew from a deli in Newburgh every Friday afternoon.

The team invited me to join their card game. They were playing bullshit, where the aim is to get rid of your cards, often by blatantly lying with a straight face about the ones in your hand. It was a game I knew well from college, only this time without alcohol.

"Bullshit," I said.

Finn cocked his head. "Are you sure you want to do that?"

I stared him down across the picnic table set outside of his trailer. "Positive." He'd claimed to drop a six facedown into the pile. I had three sixes. It was possible he had the fourth one, but my gut said he was bluffing.

He turned the card over—nine.

Emma laughed and pointed. "Busted!"

"Busted!" I repeated in solidarity with the only other woman at the table. We high-fived.

"Oh, my bad." Finn batted his eyelashes with an air of feigned innocence. "I was reading the card upside down."

Vick cackled and wiggled his silver mustache at Finn. "You're so full of it."

Finn gathered the pile of cards into his hands and winked at me.

My belly quivered, and I tried to squelch it with a bite of my turkey sandwich. Unfortunately, I had no appetite. The more time I spent with Finn, the harder it was going to be to say goodbye. I wasn't in love with the guy—*please*—but...

"Your turn, Adina."

I dropped a card facedown onto the table. "One seven." With my side vision, I could see Finn eyeballing me—a dare to lose my cool—and raised my gaze to face him head-on. I'd be damned if he called bullshit, even though it was.

"I'm going to let this go," he said. "But only because the pile is down to one card. It would be a waste."

"Thanks for clarifying your motivations," I responded dryly. My legs bounced under the table. *Damn it.* Test or no test, I liked him more than anyone else I'd "dated" in ages.

"You two seem awfully familiar for two people who just met." Emma's blue eyes passed between us with obvious curiosity.

"We're two New Yorkers trapped in the sticks for a work assignment," Finn said. "Lots to bond over. Right, Adi?"

I nodded my agreement. It was a better answer than the one I'd come up with: *It's bizarre how much you can learn about someone when your clothes are off.* "We're both staying at the B&B. Although I'll be leaving soon."

My stomach clenched. I had no love for Pleasant Hollow, but this—sitting outside on a cool autumn day, playing cards and shooting the shit with Finn's crew—was nice.

"Oh, right. Your story. Did the blueprint I showed you help?"

"Immensely," I said with a knowing look to Finn. What was the harm in Johnny thinking he'd done something positive? It was bad enough his coworkers had assigned him the moniker Clumsy Smurf. "I sent it along yesterday and am waiting to hear back from the editor."

"Anything juicy?" Emma asked.

"Let's just say I doubt Pleasant Hollow will be on anyone's list of vacation destinations if they read it." I winced. "None of you guys actually live here, do you?"

The question was met with a chorus of "No way," "Definitely not," and "Hell to the no."

"Phew." I wiped my brow in mock relief.

Finn glanced at his watch. "Ten-minute warning."

"Yes, Chef!" Emma said with a salute and everyone laughed.

For the next few minutes, Finn joked around with his staff while subtly pushing them toward finishing their lunches and getting back to work. Warmth spread through my chest. It must be challenging to be simultaneously friendly and authoritative, yet Finn made it look easy. His crew seemed to genuinely like and respect him. Maybe his past made him more sensitive, or maybe he was born that way. As if reading my mind, he looked my way and grinned.

I smiled back shyly. I would miss him. *Unless.* Unless I was wrong and Finn wasn't a replica of all the other men I'd met on Tinder, Hinge, OkCupid, and Coffee Meets Bagel. I'd dismissed Kate when she said there were definitely emotionally available men from Manhattan seeking a committed relationship, but what if she was right and Finn was one of them? If so, it might not have to end.

A text message pinged on my phone, and all thoughts of Finn left the vicinity as my heart dropped to my knees. It was Derek.

Call me.

# Chapter Twenty-Three

*I*t was easy to slip away from the construction site without much fanfare, since lunch hour was up. I told Finn I had things to do back at the hotel and would see him later, then walked to the park.

I'd turned in a great story. *It wasn't what I pitched.*

It was humorous and tightly written. *It wasn't what I pitched.*

The wind got stronger as I approached the water, and it seared my cheeks like repeated slaps across the face. My mind was spinning. If Derek wanted to talk, why hadn't he just called me? Why had he bothered with a text? Was he being respectful of my time, allowing me to call him at my convenience? *Doubtful.*

After I'd sufficiently exhausted myself with twenty questions only Derek could answer, I plopped on a bench, pulled up my big-girl panties, and called him. My pulse raced faster than a sprinter in the Olympics.

"I read your piece," he said without preamble.

*And?* I waited for him to elaborate, until the awkward silence told me he wasn't going to. "What did you think?" I chewed my lips way too hard.

"It was...cute. But it's not what you pitched."

"I know." I closed my eyes and rubbed my temples. "Here's the thing. Pleasant Hollow is nothing like a Hallmark movie town."

"I think I read that somewhere recently."

It took me a second, and the boom of his laughter, to get the joke. I blamed it on my nerves. I chuckled too, keeping it light. "Yeah, so you can see how I can't write an honest piece using the original idea. I think my substitute is entertaining and still appeals to the Hallmark audience—just turning expectations on their head." I pulled my jacket tighter to my chest to block out the wind.

"There's no emotional component. So Pleasant Hollow isn't a Hallmark town. Who cares? Most small towns aren't."

Something apparently everyone knew, besides Kate and me.

"It's not a story," Derek continued. "And it's kind of a diss, hostile even. What did Pleasant Hollow ever do to you?"

Besides not welcome me with open arms and make me an honorary townie at first sight? Nothing. I figured it was a rhetorical question and didn't bother to answer. "Does this mean you don't want to use it?" I held my breath.

"Not in its current form. It has no subject. Is there anything juicier you can use?"

"Juicier?"

"Yeah." He clucked his tongue. "Maybe something shady about the developer. The movie where the corporate guy buys a family-owned and -run ski resort? He promised the sweet old couple he'd keep it exactly the same but secretly planned to turn it into a singles resort. Seen it?"

Of course I'd seen it. It starred the late Alan Thicke and Candace Cameron Bure. But I had no idea how it related to

The Hollows. "Do you mean you want me to find out if instead of a condo, Andrew Hanes is really using the land to build…" I racked my brain for an outrageous alternative or two. "A golf course or self-storage facility?"

"If his trickery makes the townspeople *feel* something, then yes."

I went numb in the chest. I wasn't sure the people of this town felt anything but irritated by the strange and nosy visitor in town.

"I didn't uncover anything sketchy in my research." Hanes's interest in low-income housing was a new discovery, but unfortunately, it had nothing to do with Pleasant Hollow, and I doubted it would qualify as "trickery" in anyone's book.

"There's always a story. Even if it has nothing to do with the developer. You have another week. Think outside the box and find it."

I squeezed my eyes shut, desperate for an idea to spark. "I'm on it." *Fake it till you make it.*

"I'm giving you an opportunity here. Don't blow it. Later, Gellar." He ended the call.

My vision blurred as I made my way toward the B&B, my head down and shoulders slumped. What was I going to do now? A tear dropped onto my cheek and I wiped it off with a heavy hand. Blubbering wouldn't change anything.

It would be a lie to say I *never* cried, but it wasn't a natural response for me. I didn't choke up during sappy movies or each time I had a setback in life. When I shed tears, it was often during those few times a year when I felt the absence of my dad most profoundly. I barely remembered the actual human being, but I mourned the *idea* of a father.

Occasionally, and usually when I least expected it, I'd observe a girl with her dad on the street or in a restaurant or store and wonder how different my life would have been if my dad hadn't died—how different *I* would be. And I would cry. Through the years, when a boy rejected me, I would weep, not over the guy himself, but out of yearning for the unconditional love of my daddy.

Story rejections and the like had resulted in frustration, anger, even self-loathing, but never tears. Until now. I'd allowed myself to believe a full-time writing position was imminent. I wouldn't have to spend my nights combing through the freelance boards just to keep a toe in the writing game while holding down two other jobs. Those independent gigs were hard-won, and they served to add a few dollars to my bank account and amp up my portfolio while preventing my writing muscles from atrophying. But the content meant nothing to me personally and brought no joy to my life.

A position with *Tea* was the beer at the end of a marathon, a binge-watch after a long study session, a good night's sleep after a grueling day. It was everything. I'd be able to help my mother financially, or at least better support myself to lessen her burden. From the moment the idea sprang to life the morning after watching *Million Dollar Listing*, I had been so certain this was it. Then Derek's enthusiasm and the resulting contract boosted my confidence even more.

I was wrong and back to square one, only with far less money in my savings account. I failed to deliver the story I pitched, then sent Derek a piece he rejected. I had one more chance, but if I wasted his time again, I'd burn a bridge with the only true connection I had in the business.

When I entered the B&B, I averted eye contact with Lorraine, who was in the open kitchen. For the first time since I'd arrived in Pleasant Hollow, I prayed she would ignore me. To think, less than twelve hours earlier, it would have made my day if she offered me a cupcake and asked if I wanted to chat with her in the common room. Right now, her cold shoulder was exactly what I craved. *Oh, how the tides have turned.* I would laugh if I wasn't still crying. With a cursory wave, I bounded up the stairs and into my room, letting the door close behind me. My eyes were immediately drawn to my suitcase. It was by the window, open, with clothes spilling out. The room came with a closet and a five-drawer dresser, but I hadn't used either. At least it would save me time packing to go home.

Derek's words drifted through my ears: *Something juicier.* Would getting kicked out of Lickety Splits for asking too many questions count as juicy?

I had to face the reality that unless I delivered complete and satisfactory material in a week, my contract with *Tea* would be voided, I could kiss the full-time gig goodbye, and Derek would never take me seriously again.

Maybe it was time to go home. I needed to be there for Kate. I missed my mom. I even missed the city—with its unlimited dining choices, "never sleeps" mentality, and spin bikes. If it weren't for Finn, I'd leave tomorrow, but he was the only bright side in all of this. God only knew when I'd get laid again once I got home.

Unless…

What if we made it more than just a fling?

Because my day had been shitty, I allowed myself the rare

daydream about what it would be like to be part of a couple, in a committed relationship with someone I genuinely liked. With my flexible hours at the café and gym, I could spend a night or two a week in Pleasant Hollow. And he could come back to the city on weekends like he'd done for Oktoberfest. It could totally work. It wasn't straight out of a Hallmark movie, but two city folks falling in love within the confines of a small town was no less of a small-town romance than if one or both of us lived in said small town.

I shook my head. The time for daydreaming was over. I grabbed my phone and walked to the window.

When Mom answered the phone with "Hi, Squirt," tears built up behind my lids. I blinked them away. *Enough.*

"What's up?" I asked her.

I planned to confess all, but there was no need to lead with it.

"Nothing much. Just on my way to happy hour. Mama needs a glass of wine or three."

I smiled at the thought of my mom enjoying her Friday night. "Who are you going with? Is it a date?" She'd had a first date the week before that had gone well. For one thing, he'd actually shown up.

She laughed. "It's not a date, although I have one of those tomorrow. Tonight is work people. Former work people, to be more accurate." Her voice fell. "It was Carla and Rosa's last day."

I gasped. "What? Both of them? Why?" Carla had been one of the nurses in Mom's practice for as long as I could remember. And Rosa had been the phlebotomist for at least five years.

"They were laid off. Well, Carla was encouraged to retire early."

I could tell she was trying to be upbeat even while delivering bad news. I sat on the edge of the bed. "Oh no. That sucks. Please send them my love."

"Will do, Squirt. Listen, I'm almost at Hillstone, but I want to catch up. Can I call you later or tomorrow morning?"

"Sure." My stomach curdled. "Wait. Is *your* job safe?"

She snorted. "It is for now."

"Shouldn't we talk about the apartment?" I'd opened a Pandora's box. It was too late to turn back now. My voice almost a whisper, I said, "I saw the notice in your room before I left."

I was met with silence.

"Mom?"

She sighed into the phone. "We have time for that later. For now, don't worry about it, okay? I'm at the restaurant. I love you." She ended the call.

I buried my face in my hands. It was the perfect storm—an imminent rent hike, my blowing the opportunity for a full-time job, and now the threat of my mom getting laid off. We could wait until the sky opened up, or we could heed the warning and fix it now. I had no control over the fate of Mom's job or my landlord's decisions, but there had to be a way to honor my contract with *Tea* by delivering a complete and satisfactory story. *Think, Adi, think.*

An hour later, I had nothing.

The deluge was coming and there was no umbrella in sight.

# Chapter Twenty-Four

*D*on't *worry about it.*

Well, shit, Mom. Why didn't you just ask me to hang the moon while you were at it?

I paced the wood floor, each lap seeming shorter than the last, like the space was shrinking and the bare blue walls of Room E were closing in on me.

*Enough of this.* I shrugged on my jacket, grabbed my purse and notebook, and closed the door behind me. I'd figure out where I was going when I got there.

Before exiting the B&B, I stopped in the kitchen, on the hunt for a leftover muffin from breakfast. Maybe if my mouth was busy chewing, my brain would follow suit and wake up. Spotting Lorraine, I recalled my earlier conversation with Kate. I cleared my throat to make my presence known. "Um...Lorraine?"

"Yes?" Lorraine, wearing a two-piece, carnation-pink velour sweatsuit, closed the dishwasher and faced me.

"I read online you're the town legislator. Do you have time to answer a few questions for the story I'm writing on Pleasant Hollow?" Considering my other interviews went nowhere, it was a long shot. But she was a genuine source of town information, and I had to try.

A spot of color dotted both her cheeks. "The town meeting is in an hour. You're welcome to observe!"

I laughed to myself. It was the first time a local had *welcomed* me to anything, but this was the most affable version of Lorraine I'd seen since my arrival. "I'd love to! Where is it being held?"

She gave me the address of the elementary school and excused herself to get ready.

Forty-five minutes later, I sat on a folding chair near the back of a classroom, waiting for the meeting to start. Based on the painted handprints and stick-figure drawings covering the walls, and the scent of peanut butter sandwiches and smelly feet, I'd guess it was kindergarten or first grade.

I observed with interest as others entered the room, and my excitement grew as it exceeded 50 percent capacity. Maybe a boisterous argument would break out over something juicy, like feuding businesses fighting over property lines—that was always big in the movies.

Best-case scenario, someone would finally raise the topic of The Hollows. The construction noise, perhaps? An urban eyesore in a rural setting? An opposition to city folks? Guilt jabbed at me for my continual desire to find an angle directly opposed to Finn's goals, but I was a journalist first and Finn's temporary lover second. *Sorry, Finn.*

Lorraine, who'd traded in her tracksuit for dress pants and a sweater, arrived with a binder tucked under her arm. She was joined by a slightly younger man. They sat at a table in the front of the room, facing the crowd. Lorraine called the meeting to order and gestured at someone in the front row about taking minutes. It was a familiar scene, if only through my television screen, where I'd watched Taylor and Miss Patty preside over numerous town meetings on *Gilmore Girls*.

"The first item on the agenda," Lorraine said into the microphone, and recoiled as it screeched with feedback. She tapped it a few times. "Let's try this again. The first item on the agenda is the new zoning laws going into effect next month."

Twenty minutes in, I was barely staying awake. I did a sweep of the room and saw shoulders were slumped. Eyes were remaining shut for periods of time shorter than naps but too long to qualify as blinks. Was that drool on the guy next to me? Validated, I uttered a quiet, "Not just me."

"Now we'll open the floor to new business," Lorraine said.

A thirtysomething woman in the row in front of mine stood. "What's with the school supplying only healthy meals? Why is everything peanut-free, gluten-free, dairy-free? What's so wrong with old-fashioned frozen pizza and hot dogs? They were good enough for us. They're good enough for our kids!"

Lorraine sighed. "If you recall, we had the reverse conversation last year when parents complained about the lack of gluten-free and vegetarian options in the cafeteria."

"I recall." The woman sat back down and, dropping her voice half an octave, muttered, "My sister and smug brother-in-law ruined everything for *my* kids so *theirs* could eat quinoa for lunch. They're so extra."

"You can file a petition online to request more unhealthy alternatives," Lorraine said with barely restrained annoyance.

Considering Pleasant Hollow's local dining-out options were one step above fast food, the town siding with the USDA regarding healthy school meals struck me as comical. I snort-laughed.

The woman turned and glared sharp objects at me with her eyes.

I slid down my chair and, using my notepad as a face shield, scribbled notes. In terms of scintillating material, we'd likely reached the peak with the school lunch wars.

"Next item on the agenda is event permits. Any requests?" Lorraine asked.

Events? My ears perked up.

"Us!"

I whirled around as a cute elderly couple shuffled to their feet. Maybe they'd overheard me talking with the business owners and had their own ideas for community bonding.

"We need a permit for..."

I crossed my fingers.

"...the new fireplace Garrett is building for us."

The air whooshed out of me like a punctured tire. Shame on me for daring to hope.

Skipping all subtlety, Lorraine rolled her eyes. "Those types of permit applications are online."

The couple took their seats again.

I tossed a sympathetic frown their way for sitting through this boring-as-all-get-out meeting for nothing. *I feel your pain.*

The man gave me side-eye. "What are you staring at?"

I quickly looked away as I realized they were the cranky couple I'd passed on Main Street earlier in the week. Clearly "old" didn't equate with cute and cuddly grandparent types for these two.

My phone pinged with a text from Finn.

What are you doing?

My heart lifted, but I hesitated before responding. Telling him I was at a town meeting would require me to divulge my story had been rejected. I wasn't ready to talk about it yet.

Walking around. Why?

His response came immediately.

It's happy hour at Finn's Tavern.

I faced forward again. The allure of Finn's invitation had me wishing I could beam myself to the B&B instantaneously. But what if I left the meeting right before someone complained about the deer population or the nonexistent town troubadour? Unlikely, but I had one more card to play before I could bask in Finn's nakedness again. I stood and waved a hand.

Lorraine jutted her chin toward me. "Did you have a question, Ms. Gellar?"

I suppressed my surprise and delight that she remembered my last name. "Does anyone want to comment on the construction of The Hollows? Big changes are near, from an influx of residents to competition for business to the town skyline! If you have an opinion, I'd love to hear it." I presented the crowd with my practiced I'm-on-your-side expression.

"Thoughts, anyone?" Lorraine scanned the room.

It was so quiet we could probably hear a tree fall in a forest in Pennsylvania.

"Anyone? Going once, twice..." She banged her gavel. "Meeting is adjourned."

# Chapter Twenty-Five

Finn walked a few steps to the right, then to the left, circling the immediate area a few times before finally standing still on the grass. "Here it is. The perfect spot."

I narrowed my eyes. "Perfect for what? What are we doing?" It was late Saturday evening, and Finn suggested walking to the park.

He pulled a dark blue fleece airplane blanket out of his black Under Armour backpack. "Movie under the stars—Pleasant Hollow style."

My eyes bugged out. I'd have been less shocked if he said Jason Momoa had checked into the B&B. "Pleasant Hollow has an outdoor movie night? Like Bryant Park? Why didn't I know about this? Where is everyone else?" I didn't spy another person among the trees and occasional benches in the small park.

Finn placed a hand on my arm. "Easy there. Pleasant Hollow doesn't have a movie night. I do. *We* do. And no one else is invited." He brushed aside some leaves and spread the blanket on the ground before us. "Sit."

My curiosity outweighed my apprehension that it was too cold to sit outside for the duration of a movie. At least I'd worn my army jacket. I sat down, thankful I had on loose-fitting boyfriend jeans, and patted the spot next to me. The sky was a bright royal blue, and the horizon was tinged with pink. The river was still visible from here, but it would be sunset soon and our view would be limited to one another. "Where's the screen and what's playing?"

"The screen is my laptop monitor, and the movie is *Frances Ha*."

I cocked my head. "Interesting selection."

He shrugged. "It's supposed to be a love letter to Manhattan. I'm a little homesick and thought you might be too."

Considering how bad I'd wanted to escape the city a week ago, the truth in his words surprised me. But nothing made you more cognizant of the phrase "There's no place like home" than being a stranger in a strange town where no one desired to learn your name (except Lorraine, and I was paying her).

"This is nice." It was—dare I say it—romantic. I bumped my shoulder against his. "Thank you," I said, silently admiring his weekend look. His uniform of a gray hoodie and tattered jeans demonstrated it wasn't clothes that made the man but the other way around.

"I also thought we could both use a little fresh air."

I blushed. Aside from taking turns picking up food at Pinkie's, we'd spent almost every waking moment since last night tangled in his bedsheets.

"Have you seen it?"

"The movie? Nope."

"We can watch something else if you want. *Saturday Night Fever*? *When Harry Met Sally*? *Home Alone 2*?" This time he bumped *my* shoulder. "I considered *American Psycho* but didn't know how comfortable you'd be watching a movie about a serial killer alone with a guy you just met."

"Good call." Only it didn't feel like we'd just met. "You've really thought this through! Let's watch *Frances Ha*." The movie was secondary to the act of watching it *with him*.

"I also have..." He pulled a can of Pringles out of his bag and opened it with a POP. "Ta-da," he said, placing a few chips in my palm. "Movie popcorn has nothing on Pringles."

"What else do you have in there?" I asked, peering inside his bag. "Let me guess, a monkey?"

"Close." He removed two bottles of Heineken, twisted them open, and handed one to me. "Cheers."

I clinked my bottle against his. "Wait. Does Pleasant Hollow have any open container laws?"

Finn took a long swill from his beer. "Don't know. Don't care."

I chomped on a chip. "I don't think I've seen a cop since I got here. Does the town even have its own police station? A sheriff? There's always a sheriff in the mov—" I cleared my throat. "Never mind."

Finn cracked up. "You're a piece of work."

"What do you mean?" But I could tell by the expression on his face I was endeared to him. It was the *fondness* thing again.

He brushed a hair from my face. "I enjoy you immensely, Adina Gellar." Then he leaned forward and kissed me softly.

The innocent closed-mouth kiss left me dizzy. I shut my eyes until the weight of his lips against mine was gone. When I opened them, Finn gestured to his laptop. "Ready?"

"Ready." Under other circumstances, I would have been captivated by a movie featuring a young woman in New York finding her way, but...Finn *enjoyed me*. No one had ever said that to me before.

Kate and I always made fun of the couples in Hallmark movies who fell in love after a week. I wasn't *in love*. But...what was happening here?

What we had was more than sexy times. A private movie viewing in the park definitely qualified as a PG-rated bona fide date. In addition, rather than play it cool like most of the guys I dated, Finn communicated...with words...how much he liked me. Maybe my assumptions about him seeing me as a convenient but temporary fling had been premature.

"So...uh...when do you think you'll come back to the city next?" *Real smooth, Gellar.*

Finn paused the movie and turned to me. "What was that?"

My mouth opened and closed. Any "game" I'd accumulated in my twenty-five years was lost. "You said you went back home for Oktoberfest. Any plans to do it again soon?" Oh, how I longed to bury myself under the blanket or crawl into a hole in a tree like a possum.

"I'm not sure." His eyes were the shade of cognac and equally intoxicating. "Why?"

"You said you were homesick." It was the perfect opening to gauge his interest in seeing me after this was over, but I was too afraid of the answer and having too much fun to risk it. I was still reeling from Derek's rejection of my story the day before.

"I have no solid plans to go back to Manhattan, but I might visit my sister in Brooklyn."

"How nice! Are you guys close? I always wanted a sibling when I was younger. Was it like a twenty-four-seven playdate?" I emptied a few more chips into my hand.

"Maybe when we were really little." He peeled the label half-way off his beer bottle until the top half curled over. "Our adult lives are just very different." He turned the movie back on.

I nibbled on a chip, debating whether to say my next words, and then went ahead and did it. "Can I ask you something personal? Feel free to say no."

He paused the movie again and turned to me. "Shoot."

"You mentioned you were once homeless. How did it happen? How old were you?"

Finn stilled.

I fisted the blanket at my side. Perhaps the timing was off. But when would be better? During sex? Besides, if he shared, it might mean he trusted me...that I was more than a fuck buddy. If he blew me off, I'd have my answer. My eyes locked onto his Adam's apple as he swallowed.

After an awkward lull, he spoke. "I was thirteen. My mom had just died. All our money went for her treatments. Their health insurance was for shit."

"Oh, Finn." I was hit with an urge to wrap my arms around him and hold him tenderly. But I didn't dare. Instead, I scooted an inch closer and squeezed his knee encouragingly.

He curved his fingers around mine. "My dad lived paycheck to paycheck as a high school librarian but lost his job after missing so many days of work visiting my mom. We couldn't pay the rent on our fancy apartment in Westchester and were evicted. My parents...they didn't manage their money well, spent beyond our means. I couldn't live without my Game Boy, and Jill would *die* if she was the only girl in her class without designer clothes."

"Please don't tell me you guys blame yourselves."

"We don't. Jill blamed my dad. I blame poor money management and greedy pharmaceutical companies."

"How did you finally get out from under it?"

Finn smiled as if recalling a pleasant memory. "An old friend, aptly named Angelo, got my dad a job at his law firm as a legal librarian. The sign-on bonus, which I'm pretty sure came from Angelo's own wallet, gave him enough for first month's rent and a security deposit on a very cheap one-bedroom place in the Bronx. The steady paycheck paid the rest, and Jill and I learned to live with less. At that point, I didn't care about toys anymore. I just wanted a warm bed and daily showers with hot water."

My heart felt lighter. "Thank God it all worked out."

"For a while anyway."

I frowned. "What do you mean?"

He released my hand from his and took a pull from his beer bottle. "Nothing. My dad has had a lot of angels watching out for him, that's all."

I nodded, sensing there was more to the story but not wanting to push my luck. I was thrilled he'd opened up this much. It was enough for now.

He turned the movie back on.

My stomach growled. Chips weren't going to cut it. "I'm craving a Shack burger."

"Minetta Tavern is better," he said, without turning away from the screen.

"Says who?"

"*Time Out New York*, for one. Me for another." His eyes traveled in a little circle around my face. "You're not into the movie, are you?"

"It's not that. It's just…" I hugged myself. "Kind of chilly. Maybe we can move the theater indoors?"

"I think that can be arranged."

While I threw out the garbage, he shut down his computer and folded the blanket. Then we walked hand in hand back to the B&B. His thumb caressed my palm the entire time. I still had no idea if we had a future outside of Pleasant Hollow, but I did know we weren't going to watch the movie.

# Chapter Twenty-Six

Sunday morning, we opened our eyes at exactly the same time, or at least within seconds. "Morning," I said, sounding like there was a frog in my throat.

"Back at you." Finn rubbed his bare foot up my leg under the covers.

My nerve endings sprang to life at the contact, even as the rest of me remained at the edge of consciousness. I nuzzled my face in his neck drowsily. "Sleep well?" I was enjoying that moment between sleep and full awareness when my mind was slow to overthink or second-guess anything.

He mumbled, "Mm-hmm" and using one arm, pulled me into the curve of his body.

We reached for each other as if we weren't new lovers still self-conscious the morning after the first few times we'd shared a bed, as if it were the most natural thing in the world. I didn't worry about how my naked body looked in the bright light of day or fear I'd outstayed my welcome in his room. Mutual morning breath didn't stop us, although it might explain why kissing lasted only a minute before he pulled back. With my eyes shut and only half-awake, I heard the nightstand drawer open and shut, followed by the rip of a condom wrapper. Then I felt the weight of his body over mine once again.

"Is this cool?" he asked.

I confirmed my consent with all the efficiency I could muster in my half-dream state. And then he was inside me. He gave and I took, over and over *and over* again. For how long, I had no idea. It was the phoenix of fucks, a magic candle that relit itself each time we thought we were done for. A wave in the ocean that tumbled and turned but refused to crash to the shore. Maybe being only partially conscious gave us both more patience and stamina. Whatever it was, I never wanted it to stop.

Eventually, the candle burned out and the wave broke. We were panting and our skin gleamed with sweat, but we were no longer conjoined. It was a quiet peaceful moment, and I basked in complete satiation. All was right with the world.

And then, like a blow to the face, I remembered Derek's reaction to my story. Just like that, my Zen state of consciousness flew out the window, replaced with panic. The last thirty-six hours with Finn had been a blissful diversion, but we couldn't stay tucked inside this hotel room avoiding the outside world forever. What was I going to write about? I slid away from Finn and curled into the fetal position.

"Adi?" Finn patted my back. "Are you all right?"

I pressed my face into the sheet and said a muffled "Not really."

"Is it me? Did I hurt you?" His voice was heavy with concern.

"No!" He was the one thing I'd done right. I flipped over to face him. "It's definitely not you." I braced myself to say it out loud. "My editor hated the story."

Finn's mouth dropped open. "Really? Why?"

"It wasn't a story. It lacked an emotional component. It was mean. Just your basic suckage." I sat up and toyed with the zipper of the pillowcase. *Ziiip. Ziiip. Ziiip.*

"Sorry, Adi." He caressed my cheek. "What now?"

I grazed the now-hot skin where his hands just were. "I keep trying. I've compiled notes from various interviews, research, and the town hall meeting I attended, but they're like pieces from several different puzzles that don't fit together. A bunch of somethings that add up to a whole lot of nothing. But Derek says there's always a story, so I'll stay a little longer to find it." Some would say it was throwing good money after bad, but quitting now would only guarantee that every cent I'd already spent had been for nothing.

"I'm both sorry and thrilled to hear this."

I screwed up my face. "My epic fail thrills you *how* exactly?"

The corner of his mouth twitched into a smile. "It gives me more time with you."

My stomach did an Olympic-worthy maneuver—a running leap into a cartwheel followed by a somersault—before it stuck the landing. It was *time*. I shuffled under the covers. "I know it's soon...we've only just met, but I was wondering—"

A phone rang.

"Yours," Finn said, grabbing it from the nightstand and handing it to me.

I glanced at the screen and back at Finn. "It's my friend, Kate. Mind if I take this?"

He waved me away.

"Hey there," I said.

"Can you talk?"

I frowned at the distressed tone of her voice. "What's wrong?" I met Finn's concerned look with a one-second signal.

"I'm fine. I just need to tell you something." She paused. "Is someone with you?"

"Finn." I got a squidgy feeling just saying his name.

After a pause, Kate said, "You know, maybe it's not the best time."

"Screw that. It's never a bad time for you." I lowered the phone. "I'm going to take this to your bathroom," I told Finn.

"Go for it."

I climbed out of bed and walked across the room with one hand covering my naked butt.

"Shall I compare thy ass to a summer's day? Thou art more lovely…"

I dropped my hand and did a little shaky-shake for Finn, then closed the bathroom door behind me. Holding back a laugh, I said to Kate, "Okay. What's wrong? Did you tell your parents you failed the bar?"

"This isn't about me. It's about…" She sighed. "Finn."

"Finn? What about him?" I lowered the sparkling-clean toilet lid and sat down.

"You might not care. I mean, you did say you were totally fine with a fling, right?"

She was correct. I *had* said that. But things had changed since then. "I *really* like him, Kate. I think there's something there. In fact, you just preempted a DTR conversation."

"Oh."

I expected a reaction, but this wasn't it. "What's going on?"

"Did he define the relationship?"

"Not yet. You preempted it." I chuckled. When she didn't join in, a chill went through me. "Just rip off the Band-Aid."

"I searched for him on OkCupid."

"You…what? I have so many questions. The first being why

do you have an OkCupid account? Are you and Diego in an open relationship now?"

"Diego knows all about it. He says hi by the way."

"Hi, Diego!" I stood and opened the bathroom door a crack. My mouth watered at the sight of a bare-chested Finn watching TV on his bed. I closed the door again and whispered, "You've answered my first question. Now answer my second. Why?"

"I'm in denial about failing the bar and needed a diversion."

"Fair enough. But there are millions of men in the city. What was your strategy?"

"I downloaded the app and made a fake bare-bones profile. You said he was twenty-eight and lived on the Upper West Side, so I searched for twenty-eight-year-old white guys within a five-mile radius of the 10023 zip code. Diego did the same thing, but on Tinder. I also searched him on social media so I knew what he looked like. He's hot, by the way."

"Wow. You roped Diego into this harebrained scheme with you? You can tell me later what you promised in exchange for his efforts." I braced myself. "So...uh...you found him?"

"We had to swipe left on hundreds of profiles, but yes." She clucked her tongue. "Let me just say that I still think there are plenty of men in New York City craving a serious relationship, and they're not all like Leo et al., but...um...I don't think Finn is one of them. I took a screenshot of his bio if you want to see it."

I took a steeling inhale. "Send it to me." My voice came out in a whisper.

"Okay. Hold on a second." She kept talking. "This is all my fault. You were so 'If he wanted a girlfriend, he'd have one,' and I was all like, 'Maybe he just hasn't found the right girl yet. You could be her.'"

The way her voice went up an octave during "my" part would have been comical if I didn't feel like I was going to throw up.

"I sent it."

My nausea escalated. "Sorry in advance if I disconnect you by accident." With a shaky hand, I went to my home screen and to my texts. I enlarged the attachment she'd sent. It was a close-up of Finn dressed in a medieval monk outfit in front of Burp Castle, a "whisper-only" bar in the city. Something warm exploded in my belly. He was such a dork. And I would have swiped right on him immediately.

> Finn
> 28. Manhattan, NY
> Straight, Man, Single, 6'1, average build.

I pictured Finn's broad torso. We had two entirely different definitions of "average." At least no one would accuse him of overreaching.

> White, Speaks English and Spanish, Attended university, Drinks sometimes, Omnivore, Doesn't have kids.

> Looking for women for short-term dating and hookups. Open to non-monogamy.

I brought my hand to my mouth like I was going to be sick and fell back on the toilet seat. Then I closed out of the text and returned to Kate. "I'm here." I blinked back tears.

"Are you okay?"

*Not even a little bit.* "I'm fine. Just caught off guard is all."

I straddled the line between full-on honesty and completely minimizing the extent of my distress. If I said I didn't care, she'd know I was lying. But I really didn't want to cry *again*. And I didn't want to make Kate feel worse than she already did. She wrongly blamed herself for getting my hopes up that I could have something real with Finn.

"You should have banged the handyman!"

I choked on a laugh. "My bad. Though, honestly, this just confirms what I assumed about Finn the minute I found out he wasn't from Pleasant Hollow."

"What now?"

"I do what I came here to do. Write a story." I gave her an abbreviated update. "In the meantime, I have to deal with the naked man in the next room."

"Meaning?"

"I'll let you know as soon as I figure it out. Thank you for looking out for me."

"Always!"

After we ended the call, I stared at my sad reflection in the mirror. My face looked like it had been through a landslide—droopy eyes, downturned lips. I was a poster child for the heart-sick population. I had to pull myself together before I left the bathroom.

I blinked a few times to wake up my dull eyes, patted my cheeks for color, and rolled my shoulders back. Into the mirror, I said, "It's fine, Adi. *You* are fine. Now you can lower your expectations. It's *fine*."

I took a deep breath, opened the door, and stepped back into the room.

# Chapter Twenty-Seven

Finn muted the television. "Everything all right with your friend?"

"Uh-huh."

I crouched by "my" side of the bed and scanned the room for my clothes. My stomach hurt like I'd drunk a gallon of full-lactose milk—*expired* full-lactose milk with chunks—but I had options. I could take Finn's dating profile at face value and assume his desire for commitment was limited to short-term dating with exclusivity up for debate. *Or* I could ask him straight up.

He'd been kind to me—welcoming—more so than anyone else in this godforsaken hamlet. Giving him the courtesy of a face-to-face rather than relying on OkCupid was the least I could grant in return.

But the only thing worse than having a define-the-relationship conversation was having it naked. I spied my jeans partially hidden under the bed and pulled them to me. My black thong still clung to the crotch of the denim like I'd undressed my bottom half in one swift motion. Once I was clothed from the hips down, I searched for my shirt, wondering if I'd find it dangling from a lampshade or hanging outside his door like a DO NOT DISTURB sign. We'd returned from the park the night before technically sober, but drunk on lust.

"What do you want to do today? Do you need to work? If not, we could enjoy Sunday Funday at Brothers? Or coffee and pie...er, bacon at Pinkie's. Or if you want to be active outside of bed, there's a hiking trail we can take."

I stared at him. *We.* Did Adi plus Finn equal a "we"? Was it possible his dating profile was outdated? Had he written it on a dare? *Don't be a pussy, Adi. Ask the question.*

A boom of thunder sounded from outside.

"So much for the hike." He patted the bed. "Come back here."

Instead, I walked to the window, picking up my bra and star-printed long-sleeved T-shirt off the floor on the way. It was before noon, yet the sky resembled a giant black-and-blue mark. I finished dressing while watching the trees outside sway rhythmically, like a choreographed dance.

Through with stalling, I turned on my heel and sat on the edge of the bed. *Not* doing this would be so much easier, but I'd hate myself.

Finn smiled. "Finally."

I clasped my hands together. "I'm glad we met."

His lip quirked up on one side. "Likewise."

"I'm going to be straight with you," I said, running my palm up and down the periwinkle-blue comforter. "That was my friend Kate on the phone before."

"I know."

"She found your dating profile."

Finn's mouth went slack with surprise.

"I didn't ask her to, but I told her about you, and..." My

face prickled with heat. "Is it true you only do short-term dating and hookups?"

He winced.

I put a hand up. "This is not an attack. You don't owe me anything except an honest answer."

His Adam's apple bounced when he swallowed. Then he looked me straight in the eyes. "It's true."

My heart sank even though I knew this. I *knew*. "I get it." I nodded. "There are a lot of single women out there. Why tie yourself down?"

It was everything I feared from the start about crushing on the hot city dude. Would I ever learn? I tensed my muscles to keep from shaking.

A shadow crossed his face. "It's not that. It's…" He scrubbed a hand along his beard. "I'm not boyfriend material."

"What's that supposed to mean? You're made of polyester instead of flesh and blood?"

A faint smile flickered across his lips before he shook his head. "Relationships are…" He closed his eyes for a beat. "I've tried, and it's not…it's complicated."

*Complicated.* What did that mean? My mouth opened to speak. *No.* I gripped a square of the comforter. I wasn't going to be that person—the one who continued to ask the questions when the most important one had already been answered. This…whatever *this* was…wasn't my HEA.

"You don't need to explain."

He sighed. "Adi. I never meant to lead you on. I thought you were okay with…" He waved his hands around the room as if the space represented our "relationship."

"You didn't." I shook my head emphatically. "I knocked on

your door that night with no expectations, and I have no regrets. But our one-night stand has morphed into a several-night stand, and I think we should stop before someone catches feelings." Except it might be too late.

"Of course. If that's what you want." His voice was soft.

I nodded, even though it was hardly what I *wanted*. For once, I *wanted* a relationship where my partner didn't have one foot out the door while peering over his shoulder for something shinier to come along.

Finn rose from the bed and lifted a shirt over his head. The sinewy muscles of his chest tempted my restraint, and I averted my eyes.

"A committed relationship just doesn't fit into my life. But I like you," he said. "I really do."

I blew a raspberry with my lips. "Well, duh. What's not to like?"

He laughed, his smile split wide. "If I were going to get involved with someone, she'd be like you, Adi Gellar. It's not you. It's me."

I rolled my eyes. "Spare me."

I wasn't sure how much longer I could keep up the act. I glanced at the clock radio on his nightstand and fake-gasped. "It's almost checkout time." I pushed myself to a standing position and motioned toward the door. "I'd better go tell Lorraine I need to reserve for another week."

This talk with Finn had changed nothing. If anything, it made me even more determined to smoke out a story. Perhaps it was too much to ask to leave Pleasant Hollow with both a promising love life and a career, but I'd be damned if I left without at least one of them.

"Adi?"

I stopped with my hand on the knob and faced him. "Yeah?"

His face looked pained. "We can still be friends, right?"

I smiled softly. "Of course. Friends."

# Chapter Twenty-Eight

*B*ack in my room, I showered to wash the remnants of Finn—his touch, taste, smell—from my skin and tried to focus on the positive. It was better to find out Finn was exactly like every other guy in Manhattan now, so I could gird my loins from falling even deeper in...I quivered. This was *not* love.

I was still in my towel when there was a knock on my door. "Ms. Gellar."

Startled, I dropped my deodorant on the floor.

Another knock. "Ms. Gellar," Lorraine repeated.

"One second," I called before scurrying to the door, hiking up my towel on the way. My reservation didn't include flashing Lorraine my 32 barely Bs.

"This is your checkout reminder," she said from the other side of the door. "Please be out by noon so I can clean up for the next guest."

My towel fell to the floor. *Shit.* Technically, I was late to check out, but since I planned to extend my reservation, I didn't think she'd mind. Given how empty the place had been all week, I doubted anyone was waiting for my room. By the time I got myself decent and popped my head into the hallway to confirm, she was already down the hall, leaving behind only a hint of her flowery perfume.

Fifteen minutes later, I made my way to the first floor and with each step, the noise coming from the common room got louder and louder. I froze at the bottom of the stairs. The place was packed!

I felt the need to warn the poor innocents that Pleasant Hollow wasn't much of a vacation destination, but first I had to find Lorraine. I weaved through the maze of people and luggage. Spotting her near the kitchen, I said, "Excuse me" and slid between a silver-haired couple who were gesticulating wildly. I kept my arms pressed tightly to my sides to avoid getting caught in the line of fire.

*Whack.* I lurched upon impact with a little boy—correction: a *wet* little boy—who'd crashed right into me. I took a step back and tripped on an umbrella. "What the actual fuck?" I said, instantly regretting my profanity in the company of a minor, but the child either hadn't heard me or had already rushed to tell his parents about the lady who cursed.

I found Lorraine in the crowd and told her I needed to extend my stay.

Except instead of asking for my credit card as expected, she shook her head. "No vacancies. We're at full capacity." She gestured out the window. "Pretty treacherous conditions out there."

I followed her line of vision. My mouth opened and stayed that way. Never mind cats and dogs, it was raining lions and wolves. "How long is it supposed to last?"

"Long enough for people to get off the road and book a room for the night."

The hair on my arms stood up.

"Law enforcement is encouraging people to stay indoors until the storm passes."

I whipped my head in the direction of the television mounted on the wall and listened as a local meteorologist continued his warning against driving.

"We need to emphasize the danger of being on the road for the next twelve to eighteen hours," he said, pointing at the moving weather map marked almost entirely in green.

"Let me know when you're out of your room," Lorraine said before turning to another guest.

I nodded absently. What was I going to do? My stomach hardened.

"Adi." Finn appeared by my side like a friendly apparition.

I hugged myself to keep from shaking.

"Are you all right?" His brows furrowed with concern.

"Not even a little bit." I shared my predicament with my new *friend*. "Is there anywhere else to stay in Pleasant Hollow?" Based on the research I'd done back home, the next closest lodging was in a different town. "You think Lorraine would let me camp out here?" I pointed at the assortment of chairs. "I don't need much." It would be good practice for when Mom and I were out of a home.

"Why don't you stay with me tonight?"

I shook my head. "No. I...I couldn't."

"Why not? You spent the last four nights with me anyway."

"That was different." My initial comfort with a hookup had changed to optimism—some might say delusion—that it could grow into something more. Now I was stuck in this in-between place where casual sex with Finn felt dangerous. Stupid *feelings*.

I was positive he'd respect my choices, but it would be awkward and uncomfortable.

"What's going on in that head of yours?" he asked teasingly.

"It's not a good idea," I said, shifting my feet.

He frowned. "I'm not sure you have a choice. There are no other rooms available, and the roads are too bad to leave town. You can book your own room tomorrow after the weather clears and most of these people check out."

I pressed my fingers to my temples. This was a trip planned by Satan himself.

"It's not a quid pro quo offer. If that's what you're worried about."

I searched his face, finding nothing but genuine kindness. I kind of hated him for it. But he was right. I had no choice. My shoulders relaxed in defeat. "Okay. Anything to escape this shit show."

As if I needed further incentive, the woman to my right shook her head zealously and her wet ponytail slapped me in the face. "But I will absolutely pay you back," I said, wiping my damp cheek. With what or whose money, I hadn't a clue.

"The hotel bill gets passed along to my boss. Andrew has no idea how many people are actually staying with me."

I didn't ask how many others had shared his bed since he got here. I simply expressed my assent and thanked him for his generosity.

Then I said a silent prayer I wouldn't regret it.

# Chapter Twenty-Nine

Finn said to make myself comfortable while he tidied up the bathroom. He was something of a neat freak, I'd noticed. In contrast to the room I'd just vacated, all of Finn's clothes were either tucked into drawers or hung in the closet, and there wasn't a single shoe to trip over. His desk was empty of deodorant sticks, hairbrushes, and pain reliever bottles, which suggested that, unlike me, he kept them in the bathroom where they belonged. I doubted there was much to "tidy up," but I appreciated his effort. It was hardly the first time I'd been here, but the circumstances were *much* different.

Antsy, I walked over to the window. Whereas my room had a view of the backyard garden, his looked out onto Main Street. The sky was currently one shade away from black with occasional streaks of white when lightning struck. How much longer until another room would become available? I glanced at my watch and sighed. If I didn't know better, I'd think time was moving backward.

"What's it doing out there?" Finn asked.

Still facing the window, I said, "It's bad. The town's autumnal equinox parade will surely be rained out."

Behind me, Finn whined and stamped a foot. "But we can still bob for apples, though, *ri-eet*?"

I laughed and turned to face him. "I'm starving. Want to see if Lorraine put out any food in the common room?" The more time we spent outside of his hotel room, the better.

Finn agreed and we headed downstairs where guests were spread out on the couch and chairs. Others stood in the kitchen drinking coffee and eating from boxes of Entenmann's chocolate chip cookies. A din of conversation filled the air.

"Wow. It's so homey." I could hardly believe my eyes. Sure, *now* it was like a scene from a Hallmark movie, only with store-bought baked goods.

Finn handed me a cookie and a napkin. "Material for your story?"

"It's a good thing I brought my trusty notebook with me." I patted the bulging pocket of my hoodie sweatshirt. "Maybe Lorraine will organize a game of charades."

"Or hangman."

"Would you rather?"

His eyes sparkled. "Never have I ever."

"Murder mystery."

"Not it," Finn said, lifting his palms.

"To be the killer or the kill*ee*?"

He scrunched his face. "Is kill*ee* a word?"

"Victim. Whatever." With my cookie in hand, I walked to the nearest window and gave a silent *F you* to Mother Nature. But for the storm, the B&B would be empty and I'd be in my own room brainstorming my story instead of engaging in far-too-delightful banter with Finn and making a mental list of ways to avoid having sex with him again.

The only thing I had going for me was this gathering. It was a perfect time suck. With any luck, it would go late, and by the time we retired for the night, I could feign exhaustion.

"I used to be afraid of thunder," Finn said out of nowhere.

"Really?" I stole a quick glance over my shoulder at him before turning back around. It hurt too much to look at him right now.

"My dad told me to count the seconds between every boom. He said if I could get to ten, it meant the storm was almost over."

I faced him again. "Is that a thing? The ten-second rule?"

His gaze locked on something out the window. "I'm not sure, but it distracted me from my fear, which I guess was his intention."

I smiled, touched by the reminiscence. "That's a nice memory."

"The good ol' days." His face went dark for a moment, then back to normal like someone had waved a magic wand in front of it. "Want another cookie?" he asked.

"No thanks."

"Be right back."

I sighed dejectedly at the abrupt change of conversation, even though there was no reason to expect Finn to confide in me again. He hadn't voluntarily shared his homeless experience either. I'd dragged it out of him. When was the last time *I* had poured my soul out to a hookup? Why should he? But I couldn't help wanting to know more about him anyway.

It was time to mingle. I scanned the room. My lips curled into a grin when I spied a woman wearing a Peloton Century Club T-shirt. I weaved through the crowd until I reached her. "Congratulations on the milestone," I said, pointing at her shirt.

The company gifted it to members after they took one hundred of their cycling classes.

She glanced down, as if to reacquaint herself with her current outfit, and beamed. "Thank you! You ride?"

"I'm a spin instructor. For New York Fitness Club, not Peloton." I'd taken my share of Peloton classes, but I wasn't comfortable in front of the camera (or hot enough).

"What a great job. Are you certified?"

"I am. I took an instructor certification course a couple years ago but stopped at the basic level." A sour taste seeped into my mouth at the reminder my certification was due for renewal soon. More money I didn't have.

"How many levels are there?" Finn glanced between us. "Sorry to interrupt. I'm Finn."

"Debra. Nice to meet you. Tell me more about the certification process," Debra said, tilting her head to one side.

"There are master levels I could take, but they're mainly for people who want a long-term career in cycling. My mom suggested I get certified to make extra money while trying to break into journalism."

Finn smiled. "I love that it was your mom's idea."

I recalled my first-ever class. I was in high school and Mom brought me to Equinox as her guest. The instructor, Darryl, worked us so hard I thought I would die. I was hooked from then on. "She's the one who introduced me to spinning. She comes to my classes sometimes."

"Did you say you're a journalist?" Debra asked.

"I am! I'm actually writing a story on Pleasant Hollow," I said proudly.

Her head drew back quickly, and her blue eyes widened. "This town? Why?"

"Good question," I mumbled.

Finn snorted.

I poked him in the side. "Stop it."

Debra beamed at us. "You guys are an adorable couple!"

"We're not together!" Finn said loudly and forcefully.

Debra took a step back. "Oh, sorry. I just assumed."

"Yes, we're just friends," I said through gritted teeth. What was his problem?

We stood in a triangle of silence.

"Brian!" Debra tugged at her son's arm as he ran by. "What did I say about running inside?" She shook her head in frustration. "Kids. I'm sorry. Nice to meet you both!" She raced after her son, who I recognized as the little boy who'd run right into me earlier.

I laughed at the irony of her doing exactly what she told her son *not* to do and turned to Finn. My body tensed, remembering his outburst.

He looked properly chagrined. "I'm sorry for..." He lowered his gaze. "Before."

My face went hot. "I heard you the first time. You're not boyfriend material. *Blah, blah, blah.*" I placed my hands on my hips. "Don't worry. I'm not going to boil bunnies on the stove. We had a fling—a four-night stand. It was hot, but we're not in some romance novel. I get it." I spotted Lorraine by the grandfather clock. "I need to remind Lorraine to save a room for me for tomorrow." I rushed over to her, willing him not to follow me.

The crowd dwindled at the same rate as the Entenmann's

cookies and before long, guests retired to their rooms. Back at Finn's, we worked in silence. I wrote a three-hundred-word freelance article on a small, employee-owned, fair-trade organic coffee company based out of Colorado—the assignment I'd applied for before I left the city—at his desk while he stretched out on the bed with his laptop on his knees. While it didn't solve my immediate problems, snagging the coffee piece lifted my confidence that I had the potential to make more money on my writing, even without a full-time job at *Tea*, if I doubled down on my freelance efforts.

The first draft finished, I put it aside to edit the next day and resumed my search for a new angle here in Pleasant Hollow. I had my laptop open to the public financial records I could find on the town. There was data on expenditures, revenue, budget, and payroll, but I couldn't make heads or tails of the numbers. I was not one of those blessed to have the gift of words *and* numbers.

I could ask Finn to interpret, but the subscribers of *Tea* wouldn't care about the contents of Pleasant Hollow's Comprehensive Annual Financial Report from preceding fiscal years anyway. If the *locals* cared enough about The Hollows to seek evidence that its development would hurt them financially, it might be worth digging, but they didn't, so it wasn't. I also strongly suspected any further prodding would lead to the opposite conclusion.

I closed out of the window and turned my attention to Finn's desk. There were a lot of papers on it, naturally in neat little piles. My eyes scanned the documents at the top of each stack as a procrastinating device more than out of actual curiosity: *Certificate of Liability Insurance*; *Insurer: A. Hanes Ltd.*; *Workers'*

*Compensation; Name of injured party: John Connors.* Yadda yadda yadda. Fascinating stuff it was not. I glanced over my shoulder. "Maybe I should reconsider taking Johnny up on his offer for dirt on The Hollows."

Finn glanced up from his computer. "What kind of *dirt* do you expect to find?"

"I don't know. Witch trials?"

He gave a crooked smile. "Séances?"

"Orgies?"

He laughed. "Sorry to be a bummer, but unless a worker falling off a ladder because his eyes were dilated from the optometrist appointment he didn't tell me about is considered scintillating material, I've got nothing for you."

"Boooring," I teased. "I wouldn't throw your construction site under the bus for a story anyway." I was still a journalist first, and my temporary role as Finn's lover had been adjourned, but my *fondness* for him rendered the notion of betraying his trust for the sake of the story unthinkable.

"Much appreciated."

I buried my face in my hands. "But what am I going to do?"

I heard a shuffling of feet and looked up at Finn standing in front of me.

"What?" I was still having flashbacks to earlier when he'd declared to Debra with obnoxious exclamation points that "We're not together!"

Finn's eyebrows shot up, but he didn't comment on my surly tone. "Can I make a suggestion?"

I flapped a hand beckoning him to speak. "By all means."

"You tried to make the town fit into your preconceived story, and it didn't work because—"

"Because Pleasant Hollow is not a Hallmark town."

"Ding, ding, ding." He mimed ringing a bell. "And you got frustrated when you didn't get the answers you needed."

"Was there a suggestion in there somewhere?"

He gave an amused shake of his head. "How about this time you just talk to people with no specific angle in mind? Just talk to them. Find out who they are and what makes them tick. I bet you'll find your story."

I clucked my tongue. "You sound like my editor, only less fragmented."

"I don't know what that means, but I'll take it as a compliment."

"You should." I felt the color rise to my cheeks. "It's a smart idea. Thank you." Ordinarily I'd be annoyed by a man swooping in to try to *fix* things, but Finn wasn't exercising his machismo or mansplaining. He was merely staying the course of the support and encouragement he'd been providing since we'd met. His kindness was hella annoying.

"You're welcome." He sat on the edge of the bed. "Have you met Mel from Mel's Hardware?"

"Yes. I only mildly humiliated myself in his store."

The corner of Finn's mouth curled. "We get last-minute supplies from him. I can make a more personal introduction. He's a lifer in Pleasant Hollow. Might have something you can use."

"That would be great. Thanks."

Feelings of gratitude battled the impulse to question Finn's motives. But my mind was already churning with ideas. I could ask locals how they came to settle here. Maybe they were third- or fourth-generation residents who never dared to explore beyond the borders of Pleasant Hollow. Perhaps they'd ventured to other destinations and returned for an old love. Or they'd gotten lost (or lost their memories), found themselves in Pleasant Hollow, and fell in love with the town. Unlikely, but not impossible. In any event, all of these origin stories were traceable to Hallmark movies. I'd go in with an open mind and surrender my preconceived story if I had to, but it eased my stress to have a potentially fitting option in my pocket.

"I've also gotten friendly with Jan." He paused. "From Lickety Splits."

I pouted. "Too soon."

He tossed his head back in laughter. "I'm not joking. Maybe you can redeem yourself if I intervene."

"Your rep could take a beating if she knows we're friends."

"I'll risk it. You can pay me in ice cream."

"Deal. What's your favorite flavor, by the way?" For no good reason whatsoever, I hoped he'd say rum raisin.

"Mint chocolate chip. Why?"

"Just curious." I bent a stray paper clip between my fingers. "Why are you being so nice to me?"

He narrowed his eyes. "Why wouldn't I be nice?"

"I mean, what's in it for you?" A knot formed in my stomach at what I left unsaid about the discontinuation of our sexy times.

"Besides the satisfaction of knowing I helped someone?"

I raised an eyebrow.

He extended his foot to lightly kick the leg of my chair. "Maybe you'll acknowledge me in your story."

Laughing awkwardly, I said, "The pieces I write don't have acknowledgments."

"I was jok—" He was interrupted by the ringing phone on the nightstand. "You mind?"

"Of course not." I refocused on my notepad, wrote: *Get to know the town, and the story will follow.*

"Tell me what happened."

I instinctively spun around at the urgency in his voice.

"Just calm down." He ran his free hand through his thick hair while pacing the room.

I stood, desperate to know if he was okay.

He lifted his head, as if sensing me watching him, and frowned. "I'm just gonna…" He pointed at the door. "Take this in the hallway."

"Okay."

He stepped outside, and my eyes remained fixed to the door for half a minute until I forced myself to look away. I sat back down. Finn's phone call was none of my business. *He* was none of my business, and I had a story to write. But since I was following Finn's advice and not planning my interviews ahead of time, there was nothing for me to do until the next morning.

I knelt in front of my roller suitcase and moved my toiletry bag from the right side to the left, then rearranged my dirty clothes from the top to the bottom. I stared absently at a dirty sock. Where was its other half? I grabbed my toiletry bag and a pair of purple-and-white polka-dot pajama pants from my suitcase and stood.

Who was calling Finn? Andrew Hanes? It didn't sound like a business call, but what did I know? Inside the bathroom, I slipped out of my jeans and into my PJs. Then I washed my face, removing all traces of makeup, and tied my hair in a ponytail. Staring back at me in the mirror was a woman I was confident Finn would have no problem keeping his hands off. It was for the best.

I reentered the room at the same time Finn returned from the hallway. I froze with one foot still in the bathroom. "Is everything all right?"

"It's fine." He turned his back to me and toyed with something on his dresser.

"It sounded..." What word was I searching for? "Not fine."

He spun around. "Just some stuff. Work stuff. I need to deal with it tomorrow."

Something was sus, but I had to back down. He wasn't a source I needed to press for answers. And he wasn't my boyfriend.

I nodded. "Okay." I slowly stepped toward the bed in the late realization there was only one of them and two of us. "I can sleep on the floor."

Finn jerked his head back. "Why?"

"Because I told you I don't think it's a good idea for the two of us to...to..." I made the universal gesture for sex with my thumb and index finger.

Understanding washed over his face. "I think we're fully capable of sharing a bed without having sex," he said, grabbing a pillow from the bed and holding it to his chest. "But I'm happy to sleep on the floor if it makes you more comfortable. Although I think the chair might be better."

My rib cage tightened. "No. It's your room. You should sleep on the bed. I'll take the chair." I pressed the other pillow to *my* chest.

"Not happening."

We squared off, both of us holding pillows tightly to our torsos.

"This is ridiculous," Finn said at last. "There's enough room for another fully grown adult to fit between us as a human wall. Want me to ask Lorraine?"

"Gross!"

He laughed. "If sharing a bed makes you that uneasy, I'll absolutely sleep on the floor or chair, but I promise I won't touch you unless you touch me first."

I pressed my lips together. "I won't touch you."

Tossing his pillow back on the bed, he said, "Then you have nothing to worry about."

# Chapter Thirty

I woke up the little spoon, Finn curled around my back. His arms encircled my center where our hands were clasped together. I didn't remember when or how we got into this position, but I liked it. Without thinking, I settled in, adjusting my backside against him. I was already aroused.

Finn stirred and pulled me closer to him.

And then I remembered I wasn't supposed to enjoy this intimacy anymore...and Finn was hard.

I slid out of his grasp, cursing my body for betraying me in the worst possible way. "What happened to no touching?" I demanded.

Finn shuffled under the covers. He mumbled, "Sorry about the morning wood."

My face flamed.

He chuckled. "I don't recall you being so bashful, Adi Gellar." His leg brushed against mine.

I squirmed. "I'm not bashful. This is just...awkward." And excruciatingly painful. I wanted him. God, did I want him.

"It doesn't have to be. I like you. I think you like me. We've got this big bed."

I snorted.

"Fine. It's not as big as I thought it was. But as long as we're here…"

I studied his face, shining with hope, wishing I could see into his soul. He wasn't trying to hurt me. He *liked* me. The sex was great. Why not? But I couldn't erase the words on his dating profile. Or the certainty in his voice when he confirmed he wasn't interested in a long-term relationship. Beneath the pleasure of the act would be the crushing knowledge that the true connection I desired was beyond my reach. He now failed the "Will I be mentally okay if it doesn't lead anywhere?" part of my sex test. Being let down when things didn't progress with a guy was one thing, but getting my heart broken was another. I saw that potential with Finn. "I'm sorry, but no."

He nodded. "That's too bad. We're fantastic at morning sex."

*Don't I know it.*

Finn flipped his legs over the side of the bed and stretched his arms above his head. I could see the muscles of his back flex even through the T-shirt he'd slept in, probably out of respect for me. I looked away.

"I need to get an early start today," he said, now standing. "But feel free to take your time getting ready. I can bring you to Mel and Jan later if you want."

"That would be great. Thanks!"

He presented a silly grin. "What are friends for?"

After Finn left, I revised, finalized, and submitted the coffee article. Then I showered and went downstairs for coffee and sustenance. Henceforth, bacon and eggs at Pinkie's would be reserved for special occasions. Like when I pulled an actual story about Pleasant Hollow from my ass.

It was officially my second week on the road, and I shuddered at the thought of my approaching-negative bank balance. For the first time since my arrival, the kitchen was filled with fellow lodgers. I joined the crowd, prepared to battle for a muffin that wasn't oatmeal, and was pleasantly surprised to find my B&B mates hovered over several dozen assorted donuts from Dunkin' Donuts set out on the counter. Lorraine must have splurged. I removed a glazed donut and a French cruller (one for now and the other for later) from the batch and greeted Debra with a wave. Little Brian clung to the back of her leg and yawned. Like the rest of us, he was much less rambunctious in the morning. Then I confirmed with Lorraine that Room E would once again be mine after four p.m. and headed to the park.

My plan for the day was simple: talk to people and let the story find me. As far as plans went, it could use...well, *planning*, but it was all I had. However, before I exchanged niceties with strangers, I desperately needed the comfort and ear of a devoted friend. I chose a bench not far from Finn's and my "movie spot," and texted Kate.

You around?

Resting the phone in the space between my legs, I took a sip of coffee, letting the cool September breeze wash over me. The temperature had risen at least ten degrees since the last time I'd been outside on Saturday, and it was warm enough to wear my mom's purple hoodie without a jacket. The sky was bright blue and dotted with cumulus clouds. When I was about eight, I went through a stage where I was certain my dad lived on a cloud. My mom taught me the different types: cumulus, stratus, cirrus, and so on. We collectively decided my father had taken up residence on a cumulus, because they were the coziest of all clouds and we wanted him to be comfy in his new home. Seventeen years later, I stared intently at one and pleaded for my father, if he was there, to give me some guidance. *Help me find the story.* I implored him to make me forget all about Finn like I had forgotten all the other boys. I had no reason to believe my dad was listening, but what was there to lose?

I jolted at the sound of my ringtone. Kate was FaceTiming me, which was the next best thing to an answer from my dad right now. "You didn't have to call. Aren't Monday mornings busy for you?" I said, which, in our secret best-friend language, translated to "Thank God you called. What took you so long? I *need* you!"

"*Tuh!* As if I can concentrate on work when my best friend's love life is in turmoil." She scowled at me and tugged a strand of the long, straight black hair she'd worn with the same middle part since we met. It was only recently she'd gone bold (her words, not mine) with red highlights.

Even glowering, her face on my phone at this moment was like chicken soup for my battered soul. "It's bad, Kate." The sweeping statement referred to everything: my love life, my career, and the imminent rent hike. "I don't know what to do."

She pressed her pale red–painted lips together. "Tell me everything." It wasn't a request. It was a command. "Start from the beginning."

By the time I caught her up, my coffee was drained, and I was halfway through my second donut. I wiped the crumbs off my jeans, relaxed into the bench, and prepared for one of Kate's incomparable pep talks.

Her face wrinkled up. "I need to go, but will you be around later?"

My lips moved, but no words came out. "Um...yeah?" I had overestimated her. This morning's pep talk was incomparably *ineffective*. It was my fault for needing her services on a weekday. She also had her own problems, like failing the bar. It wasn't fair to expect her to drop everything.

She tilted her head to the side. "I promise we'll figure this out. For now, just do you, which is to say, be so irresistibly likable that the people of Pleasant Hollow can't help but want to be your friend and spill their secrets! Also, when I say people, I mean hot, single, twentysomething men who will restore your— *our*—faith in romance." She held up a pinky to the screen. "Promise?"

"Pinky swear." I wiggled one pinky at the phone, crossing the fingers of my other hand behind my back, and we ended the call.

# Chapter Thirty-One

Twinkly Nails was unlikely to be packed with men (single or attached), but it was my first stop, because I desperately needed a manicure. And surveys showed people with painted nails were more likely to make friends than those without. I might have made that up, but I believed it to be true—mind over matter.

With its hot-pink, black, and white exterior, Twinkly Nails was the only local business that met my small-town expectations in terms of charm. Even better, the entrance had been rigged to play the opening notes of "Nail Polish" by Sophie Beem upon entry. I stepped inside and wiggled my hips and shoulders to the music. I was still mid-wiggle with several sets of eyes on me when the music stopped. I froze like it was a game of statues and greeted the sparsely filled salon with an awkward smile. "I'd like to get a manicure."

A woman in her mid-thirties with thick, dirty-blond hair and large gold-rimmed glasses nodded. "Pick a color," she said, gesturing toward the back of the room.

The salon was set up with rows of nail stations on the right and about seven black leather chairs for pedicures on the left. Shelves with an impressive array of nail polish colors were located in the back of the room near the dryers and a private room which I guessed was used for waxing.

I ignored the pretty bottles of Essie and OPI and went straight to the selection of Bettie Pain colors. I was unfamiliar with the brand, but the owner's sister, Davina, had said customers traveled far for it. I quickly chose Vorfreude, a bright-pink base with flecks of purple and gold, and returned to the blonde, who gestured for me to sit at her station. I was glad she didn't pass me along to her colleague, the one I'd spied giving the death stare to the back of a customer's head the week before. I snuck a glimpse at her and suppressed a laugh as she yawned into her customer's back mid–chair massage.

Examining my cracked nail beds, my technician said, "You look familiar but not."

Strangely enough, I knew exactly what she meant. "I'm from out of town, but we spoke when I came in last week. I'm a journalist." Hopefully, she wouldn't remember the manicure appointment I'd canceled at the last minute.

Her light eyebrows climbed up over the top of her glasses. "Oh, right! You interviewed my sister too."

"Yes." Davina had been the ideal candidate for a character profile of a Pleasant Hollow resident with a Hallmark-movie job, minus the living in Pleasant Hollow part. My ribs tightened at the reminder of my earlier setback. *Move on, girl.* "My name's Adina."

"Laura. I own Twinkly Nails. Davina told me about the misunderstanding."

I shifted in my chair. "Um…yeah…I'm sorry I wasted her time."

"It's her fault too, because she insists on using the Pleasant Hollow hashtag on all her posts. I know she's trying to be supportive and pay her success forward, but it was bound to cause confusion." She held up a stainless-steel cuticle pusher. "Can I cut your cuticles or just push back?"

"Whatever you think is best." I instantly liked Laura, as I had her sister. "No need to play the blame game. I enjoyed talking to her, and maybe someday I'll feature her in a story. Just not this one." The direction of the conversation reminded me there was a dual purpose to being in this salon right now: a much-needed manicure *and* my new angle. Focusing on both Finn and Kate's advice to open a no-pressure dialogue, I said, "So you're not originally from Pleasant Hollow either, I assume?"

"Nope. Born and raised in the Albany area."

"Can I ask what brought you to this tiny town?"

She lifted an eyebrow and cocked her head. "You really want to know?"

"Of course! I wouldn't ask otherwise," I said truthfully.

She placed a warm washcloth over my hands and rubbed them together, instantly scoring even more points. "I got my cosmetology certification when I was eighteen. I worked in nail salons for years, slowly building up a decent clientele. But I didn't always agree with the owner's choices—what gels they used, what products they invested in, and such. I dreamed of opening my own shop."

She massaged my right hand with a soothing yet firm touch. "I didn't come from money, had no degree beyond high school, and property is mad expensive. But then a real estate agent showed me this space. I had never even heard of this backwater town, but the price was right, and unlike most cities, where there's a salon on every block, there was zero competition here. I jumped on it and never looked back." She finished massaging my left hand. "Do you want to pay now?"

"Sure." Pushing aside worry about my increasing balance, I handed her my credit card, which she walked over to the front desk for processing. Knowing I wouldn't be able to use my hands for a while, I peeked at my phone. There was a notification from OkCupid:

Your profile is about to become inactive. You haven't been online in a bit, so we'll stop showing your profile soon. Still want to connect? Log in today.

I slouched in my chair with a low whimper. Why had I allowed my hopes to soar that Finn could be more than a temporary hookup? Would I be chained to these hellish dating apps forever? If given the choice right now, I'd rather walk Main Street body-painted with nail polish than go on another blind date with a city boy, but I knew those pesky *needs* would rear their evil head at some point. For the sole purpose of keeping my profile active for when the time came, I opened the app and swiped left on the first two bios without even reading. Then I clapped my hands together to be done with it.

When Laura returned with my card, I pushed thoughts of sex, Finn, and sex *with* Finn to the side and beamed at her. "Your success story is super inspiring. Would you mind if I mentioned it in my piece?" I signed my name on the bill and leaned in conspiratorially. "Between you and me, I'm not sure what the story is about yet. I want to talk to some locals. Maybe other business owners' dreams coming true in this relatively unknown town can be the common thread."

Laura's friendliness inspired confidence that others would do the same if I took my desperation down a notch. At this point, I put minimal stock in an angle involving Andrew Hanes, but I wouldn't be a good journalist if I didn't bring it up again in this more casual atmosphere. "Are you afraid a salon going up in The Hollows will affect your clientele?" Perhaps her original answer from the week before would change now that we'd bonded.

"Not really. These hands"—she wiggled them—"are magic." Her eyes glinted. "I give the best manicure in Orange County, probably Dutchess too. I even have clients who drive in from Albany and Schenectady for my fillers!" She jutted her chin at my own newly sparkly nails. "You'll see what I mean in a few weeks when this manicure is still going strong."

My manicures were lucky to last five days before chipping. Whether the culprit was continuous tapping of computer keys or excessive sweating in my spin classes, I didn't know. Either way, I kept my doubts to myself.

"My clients are loyal, and I bet my prices are more competitive than whoever The Hollows brings in." She shook a bottle of Essie top coat. "I might not win over the people who live there. It's hard to compete with the convenience of a nail salon in the lobby, especially on rainy days like yesterday. But my mortgage is paid off, and I make more than enough with my existing clientele to handle my overhead."

"Final question. What's your favorite part of owning a nail salon?"

She grinned. "That's easy. Giving people a break from the daily grind of their own lives. For a relatively low price, my clients are pampered and leave far more relaxed than when they entered."

"Fantastic answer." Her reasons were similar to why I chose to be a lifestyle journalist, offering alternatives to the hard-hitting news by sharing uplifting stories that brought smiles to people's faces instead of fear. While my stories might not make readers feel pampered, if done right, they'd at least provide an escape from the stresses of their own lives for a little while.

We continued to chat until it was time for the dryer, and it was the most enjoyable conversation I'd had with anyone in Pleasant Hollow, besides Finn, since arriving. Twenty minutes later, she assured me my nails were smudge-proof. With Laura's permission, I snapped several photos of her and the interior of Twinkly Nails. Then I said my goodbyes, with no regrets over leaving a generous cash tip I couldn't afford.

I stepped out onto Main Street and searched for my dad's cloud in the sky. Laura was right. I felt relaxed . . . like things would be okay.

For the first time in over a week, I remembered what it was I loved about being a journalist. I was excited to talk to more people. Laura was passionate, ambitious, competent, and warm. I was surprised she'd lasted so long in Pleasant Hollow, where, at first impression, like-minded people seemed in short supply. If the second impression was the charm, I looked forward to getting it.

I didn't have a story yet, but I was confident that when I revisited my notes in a couple of days, the answer would stare back at me like a hidden message revealed at last.

# Chapter Thirty-Two

Motivated by my success at Twinkly Nails, I was eager to keep the momentum going. I had no destination in mind other than skipping over Mel's Hardware Store and Lickety Splits for now.

I skulked past the latter with my hand shielding the side of my face in case Jan was watching out the window. If Finn paved the way, I could make my own better second impression at both businesses later.

Only, that got me thinking about Finn and the strange telephone call the night before that had driven him into the hallway. From there, my mind wandered to waking up in his arms with his erection pressed against me. I felt an ache in my gut. I could have him, just not how I wanted. Best not to think about Finn at all. Redirecting my focus back to my journalism career, I walked two blocks down Main Street and through the doors of Books on Main.

Although not nearly as expansive as the Strand or various Barnes & Nobles in the city, Books on Main occupied a decent-size space for a mom-and-pop bookstore, and carried all of the typical categories like general fiction, mystery, young adult, nonfiction, biography, self-help, and romance. The owner, a statuesque Black woman with chin-length dark hair, was busy talking to another customer.

Like in Twinkly Nails, I didn't have a prepared roster of interview questions. Rather than repeat the mistakes of my past, the new plan was to engage in conversation more organically and see where it took me. Perusing the bookshelves would loosen me up like a pre-date cocktail. I uttered a quiet hello and marched right over to the romance section.

My fingers brushed the book covers with attractive couples embracing under a blue sky or in front of a body of water, mountain, park, or some other rural backdrop. Clearly, romance authors and publishers found a small town to be a more enchanting setting than a big city. Yet drop *me* in a small town and who did I fall for? Finn Adams from the Upper West Side, of "seeking short-term dating or hookups" fame—the opposite of romantic. Was it typical or ironic? I snorted. Probably a little bit of both.

Since turning off all thoughts of Finn was working (not) so splendidly, I removed *Waiting on You* by Kristan Higgins from the shelf and opened to a random page. Featuring estranged high school sweethearts Colleen and Lucas from the picturesque fictional town of Manningsport, New York, which was nothing like Pleasant Hollow, it was my favorite of the five-book Blue Heron series. While doing my buddy read with Kate, I'd ignored the descriptions of the main characters furnished by Higgins and pictured my parents instead (except during the sexy times, obviously).

"Can I help you with something?" came a friendly voice behind me.

I returned the book to the shelf and greeted the owner with a smile. "Out of curiosity, has Books on Main been the setting of any real-life meet-cutes?" I cringed as heat rose up my neck. The question had slipped out without any forethought.

The woman scrunched up her face in obvious puzzlement.

I pushed aside my initial reaction of embarrassment and trusted my instincts. I'd asked it for a reason, even if I had no idea what it was yet. "Pardon my goofiness." I chuckled nervously. "I'm a city girl who devours romance novels and Hallmark movies set in small towns." I made a sweeping motion around the store. "Charming indie bookstores like this often play a big role in how the couples meet, and I was just wondering if there's any truth to that here."

The woman continued to stare at me as if debating whether to call the town doctor—whom I'd yet to meet—for a consult. Then she threw back her head in laughter. "As the owner of a bookstore, I get asked a lot of questions, but this is a first."

"The change of scenery has brought out my quirky side, that's for sure," I said with a sheepish shrug.

She smiled warmly. "I've never witnessed a love match here myself, but in a sense, it's where my parents met."

"Do tell!"

The front entrance sounded the arrival of a new customer, whom she welcomed cordially before turning back to me. "Before the store was even built, when it was just unoccupied land, my dads put separate but matching bids on the property. While scoping out the competition, they discovered they both planned to use the space for the same purpose: a bookstore. They partnered up and fell in love." She surveyed the store with visible pride. "And the rest is history."

Goosebumps rose on my skin. "Wow. I'm full-on choked up here! What an amazing story."

Her eyes danced. "Isn't it?"

"I'd love to talk to your dads if they'd be interested." I removed my business card from my purse. Along with my name, phone number, and email address were the words COACH, ENERGIZER, STORYTELLER to correspond to my three vocations as a cycling instructor, barista, and journalist. "I'm a journalist from the city. You might recognize me from when I was in here last week."

She nodded. "I do. We don't get many new faces. I'm Grace."

I shook the slender hand she extended. "My original story angle fell through." I immediately regretted letting that detail slip. Oh well. Too late now. "Although I'm not sure what direction the article will take, the more material the better." My stomach cramped with the knowledge I'd eventually have to figure it out. I *would* figure it out. "Even if they don't want to be featured, serendipitous love stories like your fathers' are good for the spirit."

"I agree." Grace dropped her voice to a whisper. "Between us, I love Hallmark movies too. Pure fantasy."

"Totally. Like a dreamworld. A utopia! Nothing like real life." I cleared my throat. "You mind if I take some photos before I go?"

"Not at all." She waved my card. "I'll pass this along to my parents."

"Thank you!"

I took some pictures and, not wanting to leave the store empty-handed, selected a random romance novel from the shelf to purchase on my way out. A few minutes later, I stepped out into the sunshine in bright spirits. Derek was right when he'd said there was always a story. Little by little, I was finding mine.

Deeming a break well-deserved, I went back to the park to read my new book: *Rescue Me*. Less than a sentence into the back cover, I discovered my mistake. The hero's name was Finn McAllister. *Finn*. I shoved the novel back in the bag. Break over.

I was a block away from the B&B when Kate called. "Perfect timing!"

"Where are you?" she asked.

"Pleasant Hollow."

"Obvi, but where? Any chance you're near the B&B?"

"As a matter of fact, I'm..." I let my voice drop off as my eyes locked on a familiar face about twenty-five feet away. I squealed—*loudly*. Seriously, guinea pigs had nothing on me.

Like lovers reuniting, we ran into each other's arms and rocked back and forth. A tear fell from my eye.

"You're here," I said into her apricot-scented hair.

"I'm here," she repeated, squeezing me tight.

# Chapter Thirty-Three

*I* can't believe you're here." Standing outside the B&B, I studied Kate's face as if she might turn into someone else if I blinked.

Her light brown eyes held my gaze. "You sounded so lost this morning. I told my boss I had a family emergency and took the rest of today and tomorrow off."

I shook my head slowly with a close-lipped smile. "I did not see this coming. You cut off our call so quickly."

She placed her hands on her hips. "Yes! So I could borrow Diego's car and be here in time for a late lunch. Say hi to Mia the Kia," she said, jutting her chin to where her boyfriend's silver Kia Soul was parked across the street.

"You're amazing." I grabbed the handle of her small purple-paisley roller suitcase. "If my room is ready, we can drop this off and I can show you around."

Kate's sustainably sourced tan suede booties lifted two inches off the ground. "I can't wait."

I giggled. Her overenthusiasm reminded me of mine that first day. I hoped she would take the disappointment in stride.

Kate followed me inside the B&B, and I checked into Room E

for the second time in as many weeks. It took longer than it had to, thanks to Kate's numerous unsuccessful attempts to suck up to Lorraine.

Afterward, I said, "I told you she's not the warm and fuzzy type."

"What a letdown." Kate looked like she might cry.

"I have something to cheer you up." I removed *Rescue Me* from my purse and handed it to her. "A gift."

She stood in front of where I sat on the edge of the bed and hugged the book to her chest. "For me? Is it steamy?"

"I wouldn't know. Read the blurb." I watched her eyes scroll the back cover copy and then widen.

She burst out laughing. "Out of hundreds of romance novels you could have picked with heroes named Josh or Logan, you chose one with Finn. Hilarious."

I pouted. "The universe is cruel."

"No worries. I'll take it off your hands." She pulled me to a standing position. "Time for my tour."

Outside the B&B two minutes later, I said, "What do you want to see first, bearing in mind a tour of this town will take all of a half hour and that's including the residential area?"

"I'm starving. Have you had lunch?"

"I'm hungry too. Now's as good a time as any to show you Pinkie's Diner. It's my favorite spot, which isn't saying much considering the competition."

"How do they feel about bringing your own food?"

I froze, just now noticing the brown paper bag in her hand. "What's that?"

"Nothing. Just bagels from H&H." She kept walking as if

bringing me the holy grail of New York City bagels was no big deal.

I doubled my stride to catch up. "You didn't."

"Oh, I did. I assumed you might be jonesing for one."

"I am. I *so* am." I'd been in Pleasant Hollow less than two weeks, but it might as well have been two years where my taste buds were concerned. My mouth watered with anticipation. "I love you!"

She raised her chin high. "I know."

I led her away from the shops on Main Street toward the river. Kate's head swayed back and forth as she took it all in, and I tried to see it from her eyes—the flat grassy areas and concrete walking path that ran through it, a small kids' area with a swing set and jungle gym, benches every twenty or so feet, the statue of Natalie Schull. "It's pretty! Is there a gazebo?" Hope sparked in her eyes.

"Sorry." I smile-frowned at her. "Let's sit here." I stopped at a park bench, where I relished my scooped-out sesame bagel with veggie cream cheese and tomato, and gave her a status update. "It turns out not everyone in this town is standoffish and completely lacking in passion," I said, and filled her in on Laura and Grace.

"Yay! I knew you could do it. But what's the deal with Finn?"

I stopped mid-chew. "McAllister or Adams?"

She gave me a pointed look.

I kicked a pebble at my feet. "He's probably at work."

"Are you okay?"

At the sensation of her hand on my arm, I opened my mouth to tell her I was fine. What choice did I have? But I wasn't fine, and if I couldn't be straight with my best friend of almost twenty years, what was the point of her driving all the way here?

"There's something there, Kate. I know it. So much so that I let go of my cynicism and fantasized about our future!"

I took another, more aggressive bite of my sandwich before making a conscious effort to slow down and actually taste it. I'd be damned if I let Finn's lack of feelings for me ruin my bagel-eating experience.

"Why doesn't he want a girlfriend?" she asked.

"How would I know?"

"You didn't ask?"

"I didn't want to be that girl who's fine with a hookup right until the morning after, when she's suddenly all up in his business," I said in a quiet voice.

"Weren't you?"

I glared at her. "It took a little longer than that! The first couple of times, it was just casual sex with a really cool guy." I tapped my feet. "It was at least a day before I started questioning my feelings."

"A whole day!"

"I hate you." I laughed despite myself. "Around the time you showed me his OkCupid profile."

"Right." She ducked her head.

I nudged her shoulder. "It's not your fault!" I could tell she felt guilty, but it wasn't like she'd written Finn's dating profile. She just happened to be the one who'd brought it to my attention.

"I know." She sneezed.

"I own my initial decision to sleep with Finn, and I'm not kicking myself over it now. But I also stand by my right to cut off future encounters if it no longer feels healthy to me. Either way, Finn doesn't owe me an explanation."

"True. But what if he wants to give you one?"

"I'm guessing he doesn't, since he didn't."

She sighed. "All I'm saying is there's no harm in asking. You're a journalist!"

"I guess."

Kate was right, but the appropriate time to delve further into Finn's motives had been during our initial conversation, before I ran back to my own room. This morning, after we woke up in bed tangled in an embrace, would have been fine too, but Finn had rushed to get in the shower. And, honestly, did it really matter *why* he chose to remain a bachelor?

"Let's change the subject," I said. "Did you tell your parents about the bar yet?" Kate would probably claim that dropping everything to be here for me despite her current personal strife was a form of procrastination, and I'm sure it was, but it was *also* because she was the best friend on the planet.

"Uh-huh." She hung her head and let her dark hair curtain her face.

"How'd they take it?" I asked, my voice soft.

"They were outwardly cool about it, but I doubt they'll brag about their daughter the lawyer anytime soon. Not until I pass, at least." When she raised her head, her eyes lacked shine.

"Which you will!" I hated to see her so sad. "Your parents love you no matter what." They were both first-generation Americans who resented the pressure their Korean parents had put on them and made a point of going easier on their own children. Sure, they'd be saddened she didn't pass on the first try, but they'd both get over it and implore her not to give up.

"On to more important matters," she said, her face lighting up. "How was the sex with Finn?"

"Best sex of my life, Kate." I didn't know whether to laugh or cry.

"Yaaas!" Her hand, which she'd raised to give me a cheesy congratulatory high-five, paused in midair as she focused on something behind me. She widened her eyes like a flushed-face emoji, and her mouth dropped open. "Who's the hot Hemsworth? He looks familiar. Is that…"

I glanced over my shoulder. A man was jogging our way. A red plastic ball landed at his feet, and he stopped and bent at the waist to pick it up. He tossed it to a little boy a few inches away, using a soft touch to ensure it would be caught. He smiled as the boy toddled away toward his guardian and wiped his face with the bottom of his white T-shirt, giving us a glimpse of tight abs and a trail of hair leading under the waistband of his black runner shorts. "You're drooling."

"With good reason!" she said, still gawping at him.

Spotting us, he called out, "Adi!" and walked our way.

I shivered traitorously with pent-up desire. "Finn. Meet my best friend, Kate. Kate, this is my…Finn."

Finn smirked and extended his hand to Kate. "Nice to meet you, Kate. I'm her Finn."

# Chapter Thirty-Four

*J*ogging on your lunch hour?" I asked, careful not to let my eyes linger on his muscular calves or the sweat-soaked T-shirt clinging to his chest in the most delicious way.

He stood in front of our bench with his feet hip-width apart. "I just got back from Middletown. I'll go in later."

"Errands?" If my favorite television shows were any indication, many small towns relied on the adjacent larger ones for products they didn't supply locally.

"I visited my dad," he said, rubbing the back of his neck.

"Oh." I frowned. "Wait. Your father lives in Middletown? Isn't it less than a half hour away? Why wouldn't you stay with him instead of the B&B?"

"It's complicated."

*Complicated.* I hated that word. I stared him down, willing him to elaborate.

He stared back, either not getting the message or ignoring it, and said nothing while tightening and loosening his fists.

"Why crash with your dad when your boss will shell out money to let you stay in a cozy B&B within walking distance of work?" Kate said.

Finn grinned at her. "Exactly. Although as Adi already discovered, 'cozy' is questionable." His eyes glowed with mischief.

She gave me a knowing look. "Yes. *Adi* told me *all* about it."

I shot missiles at her with my eyes, which she ignored. It was becoming a trend.

"How long are you staying?" Finn asked Kate.

"Until tomorrow."

He nodded. "Adi can show you all the hot spots."

"Pinkie's and Brothers," she said proudly.

"That pretty much sums it up." They grinned at each other. *Again.*

"It might be a weird question given we just finished lunch, but what do you want to do for dinner?" Kate asked.

As thrilled as I was to interrupt their bonding moment, I was lost for an answer. "I know you want to live the whole Pleasant Hollow experience, but I figured we'd go to Pinkie's for breakfast or lunch tomorrow. I can't subject you to the pizza here." I fake-gagged. "I won't."

Finn laughed. "Good friends say no to bad pizza."

"Unless you want ice cream or beer for dinner, we're out of options in town. Should we order delivery from somewhere else?" I worked to focus on Kate, but found it hard to tear my gaze away from Finn in all his post-run sweatiness. My fingers ached to caress his muscular forearms and biceps.

"Why do we have to stay here? I have a car. Let's drive to . . ." She looked at Finn. "Is there anything good in Middletown?"

He nodded. "I like Lakeview House in Newburgh. It's also close. It's a little pricey, but the food is more than decent, and there's a nice view of a—"

"Let me guess. A lake?" I suggested smugly.

"You're too clever," Finn said.

Kate darted her eyes between us. "Does that work for you?" she asked me.

"Yes!" My skin buzzed with excitement to escape this town and eat yummy food with my best friend. The "little pricey" comment scared me, but the fear was nothing compared to my epic need for a quality meal. Physical distance from Finn...in the form of another town...would be nice too.

"Want to join us, Finn?" Kate asked.

Wait...*what*? I blinked furiously at her. What was she doing?

His lips formed a broad grin. "I'd love to."

"Great!" Kate said.

"Great," I repeated with a fraction of her exuberance.

"I should get back and shower," Finn said.

"We'll go with you." Heat crawled up my back. "Not in the shower!" I dropped my napkin for an excuse to bend down and hide my face. When I raised my back a moment later, I'd composed myself. "I need to grab my suitcase from your room."

Finn gave an exaggerated pout. "I like your first idea better, but fine."

While Kate giggled, I swatted him with my bagel bag before tossing it in a public trash can a few feet away.

Later, while Finn presumably showered in his room, I chastised Kate in mine. She sat on the edge of the bed with her feet dangling while I paced the room. "As the overprotective bestie in this triangle, you're supposed to hate Finn, no questions asked. You're not supposed to make googly eyes and invite him to dinner with us."

"If Finn had been a dick to you, you can be sure I'd hate him and he'd know it. But from everything you've told me, he's been super nice! Besides," she said, cocking her head, "it's obvious he likes you."

I gnawed the inside of my cheek. "As a temporary hookup. I was great at my job."

She stood and placed her hand on my shoulders. Shaking them lightly, she said, "There's a method behind my madness. Inviting him out with us is a way to get to know him better and find out why he doesn't want a relationship. You said you found nothing juicy online, right?"

I'd told her I caved and Googled Finn, but aside from his social media accounts—all private—I didn't find anything except a brief mention in a story about The Hollows and a photo on the website for Habitat for Humanity's Global Village program. (He was photogenic AF.)

I raised my hands to *her* shoulders, and we stood head-to-head like a pregame huddle. "Just promise me it's not because you hope he changes his mind. That he'll magically want a girlfriend after having dinner with us. As already established in clear, bright Technicolor, my life is not the stuff of romantic comedies, and Pleasant Hollow is not Angel Falls or any of those other magical TV towns. I've accepted it. You need to as well." I gave her a light headbutt.

"I promise." She dropped her hands. "And after dinner, we can always ditch Finn and go to Brothers. I can be your wingwoman."

I shook my head impatiently. "Except the married mayor doesn't even live here, the handyman is more interested in getting to know Manhattan than me…" To avoid discussing the irony, I quickly moved on. "And if the town has a single male doctor, lawyer, chef, or devoted schoolteacher, I haven't run into him yet."

"That's because you haven't had me to help you." She lifted an eyebrow.

"Kate." I dragged out her name.

She mimicked, "Adi," but then her face brightened.

My body went rigid. "What?"

"Finn calls you Adi."

"What's your point?"

She tossed her hair back and smirked knowingly. "You're blushing."

Considering my nipples hardened every time he used my nickname, I wasn't surprised. A subject change was in order. "What does opening a successful nail salon have in common with falling in love while fighting over a plot of land?"

"Is this supposed to be a sample question for the bar exam, because it hurts my head as much as one of those." Kate pressed her fingers to her temples as if to emphasize her point.

"It's for my story! I keep waiting for my aha moment." The bagel I ate for lunch sat like a log in the pit of my stomach. I wasn't sure what I dreaded more: my worlds colliding at dinner tonight or Kate going back home tomorrow, leaving me out of reasons to procrastinate.

"It will all work out. I promise!"

"Your optimism is most appreciated." I didn't share it, but the absence of a sneeze after she said it was comforting. "Do you want to check out Main Street or not?"

She was halfway out the door before I finished the question. "Is there an antique store? Can you introduce me to Doreen? Are you *sure* there's no bakery?"

It was going to be a long night.

# Chapter Thirty-Five

It was surreal being at a table with both Finn and Kate, but I tried to act normal. Except for practically jumping out of the car before it was barely parked outside Lakeview House, a two-story bluish-gray estate with a wraparound porch on both floors. I needed to escape the feel of Finn's breath against my neck as he leaned in from the backseat to be our human GPS. If either of them noticed my haste, they didn't say anything.

Now we were seated at one of the approximately ten tables amply spaced around the room. It was too cold to sit at the restaurant's outside dining area, but our table on the top floor afforded us a clear view of the lake through the floor-to-ceiling windows. The sky was tinged with pink and orange and reminded me too much of the sunset on my movie night with Finn. But it was beautiful.

The waitress had just delivered our drinks. I took a large sip of mine, a cucumber mint cooler, and smacked my lips in pleasure. "Aah."

"You enjoying that?" Finn asked, a glint in his eyes.

I placed the gin-based cocktail on the white tablecloth. "It beats Brothers dark."

"And you never tried Brothers light." He brought a tumbler housing an old-fashioned to his lips. "Did you make any progress on your story today?"

"Your suggestion to take a more casual approach led to interesting chats with Laura at Twinkly Nails and Grace at Books on Main, but I still don't know what I'm writing about. I'm hoping once I talk to a few more people, I'll find a common thread."

The knots in my belly tightened. With Kate here, it was easy to forget the real reason for this trip. My feelings for Finn didn't help either. But Derek was waiting. *I'm giving you an opportunity here. Don't blow it.*

Our rent increase wasn't going anywhere either, and I had yet to talk to my mom about it. I took another gulp of my drink. "I'm taking the night off," I said, less for Finn and Kate's benefit and more to justify putting it out of my mind for now.

"We can go to Lickety Splits and Mel's Hardware Store at lunch tomorrow if you want." He glanced between me and Kate. "Unless you two want to spend the day exploring. What do you think of Pleasant Hollow so far?" he asked Kate.

"Adi had prepared me to hate it, but I don't. Granted, it's not quite the stuff of storybooks, but it's still a small town!" Her face shone with glee.

Finn chuckled. "What is it with you guys and small towns?"

Kate took a sip of her mocktail. As our designated driver, she was waiting until Brothers to drink. "We've both lived in the city our whole lives, where we're surrounded by strangers. Imagine knowing all your neighbors beyond a curt nod of acknowledgment in the elevator. Having the mayor on speed dial. Your doctor knowing your name without slickly scanning your file before entering the examination room." Kate beamed.

"I'm technically from a small town," I argued.

Kate rolled her eyes. "You left Indiana before you could read. Doesn't count."

I gave her the side-eye. She never let me own my small-town origin.

"Where did you grow up, Finn?" Kate asked.

"Westchester, originally." He fiddled with his silverware. "We moved around a lot," he said with a questioning look at me.

I gave a quick shake of my head to signal that Kate didn't know he'd been homeless. It was nothing to be ashamed of, but it wasn't my story to tell. "You said your dad lives nearby. Do you see him often?"

"Too often." He laughed, but it lacked sincerity.

"What about your sister?"

He muttered, "Not if she can help it." Seeming to regret his words, he smiled and pointed his fork at me. "I know why Kate loves small towns, but what about you? You said you were living the city-girl-in-a-small-town fantasy. What's that about?"

I blinked at him, momentarily stunned he remembered what I'd said during our initial meeting. "Falling in love in a small town, maybe with someone you've known all your life and just never noticed *that* way, is so much more organic than dating in the city. In a small town, there's no getting-to-know-you phase, because you've always known each other in some capacity. No bait and switch after three months. When it doesn't work out, I'll bet there's a mature conversation, as opposed to seeing the person you thought was your boyfriend kissing another woman on Instagram." I shook my head in disgust. "Wouldn't it be nice to settle down without all the trials and tribulations that come with it in Manhattan? No more weeding through thousands of dating profiles, wasting time with nonstarters. The men in small towns are more straightforward and honest." I took a sip of my cocktail. "I just want…" I stopped talking, thankful the waitress took that moment to bring over our food.

"What do you want?"

My eyes met Finn's across the table. Why would he, of all people, ask me that? "Never mind." I took a bite of my salmon, both to keep my mouth occupied and to successfully steer the conversation away from my sappy romantic aspirations. "It's delicious!" It was, although anything other than a prepackaged pastry or artery-clogging breakfast might taste like Michelin-star quality by now.

"Pleasant Hollow could use an upscale restaurant," Kate said, reading my thoughts.

"Maybe they had one," Finn said, "but it closed because after the owners retired, their daughter refused to give up her big-city job as assistant to a designer chef in order to carry on the family tradition. It's temporary, though. She'll be back. They always come back." He took a sip of his old-fashioned.

Kate and I exchanged a silent glance.

She squealed. "O. M. G."

He looked at us, all innocent-like. "What?"

"I think you know more about Hallmark movies than you let on, Mr. Adams," I said accusingly.

He made the "little bit" gesture with his thumb and index finger before taking a bite of his steak.

I watched him for a beat, having second thoughts about my earlier hesitation to share what I really wanted. After all, there was no shame in dreaming big. I drained my cocktail, motioned for the waitress to bring me another, and placed my fork on the edge of the plate. "You know what I want?"

All chewing and clanking of utensils ceased.

Since it was a rhetorical question, I plowed straight ahead. "I want someone who wants to be with me and only me. Who thinks I'm enough—more than enough."

Finn's fork froze halfway to his mouth.

Kate raised her glass. "Preach!"

But I wasn't done yet. "I want someone strong enough to let his guard down and be vulnerable, someone who doesn't take himself too seriously. I'm over the hypebeasts who care more about how they look on social media than about being with me. You want to know why I love Hallmark movies?" I didn't wait for an answer. "In Hallmark towns, the dates aren't just preludes to sex. Hallmark heroes scream their faces off in joy while sleigh-riding down the hill in the local park. They stop mid-stride on their walk home from...wherever...to initiate a snowball fight. They're not too self-conscious to ask their love interest to dance somewhere other than a dance floor. And they're all about the grand gesture. And not for the purpose of going viral on TikTok or YouTube, but to demonstrate the intensity of their feelings. That's what I want."

I took a much-needed gulp of the fresh drink the waitress had placed before me, as it occurred to me my dining mates hadn't said anything. Kate's mouth was agape, and Finn was staring at me with a strange look on his face. Maybe I'd gone a tad too far with my proclamation. My knees wobbled under the table, and a bead of sweat dropped between my breasts. My eyes pleaded with Kate. *Help me.*

Recovering from her stupor in record time, she placed one of her hands over mine. "You deserve all of those things!"

I gave her a grateful smile. "Thank you." I felt Finn's steady gaze on me but kept my eyes on Kate.

"What about you?" Kate asked Finn. "What are your feelings on true love?"

I reluctantly turned my attention to him, just as he looked away from me.

"I don't think any of what Adi mentioned is too much to ask for, although I'd argue against the relevance of geography." He fiddled with his napkin.

Kate leaned forward. "You're not anti-love, then?"

Finn scrunched his face. "Of course not." His phone rang, and he grunted before standing up. "Excuse me a second."

When he walked away, I glared at her. "What are you doing?"

She responded to the question with a blank expression.

"*My* verbal diarrhea on the topic of romance was bad enough. Please don't make it more awkward by probing Finn for *his* thoughts on the matter."

She hmphed. "I'm super curious about his story. Aren't you?"

Finn rejoined us. "Sorry about that. What did I miss?"

"Nothing," we replied in unison. I kicked her under the table as a warning to cut it out.

Blessedly, she listened to me, and the subject was closed. Finn went back to eating his steak, Kate continued to sneak peeks at me in between bites of pasta—which I pretended not to see— and I replayed Finn's uncomfortable, almost pained reactions to the questions about his family on a loop.

Something was off. But did I have the nerve to confront him? Was it any of my business? I'd insisted to Kate that trying to change his mind was pointless and could only hurt me. I'd put myself out there, didn't get the answer I wanted, and had moved on with my dignity. I was proud of myself. Our story—our *love* story, at least—was a nonstarter.

Except the way Finn still looked at me with *fondness* when he thought I wasn't looking, like right now, made me question if it wasn't really over after all.

# Chapter Thirty-Six

Brothers was jam—butt-in-every-seat, standing-room-only—packed.

From the entrance, I regarded Finn, who we hadn't had the heart to ditch after dinner. "This *is* Brothers, right?"

"It is," he confirmed, his eyes scanning the bar in surprise.

"And Andrew Hanes hasn't taken over and replaced the cousins with a famous crowd-drawing mixologist?"

He snickered. "He has not."

"Is the beer free or something?" Kate asked. I had told her the place rarely reached 50 percent occupancy.

I snorted. "Considering the cousins' lack of business aptitude, I wouldn't be surprised." I was still holding a teeny-tiny grudge against them for their dismissal of my brilliant idea for an Oktoberfest.

We pushed through the crowd and over to the bar, where, despite our objections, Finn ordered a pitcher of Brothers dark and three glasses. Taking freebies from Finn felt wrong, given he wasn't my boyfriend or my fuck buddy, but the upscale dinner and two fancy cocktails at Lakeview House had run me seventy dollars after tax and tip. It was either accept his generosity or drink water, and my pride wasn't that thick.

I pointed out Aaron and Greg to Kate. The black letters on Aaron's gray T-shirt said, "It's my birthday. Buy me a beer," which I suspected was the reason for the swarm of patrons. It wasn't clear if it was a purposely ironic choice to wear it at his own bar tonight.

Finn poured us each a glass of beer and said he had to use the bathroom. I was just pleased to learn there *was* a bathroom. An outdoor Porta Potty would not have shocked me, especially if someone other than the cousins was responsible for keeping it clean.

As soon as his back was turned, Kate grabbed me by the elbow. "Let's go."

"Where are we going?"

"To flirt." She pointed at the crowd of men surrounding us.

I didn't know where they'd all been hiding until now, but there were *a lot* of twentysomething guys. Since Kate had a boyfriend, I assumed her intention was to observe while I was expected to do the flirting. "I thought you liked Finn."

She frowned. "I do. He's perfect for you, except for that one glaring flaw. He's not looking for a relationship, and..." Her head swung back and forth, taking in the bar. "There are so many boys here—local boys! Live the small-town single scene. If not for you, do it for me!" She pushed out her lips and rounded her puppy-dog eyes at me.

"Pouting won't work," I said. "You're not my type." Then I contradicted myself by following her into the crowd.

Twenty minutes and a beer later, I was chatting—for Kate— with Chase, a white man in his late twenties with dark blond hair worn slicked back on top. He had a lean build—Finn was broader, not that I was comparing—and blue eyes. After accidentally walking into his back, Kate had introduced us before conveniently receiving an urgent text from Diego, which I was willing to bet had been prescheduled. Thankfully, Chase was easygoing and friendly, so I didn't mind being left alone with him. He was a single music teacher and volunteer firefighter, born and raised in Pleasant Hollow. Most notably, the questions he directed at me didn't suggest an obsession with New York City and its famous inhabitants but merely a genuine keen interest in me as a person.

"I don't mean to be rude checking my phone, but I really want to make sure Bogie is okay at home," he said.

And he was polite to boot. My heart zinged. "Who's Bogie?"

"My rescue dog," Chase said, his light eyes twinkling. "It's my first night out since I got him a month ago, and I can't help checking his status every few minutes."

I gasped excitedly. "Which pet monitor app do you have? Furbo? Bites 2? Pawbo?"

He did a double take. "You were right the first time! Do you have a dog?"

"I don't. But I wrote a piece last year for a digital magazine on the best pet-monitoring apps." I relaxed my smiling cheeks. It was rare I had an opening to tout one of my own articles, and it made me overly giddy. "Can I see a picture of Bogie?" I took the phone he held out and cooed at the multitude of photos. "Is he a German shepherd mix?"

Chase scratched at the hint of reddish-blond whiskers along his jaw line. "We know he's a mutt, but more than that, we're not quite sure. He was left at the firehouse. No collar or chip."

"How sad." Then I remembered something. "I haven't seen

many pets around Pleasant Hollow. I was beginning to think there was a town-wide dislike of furry friends."

Chase looked horrified. "There are definitely dogs in town, although not as many as I'd like. I volunteer at an animal shelter in Goshen once a week, and the number of dogs who don't find even temporary homes tears me up inside."

I grabbed onto his muscular forearm. "Wait. You have a full-time job, yet you volunteer at the firehouse *and* an animal shelter?"

"Yes." He smiled shyly.

I squinted at him. "Is it to impress women?"

He laughed. "No, but if that happens, I'm okay with it."

In almost slow motion, I swiveled toward Kate and widened my eyes in disbelief. Forget Garrett, Chase was a romance hero come to life.

She gave me a thumbs-up with her free hand and held out her glass to Finn for a refill with the other.

Only Finn didn't see her. He was too busy giving Chase a once-over. The pinched expression on his face indicated he didn't like what he saw. I did a slick appraisal of my own and tried to see Chase through Finn's eyes.

By all definitions, Chase was an attractive guy—a *very* attractive guy. Yet there were no butterflies in my belly, my temperature hadn't risen, and my heart was beating at a steady pace. In other words, I felt nothing. I refocused on Finn and had the opposite reaction. Seeing him jealous should have made me feel victorious. Instead, I was frustrated and confused.

"Can you excuse me a second, Adina?" Chase said, interrupting my subtle scrutiny. "Aaron just called me over for birthday shots."

"By all means. Cheers!"

"He seems nice!" Kate said, joining me with Finn on her heels.

"You have no idea." I told her about his volunteer activities.

"No way." Her eyes grew wider with each word. "I *knew* it. I can already see Trevor Donovan in the role."

"Totally." I'd been working hard not to acknowledge Finn, whose lips were clamped together in what appeared to be suppressed amusement, but I couldn't take it any longer. "What's so funny?"

He pressed his fist to his mouth. "Nothing."

I glared at him. "You could have fooled me."

He dropped his arm to his side and clucked his tongue. "I think it's great you've found yourself the 'romantic and straightforward' boyfriend of your small-town dreams. Kudos," he said, clapping his hands. "But I'm confused as to how it's going to work."

"Meaning?"

"Are you planning to move to Pleasant Hollow? Or will this be a long-distance relationship where you bus it here every weekend? You can probably get a frequent rider pass from ShortLine." His eyes danced with undisguised mirth.

I rubbed the back of my neck. Finn had a point. Chase wasn't the small-town boyfriend of my dreams, but even if he had been, I hadn't given the logistics much thought. Apparently, Finn had, though, which raised another question. "Why do you care? It's not like I mean anything to you. We were just a casual hookup. Right?"

Finn's cheeks flushed red.

Kate darted her eyes between us while biting her lip. "I'm going to…uh…use the bathroom. Yeah, I need to pee. Bad. Real bad." She turned on her heel and shuffled away.

*And then there were two.* "Small-town hero or not, *you're* the one I like. Not Chase," I hissed, glancing behind me to make sure he was out of earshot. "But you're not an option. You've made it clear the best I can hope for is short-term dating with monogamy up for debate. That's all well and good for you, but I want more." My face went hot. I never would have confessed my true feelings for Finn so boldly if I hadn't drunk two cocktails at the restaurant. I felt weak, vulnerable, and simply wretched.

Finn's eyes softened. "I like you too. I just..."

"You just what?" My breath bottled up in my chest. "Talk to me." I took a cautious step toward him.

"It's compl—"

"Do *not* say it's complicated!"

He blushed, glancing over his shoulder and from side to side.

"No one's paying attention to us." I lowered my beer onto a nearby table and crossed my arms over my chest. "Either tell me why it's so *complicated*, or hold your peace while I go back to Chase. You can't give me what I want. Maybe he can."

Neither of us said anything for a second. Out of the corner of my eye, I caught Chase's eye and waved. "I'll count to five." I stared Finn down. "One. Two. Three."

He growled. "Fine!" His shoulders dropped in defeat. "You know that saying 'not the guy you bring home to your parents'?"

"Of course," I said, my hands in fists. Where was this going? I'd be proud to bring Finn home to meet my mother. Unless he was suggesting *I* wasn't the kind of girl he could introduce to his dad. My pulse raced. Was it because I still lived with my mom?

"My dad is the parent you don't bring the girl home to."

I blinked. "I don't understand. Which is to say, *huh?*"

This earned me a smile, but it was strained compared to the easy grins I was used to. It was obvious this wasn't natural territory for him. "You can tell me anything," I whispered.

He closed his eyes for a beat. When he opened them, he said, "I really don't want to have this conversation in here, especially when you're drunk."

I opened my mouth to defend my sobriety, but I knew that he knew I was on my fourth drink. Still. I wasn't about to vomit or pass out. "I'm just buzzed," I insisted as his phone rang.

He glanced at it and muttered, "Here we go again," but didn't answer.

"Maybe you should take that." It wasn't the first or even third time his phone had rung tonight. He'd excused himself from the dinner table at least twice. Besides, it was like a curtain had gone down and I knew I wasn't going to get anywhere with him tonight anyway. "Especially if it's the same person who's been calling all night. We can continue this discussion later...when I'm *sober*." It was no use. He'd already walked away. I threw my hands up in surrender and released a heavy sigh.

Speaking of phones, I hadn't even looked at mine all night. I removed it from my purse. My mom had texted twice.

> What time do you think you'll be home tomorrow?

I cocked my head. I was going home tomorrow? Was I so drunk I didn't remember finishing my story?

> Can you guys stop and pick up
> a jar of honey and maybe
> another bottle of wine on your
> way? I'm working in the morning
> and then cooking all afternoon.

"Is it safe to rejoin the conversation?" Kate said, scanning the room, presumably for Finn.

I glanced up from my phone. "What's tomorrow?"

Kate blinked rapidly before slapping her hand against her mouth. "I forgot to tell you! I'm giving you a ride home, so you won't miss Rosh Hashanah dinner. Don't worry, Diego and I will drive you back later."

"Oh shit." Mom and I weren't observant enough to go to temple, but we did honor all the major holidays, the Jewish New Year being one of them. We always invited friends, including Kate, over for a celebratory dinner. I'd forgotten all about it, too wrapped up in my business in Pleasant Hollow and Finn, who hadn't come back yet. "Where's Finn?"

Kate smoothed a hand through her ponytail—the hairdo a clear indication the night was on its last legs. "When I left, you guys were in heated conversation over the status of your relationship." She raised her eyebrows. "What did I miss?"

*My dad is the parent you don't bring the girl home to.* "So much, and yet not nearly enough."

She scrunched her nose. "Huh?"

"My thoughts exactly."

# Chapter Thirty-Seven

You were right about the bacon." Kate chomped loudly for emphasis. "Tasty!"

"You can have the rest of mine," I said, sliding my plate across the table. It was the next day, and we were having an early lunch at Pinkie's. Only, I had no appetite.

Kate studied me, her lips pursed in concern. "Are you okay?"

I slunk into my seat. "I'm so tense, it's like someone threaded a needle through the length of my body and is pulling it at regular intervals."

What was I going to say later when Mom asked how the story was going? Sure, my visits at the nail salon and bookstore the day before had been pleasant, but I was still no closer to finding a good angle. I was entirely blocked for inspiration and completely devoid of hope I'd be able to deliver a publishable article in a week's time. Any minute now, Derek would call for an update, and I had nothing to tell him.

On top of that, it felt like rocks the size of Stonehenge had lodged inside my throat over the clock ticking on our rent hike.

Then there was Finn, who'd basically confirmed the reason he was anti-relationship was somehow related to his father. Was I supposed to just clear what he'd said from my memory? Pretend it didn't happen?

I rubbed my temples. Unlike a hangover, none of what ailed me could be cured with Gatorade, caffeine, and greasy food.

Kate tapped my hand, pulling me out of my thoughts. "Finn just walked in."

I groaned and instinctively looked behind me, immediately recognizing Finn waiting at the counter, thanks to his black leather jacket and perfect ass. Wasn't there anywhere else to eat in this stupid town? I groaned again. It was a dumb question.

"Are you going to say hi?"

"Only if he sees us first." I took a piece of bacon from my previously abandoned plate and broke it in half.

"Should we ask him to join us?"

I groaned for the third time. "Please, Kate."

We had a couple of hours before we needed to head back to the city, and I wanted to use it wisely by talking to more locals for my story. A part of me wondered if the timing of the holiday was a sign I should stay back in New York City after dinner rather than obligate Kate to make the trip three times in one day. But I wasn't ready to give up. *Yet.* I'd put too much effort into these last two weeks to leave with nothing. But how could I focus on my work with Finn at the forefront of my mind?

"We aren't a trio. Let it go for now." I raised my coffee to my lips.

"How are you two feeling this morning?"

"Finn. Hi." I turned to face him too quickly, spilling coffee onto the table.

"Sorry. Didn't mean to startle you." His eyes locked with mine, and his expression mirrored my own distress.

Ignoring the two-way tension, I wiped the wetness with my napkin, then gestured at the white Styrofoam box in his hand. "Take-out?"

He nodded. "BLT and onion rings."

"Healthy!" I joked.

"Hey, it covers most of the food groups." Turning to Kate, he said, "I won't keep you. I wanted to say goodbye."

Her face lit up. "It was so nice meeting you!"

I refrained from rolling my eyes. She was the one who'd discovered his dating profile, yet she was now his biggest fan.

"I'd say come back soon, but Adi won't be here for much longer anyway," Finn said.

I squeezed the napkin still in my hand. He didn't seem thrilled at the prospect of my leaving. Was he sorry to see me go? I steadied my gaze on him, but he didn't meet my eye.

"True," Kate agreed. "And thanks to the Jewish calendar, I get to hang with her tonight too."

At the obvious confusion on Finn's face, I clarified. "Tonight's Rosh Hashanah. I forgot all about it, but I'm going home for dinner and returning late tonight." I blew a stream of air out of my cheeks. "If I'd finished this damn story, I wouldn't have to come back at all." Worried Finn might take the statement personally, a wave of guilt rushed through me, followed by a sinking feeling from caring too much what Finn thought.

"The Gellar Rosh Hashanah is epic," Kate said.

Finn cocked his head. "Really, why's that?"

"Can you sit a minute?" I asked, ignoring Kate's smirk. My neck ached from peering up at Finn while he hovered over us.

"Sure." A moment of awkwardness ensued while he decided on whose side of the booth to sit, ultimately sliding in next to Kate. "Do you mind if I eat my sandwich? No one likes cold bacon. Aside from Adi." He gave me a teasing grin. "I don't think she's picky when it comes to bacon."

"Except when she's too upset to eat, like now." Kate bit down on her lip.

Finn's eyebrows drew together. "What's wrong?" He took a bite of his BLT.

I gave him a *look* across the booth. Maybe one of us *had* cleared our talk out of his memory.

Kate glanced between us. "As I was saying, Rosh Hashanah at the Gellars' is like Thanksgiving junior. So. Much. Food. And really good company, of course." She winked at me.

"It sounds like a great time." Finn licked a dab of mayonnaise from the corner of his mouth, managing to make the gesture sexy instead of sloppy. "Tell me more. What's the main course?"

"Why don't you come?" My mouth went agape. *What did I just say?*

Kate gasped.

The sandwich in Finn's hand dropped to his plate.

"I mean it." A voice in my head—the sane one—shouted, *Abort! Abort!*, but there was no turning back now, and he'd probably say no anyway.

"I'm not sure it's a good—"

"Not as my date or anything," I rushed to explain, guessing where his mind had wandered. "I think there are nine or ten of us this year. One more won't make a difference, especially if you bring a bottle of wine." I gave him a penetrating stare, almost daring him to accept the invitation.

He chewed his food so slowly, I suspected it was a tactic to stall.

"She's right," Kate said. "It's more of a party than an intimate dinner. You should definitely join us." She turned to me. "Not that it's my place to extend invitations to *their* party, but since Adi already—"

"Shut up, Kate."

Finn laughed, choking on his food. After a brief moment, he said, "I'd love to."

"Then it's settled," I said, with a nod to seal the deal. "Dinner is at seven, but we'll leave here at four in case of traffic."

"I can follow you in my car and drive you back later."

"You have a car here? I had no idea."

The look he threw me across the table translated to: *There's a lot you don't know about me.*

To which I responded in my own nonverbal way: *No shit.* But in exchange for a delicious Gellar feast, the least he could do was divulge some of his own family secrets.

# Chapter Thirty-Eight

*L*ater that night, sounds of amusement echoed across our dining-room table in Manhattan over my misadventures in Pleasant Hollow. I wasn't offended by their laughter, because it came from a place of love—at least with respect to my mom, Kate, Diego, Aunt Heather, her partner Regina, and our long-term neighbors and former sometime babysitters Charles and Tesibelle. Finn laughed at me too, but fondness didn't equal love.

I spooned more tzimmes, a traditional Jewish dish consisting of honey-glazed carrots, dried apricots, prunes, and other sweet ingredients—my favorite of all the sides—onto my plate.

"The results ranged from mortifying to humiliating, but thankfully, nothing was caught on video," I said, referring to my fruitless attempts to convince local business owners to host cooking contests, beer festivals, and ice-cream socials.

Finn muttered, "That you know of."

I narrowed my eyes at him and subtly scratched my nose with my middle finger. If he felt shy or out of place, like I'd feared, he faked it well.

Across the table, I caught senior citizens Charles and Tesibelle glancing between Finn and me with hearts in their eyes, and I quickly looked away. Finn was the first guy I'd ever brought home for a holiday dinner, which meant starting tomorrow, they'd probably check their mailbox every day for the save-the-date card. They'd be disappointed, but there was a lot of that going around.

"Maybe you should create a Google alert under your name in case the video evidence goes viral." Diego cocked one of his dark bushy eyebrows.

While Diego and Finn bonded in their mockery, I sliced into a piece of brisket. "Ha ha. You guys are *so* salty."

Not to be bested by the younger generation in the teasing competition, Tesibelle said, "Who remembers the chocolate-covered bananas Adina made for Valerie's thirty-fifth birthday?" before breaking into a fit of laughter.

"You mean her phallic pops?" Mom said.

Aunt Heather coughed "Dick pops" into her hand.

While Finn cracked up next to me, I side-eyed Heather, the memory of her deep-throating an inadvertently cock-shaped frozen chocolate banana coming back to me with clarity. The demonstration, though shocking to my virgin eyes at the time, had its educational virtues a few years later.

"Maybe we can go easy on the 'embarrass Adina in front of her new friend' portion of the evening?" Charles suggested.

"Thank you, Charles." I glared at my mom and my found-family members one at a time, avoiding eye contact with Finn. Given our current platonic status, the last thing I needed was a reminder of his white-chocolate banana in my mouth earlier that week.

"Is your family this obnoxious at holiday dinners, Finn?" Mom asked.

I perked up at the question. Thanks to Mom's inquiring mind, I might finally obtain some intel about him. When I'd called her on the drive over to say I was bringing a guest for dinner, she'd been too busy cooking to ask for details. She was better off asking Finn directly than funneling questions through me anyway, since I had so few answers.

"Not quite," Finn said. "It's just me and my dad."

My head lurched back in confusion. What about his sister? Didn't she come to their family dinners? And, if not, was the reason related to the breadcrumb he'd dropped about his father the night before? I observed him with curiosity. He pretended not to see me, but the clench in his jaw as he stared straight ahead gave him away.

"Quiet is nice," Mom said at the same time Kate said, "Obnoxious doesn't require a crowd."

Finn laughed. "As long as there's pie, I'm happy. Right, Adi?" He kicked me playfully under the table.

I chuckled at our private joke, even as it occurred to me how often he skillfully swerved questions away from his personal life.

Kate huffed. "Pleasant Hollow might have been a bust, but I'm not ready to let go of the fantasy. I'm sure there are actual quaint small towns with gingerbread cookies and pumpkin farms somewhere. We'll just have to take another road trip."

"Kate's right. Can you write this story about another town?" Regina asked.

"Not by next week, I can't. Besides, it was the big-city developer coming in that made the pitch work. Or not, as it turned out." I shot an accusatory glare Finn's way even though it wasn't his fault.

"Can we beat up your editor until he gives you an extension?" Heather shook her fists.

"With what, your fingernails?" Regina joked.

"I'd never get my own hands dirty," Heather said, her mouth gaping. "I'd hire someone, of course."

I laughed. It was an effort to picture my lithe, blond-haired and blue-eyed pseudo-aunt hitting anyone. Hitting *on* someone, maybe. She'd even been on the beauty-pageant circuit back in the day, having made it to the top ten in the Miss New York pageant of nineteen ninety-something.

"It's fine. I have a few more days. I'll whip something up." There was no conviction in my voice, resulting in eight pairs of unconvinced eyes on me.

"You win some, you lose some, sweetie."

"Heather's right," Kate said. "You'll find a better story, I'll pass the next bar exam, and in six months we'll both recall this time and laugh."

If only it were that simple. With this article came the promise of more entertainment and lifestyle story opportunities and a steady paycheck from *Tea*. Without it came more hustling for spin classes and shifts at the café, and cold-pitching articles for fifty cents a word if I was lucky enough to sell any. The only other avenue for making money using my writing skills was to take on more freelance assignments regardless of content, but technical writing left me uninspired. Also, building a lucrative career with freelance jobs didn't happen overnight. It took patience and time. My time had run out. I didn't know where I'd be living in six months. "We need the money now," I mumbled.

"Don't we all," Regina said, making it clear my words had come out louder than I intended.

"I hate to break it to you, Squirt, but even our current rent is more than five hundred dollars a month."

Kate pushed out her lips. "I'm so sorry I wasn't able to find anything illegal about the rent increase."

I mushed a dried apricot with my fork. "Me too."

"It isn't fair that you're in this position and we're not," Charles said.

"We feel awfully guilty about it," Tesibelle agreed, twiddling with her napkin.

Mom and I yelled, "No!" at the same time.

The possibility of my favorite seventysomethings being tossed out on the street made my blood turn hot, and I was relieved they'd been spared the rent hikes. As a child, I'd performed countless fashion shows in their living room with sample clothes Tesibelle, a retired buyer for Ross, brought home. And before his thick dark afro dwindled in the center to a thin smattering of gray wisps, Charles used to let me style his hair with bobby pins in his home office/beauty salon. It would be a shame if they couldn't live out the rest of their lives in that apartment.

"We're both happy for you. And maybe all's not lost for us either. I just picked up another freelance assignment, and if I miraculously land the staff position at *Tea*—"

"Unless it pays upward of six figures, it won't make a difference," Mom said. "We have to move."

I stilled, gripping my wineglass like a vise. It was a conversation I didn't expect to have in front of an audience, even one as close as family...and Finn.

From the seat next to me, he patted my back in a show of sympathy.

Talking about such personal information with a virtual

stranger was weird yet not. Maybe because Finn already knew about the rent hike, but I suspected it was because the last time he had felt like a stranger was the day we met, minus his irksome penchant to withhold information about himself. Our arms brushed together, not for the first time, and a delicious jolt of electricity ran through me. Logically, I knew the frequent grazing was because I was right-handed and he was left-handed, but neither of us acknowledged it or increased our own personal space to prevent its recurrence.

Mom continued. "We can't swing the four thousand dollars a month it will cost, *minimum*, to stay in this apartment, even if you get the job at *Tea*."

Even though I knew it was coming, hearing the words felt like someone was scooping out my insides. "What are we going to do?"

"We'll figure it out. I'll find a one-bedroom, hopefully around here. You'll move in with a roommate or rent a studio somewhere."

"You must stay in the neighborhood," Tesibelle said, her voice stern. "We have traditions to hold up. Christmas and Easter at our house. Passover and Rosh Hashanah at yours."

I half listened to Charles echo his wife's sentiment and Mom promise she'd do her best. I was struck by her calm demeanor in the face of all these changes. Why wasn't she angry about losing our home? Or sad we wouldn't live together anymore? My armpits dampened. Was she happy about it? Relieved? Had her patience with me getting my own place been an act?

She reached for my hand across the table. "Don't stress. We have time. And you have an open invitation on the couch.

I promise you will always have a place to stay as long as I'm alive."

Finn stared at my mother with a distant look in his eyes.

A heavy, leaden feeling overcame me. Was he thinking about when his father had been unable to say the same to him and his sister?

As if sensing me watching him, he blinked himself back to normal and stood. "If you'll excuse me, I need to use the bathroom."

Less than a second later, Tesibelle whisper-shouted, "He's adorable."

"When's the wedding?" Charles joked.

"He's not my boyfriend," I said quietly, before getting up from the table to check on him. Here I was, swimming in self-pity without any thought to how this entire topic of conversation might be affecting Finn. What if we'd inadvertently triggered him with all our talk about having a place to live? I stopped outside my bedroom when I heard his voice coming from inside the closed room.

"Probably another couple of hours. I'll call if it's not too late." His voice grew louder, then softer, then louder again, as I imagined him pacing the room.

I pressed a finger to my lips. What was I doing eavesdropping on his call? This was not the way to gather information. That was what the car ride home was for. I started to turn back.

"A woman at work." Silence. "Not just me. A bunch of us are here."

I frowned. Was he talking about me? Was *I* supposed to be the woman at work? Who was he talking to, and why was he lying? My brain whirred with questions. Was it his dad? Or was it one of Finn's other hookups and he was covering his ass? My heart drummed in my chest.

"I should get back." The door opened a crack. "I'll call you later."

I sprang into the bathroom like there were ants in my shoes and closed the door behind me. I leaned over the sink to regain my bearings and tried to make sense of what I'd overheard.

Who was Finn talking to, and why had he lied about who I was? Normally, I'd be all over him until I got answers, but Finn wasn't a story. I'd been so desperate for him to confide in me, but it was becoming clear unearthing his secrets wouldn't change what we meant to each other, which was nothing. Even if I hadn't imagined the *fond* way he looked at me— even if he did really like me, as he'd professed—what good were the feelings if he lacked the intention to back them up with action?

Inviting him to dinner had been a mistake. Leo, whom I'd casually dated for almost a year, had never made an appearance at a holiday celebration, so why had I asked Finn, who I'd stopped sleeping with and would never see again once I left Pleasant Hollow? Why was I trying so hard to learn about a man to whom I meant so little he passed me off as a colleague... not even a friend?

And if it was another woman on the end of that call... screw that! He didn't matter. The people who *did* matter were waiting for me at the dinner table. Before my prolonged absence raised suspicion, I left the bathroom and joined them.

During dessert, I passed on a slice of apple cake, choosing a chocolate rugelach because it didn't require using utensils that might result in arm-against-arm contact with Finn. Conversation blessedly turned to subjects not requiring me to acknowledge him directly at all while I was still resenting his attendance in the first place.

The firm where Diego worked as a defense attorney had taken on a client who was charged with bribing his daughter's way into admission to a fancy private high school. Despite not being the most righteous of cases to defend, it was very exciting in a "ripped from the headlines" way. Kate wasn't thrilled with the long hours Diego would be working over the next month, but we collectively decided she would use the time away from her boyfriend to study for the bar.

Later, while our guests talked among themselves, I helped my mom get a head start with the cleanup in the kitchen, rinsing the dishes and handing them to her to place in the dishwasher. "Everything was delicious, Mom. So much better than last year."

The previous Rosh Hashanah she'd had catered by Fairway, the supermarket, under the assumption it would be worth the extra cost to forgo cooking all day. The consensus was nothing beat my mom's cooking—a talent not passed down to her daughter—and the prep was almost just as time-consuming.

"I aim to please, Squirt."

I stopped rinsing and observed her stack the dirty utensils— handles up for knives and forks, and down for spoons. This level of conscientiousness was another trait she didn't pass down, but her house meant her rules. "I was so overconfident about this damn story. I hate that I wasted so much of our...*your*...money, especially now." I aggressively scrubbed the sticky remnants of honey off a plate.

"It was an investment in your future. Like all investments,

there was a risk." She closed the dishwasher door and leaned against it. "But why are you talking like it's over?"

I turned the water off. "Because it pretty much is. In fact, I'm tempted to pack up my things and hop on the bus back here first thing in the morning. Why bother talking to more people? So far, I have a hodgepodge of material with no common thread. I seriously doubt talking to the owner of the ice-cream shop will make a difference. And she hates me," I mumbled to myself. "Like you said, five hundred dollars isn't enough to keep us in this apartment. It's high time I get my head out of the clouds and start adulting for real." The morning I'd prepared my pitch for Derek, so certain this story was *it* for me, felt like a lifetime ago.

"You *are* an adult!"

"*Riiight.* I live with my mother, who pays for my health insurance, and I work two part-time jobs with no room for career growth at either."

She chuckled. "Fine. Some adulting might be in order, but be kinder to yourself. You're working toward a dream, and I support it and you wholeheartedly."

"What you're not saying is that it's about time your grown-up offspring snapped out of her quarter-life crisis and got her shit together like Kate." The same age as me, my best friend already had her own apartment, a serious boyfriend, and a solid career.

Immediately following my whiny internal monologue came feelings of guilt and shame. Kate didn't exactly live on Easy Street either. She'd had her share of shitty, half-assed romances before Diego. She'd more than paid her dues. She'd also worked tirelessly in law school only to fail the bar anyway.

"No. I don't think that at all. In my selfish fantasy world, we'd live together forever. The Gellar girls against the world."

I rolled my eyes even though I knew she meant it, at least the part about not counting the minutes until I left her nest.

"I don't want to hear any more talk about giving up. Quitting is not in the Gellars' dictionary."

"I know but—"

She wiggled a finger at me. "No buts. No excuses. *Tea* gave you a platform to tell a story. Use it. But don't write it for me. Don't write it for us or our housing situation. Write it for *you*. Then, if it doesn't work out and Derek says no, at least you'll know you gave it your all."

My eyes stung with unshed tears and my chin trembled, but I nodded my agreement.

"By the way," she whispered, "how impressed are you that I haven't asked a single question about Finn?" She grinned knowingly.

I recoiled at his name.

"Uh-oh. That doesn't look good."

I glanced behind me to confirm the coast was clear. "He's just a friend." *Or a colleague, depending on who you ask.* Normally, I'd tell her everything, but there was no time.

"If you say so," she said, one eyebrow raised skeptically. "I'm tired. Time to kick everyone out."

I followed her back out to the living room, where we started the process of saying goodbye, which I prolonged as much as possible to put off being alone with Finn in the car. I circled the dark wood dining-room table we'd had forever. It occurred to me it was the last time we'd celebrate Rosh Hashanah in this apartment. It might be the last major dinner party we'd ever hold here.

"Remember the time I left a gob of macaroni and cheese under the table to eat later?" I asked Mom.

"You were a disgusting child," she said.

Everyone laughed. Finn the loudest. Until his phone rang again and he stepped to the side.

*I don't care who it is. I don't care who it is. I don't care who it is.*

Aunt Heather drew me into a hug and whispered, "He's a keeper." Her fragrance was a mix of brisket, chocolate, and floral perfume. On anyone else, it would be gross, but Heather made it smell like home.

I squeezed her back. "He's not my boyfriend."

"Not yet." She waved at Finn, who'd rejoined us, and stepped into the hallway arm in arm with Regina.

Next out the door were Charles and Tesibelle, who exclaimed, "We like your boyfriend," with the subtlety of a police siren.

Not daring to check Finn's reaction, I kissed their wrinkly cheeks and squeezed them tight. They were the antithesis of the elderly couple from Pleasant Hollow.

Finally, I hugged Kate, thanking her once again for coming to my rescue in Pleasant Hollow and ordering her to study hard.

"Come back to break the Yom Kippur fast next week!" Mom's voice rang out from the kitchen.

"Bagels from Ess-a-Bagel as a reward for a fast I won't be engaging in?" Kate smiled mischievously. "Yes, please."

"I'll be there as long as I'm not working." Diego gave me a one-armed "bro" hug. "See ya." He shook Finn's hand, but Kate pulled Finn in for a true embrace. "Drive safely, dude. You're delivering precious cargo."

"I'll do my best," he promised.

Then it was just the two of us left with my mom. *Awkward.*

My eyes locked on a portion of the wall right outside the kitchen, and I touched it with a finger. "Was I ever this short?"

She came up beside me. "Yes. Before Pinterest and fancy DIY height charts, I used a pencil, a ruler, and a blank wall to measure your growth."

"I stopped growing almost a decade ago. I can't believe you never painted over it."

She draped an arm around me and squeezed me into a side hug. "You can't paint over memories, Squirt."

I sniffled. "That's the thing. I have so many memories here."

"Nothing gold can stay, Ponyboy."

"We watched *The Outsiders* on that couch." My voice broke.

"The couch will come to my new place."

Addressing Finn directly for the first time since my snooping session, I said, "My mother has an answer for everything."

"I can see where you get it from," he teased, not unfondly. He'd been so quiet during this exchange, standing back with a faraway look on his face, and I still wanted to know why. *Damn it.*

"Isn't it comforting to know some things don't change?" Mom said, pulling me closer into her crook.

"I suppose." I turned to Finn. It was time. "I guess we should be on our way."

He nodded. "I'm ready when you are."

My heart skipped a beat. Two hours alone in a car with Finn loomed before me, and I was anything but ready.

# Chapter Thirty-Nine

The black leather passenger seat in Finn's coppery brown Toyota Yaris was comfortable, which was more than I could say for the first half hour of the drive home. Finn pretended to be intently focused on navigating the traffic on the FDR Drive, and I feigned believing he needed complete silence to concentrate.

But the quiet in the car was anything but peaceful. Finn wasn't my Uber driver. He was my...I shook my head. What was he? My gaze landed on his hands—those perfect hands that had touched every part of my body so proficiently.

Was it worth asking him to elaborate on the conversation we'd started the night before—about his father? Should I come clean and admit I'd overheard him call me his colleague and ask why? Did it matter? Did *any* of it matter? Observing him through my peripheral vision, I laser-focused my thoughts: Say something. Say something. *Say something!!*

Finn turned his head toward me and quickly back to the road. "Did you say something?"

I gave a sigh of satisfaction that my mental telepathy had worked. Only now, the onus was on me to break the ice. "I shouldn't have invited you tonight."

"What? Why?" Finn turned to me in surprise, then quickly back to the road.

Lost for an easy explanation, I dropped my gaze to the black fabric floor mat at my feet.

"I'm glad you did. Everyone was great." His voice nearly broke on his next words. "Seriously, you have a special family. Loving…supportive…" He sucked his lip into his mouth. "Did I do something to offend them?" His forehead wrinkled with worry.

"Not at all. It's just…I invited you for selfish reasons." I clucked my tongue. "I had this stupid idea that if I nurtured you with enough brisket and noodle kugel, you'd come clean with me about your dad and why you don't want a girlfriend, especially if the two go hand in hand, and why it's so *complicated.* It was stupid." Now I was repeating myself. "But I've changed my mind. I don't want to be with someone so secretive anyway. I need trust that goes both ways. So we're good. It's all good. I just wanted you to know."

I fanned myself, then rolled down the window and stuck my head out like a dog before sliding back into the seat against a backdrop of silence.

The unpeaceful quiet resumed. Finn snuck glances at me every few minutes, but I pretended not to notice. I fiddled with the radio, settling on an episode of NPR's *Hidden Brain* podcast, and passed the time privately mocking pretentious vanity plates on the George Washington Bridge. My faves: HTMESS and GR8DOC.

"All the phone calls—not just tonight but at Brothers and in my hotel room? It's always my dad. Or about my dad."

My body went rigid. I'd given up on him sharing by now,

but who was I to censor self-expression? "Go on," I said. Not wanting to sound bossy, I added, "Or not."

"He's a functioning alcoholic. Except when he's not functioning, which is much of the time." He gripped the steering wheel. "The first time you and I had drinks in my room, it was my sister calling. My dad, who she stopped talking to a decade ago, called her crying about our mom. The night of the storm, it was his coworker. My father fell asleep on the job—he works the reference desk at the Middletown Township Public Library—and she put him in a cab home before his boss found out." He turned my way for a beat. "Someone's always coming to his rescue. Usually it's me."

I stared at him, wide-eyed and speechless.

He glanced through the rearview mirror. "Most of the time, though, it's him calling—rambling about something or needing my help. Tonight he was lonely and wanted to talk. It's hard to say no."

"Wow. Finn. I had no idea." It was a side of his world I'd never even fathomed.

"He's been like this since my mom died. He held it together, barely, for us, but just never fully recovered. My sister married right out of high school just to get away. Her husband's an arrogant prick, but he takes care of her financially, which is the only thing she cares about. She's afraid to stand up for herself, much less leave him and risk being out on the street again. My escape hatch was college and a career—I applied for scholarships and took out loans—I pledged to make it my literal business to help others. But my dad...he needs me. Our relationship is pretty one-sided: all him, all the time. I don't volunteer anything about myself, and he doesn't ask."

"Who do you talk to then...about your own stuff?" I had Mom and Kate. Who was Finn's person?

"No one. It's easier that way. I don't want to be a burden." He rubbed his eyes with one hand. My heart twisted at his pain. I stared at him while I struggled for the right words to express empathy without crossing over into pity. He didn't want my pity.

"Compared to us, your family belongs in one of your favorite movies." Traffic had slowed, and he stared at me before breaking eye contact and returning his eyes to the road.

I bit back the instinct to protest. My family life wasn't rainbows and unicorns all the time, but it was damn close compared to Finn's. I'd never been so aware of my privilege and plain good luck as I was in this moment.

"So you see? I'm not boyfriend material, Adi. I could never bring you home to my family like you did with me tonight. Trust me, you wouldn't want me to."

Over the years, I'd heard a lot of reasons for being single, but nothing like this. "That's not fair. I don't want to date your father, Finn! I don't care about that." I pressed my palms up and down the length of my thighs. "Well, of course I care, but for you. I wish it was better for *you*. That's all." I stared at the side of his face. "I would never judge you because of your father. A television sitcom dad wouldn't make me want you any more than a messed-up alcoholic dad would make me want you less."

"Are you sure about that? My dysfunctional family doesn't exactly match up to the ones in those wholesome small-town shows you love so much."

"Life isn't TV!"

Finn snorted. "Oh, that's rich coming from you."

I flinched. "That's not fair. Just because I'm a sucker for a sappy romance doesn't mean I expect real life to be that simple."

He moved his eyes from the road to me for a beat. "Your speech at Lakeview House says otherwise."

I fought the impulse to respond immediately. Yes, part of me believed life in a small town mirrored what I saw in corny made-for-TV movies. And yes, I had gone into my trip to Pleasant Hollow yearning for that. But that was after being let down by yet another Manhattan bachelor.

And more importantly: "I didn't know you then," I said.

Before Finn, I didn't think it was possible to fall for anyone I met in the city. I dated anyway, just in case and because...well...*needs*...but I didn't really believe love would happen. Maybe my feelings were on the fast track because of how much time we'd spent together almost daily (and nightly), but less than ten days into knowing him, I was absolutely falling in love with Finn Adams.

He laughed sardonically. "You've never seen my dad on a bender. The things he says could make a sailor blush. Ask my ex-girlfriends. They couldn't handle it. I wouldn't expect you to either."

I froze at the mention of his past relationships. Someone out there had called Finn her boyfriend, and their breakup had driven him to change his dating preferences. Was I angry at her for not standing by Finn's side, or was I jealous she had the opportunity in the first place? I absently opened and closed the glove compartment on repeat until I felt Finn's eyes on me. I snapped it shut. It didn't matter.

"I don't scare off that easily."

Drunk losers who couldn't fathom me not wanting to take

them home from the bar had called me a lot of things over the years—I was a prick tease, a desperate slut, too fat to be a spin instructor, lousy in bed (my personal favorite, since I'd refused to sleep with him), a dog who'd be so lucky to have his dick in my mouth—I knew better than to take it personally. There was nothing Finn's father could call me that would make me think less of his son.

He gave me a sad smile. "You say that now."

"I do." And I'd say it tomorrow and the day after that, if he let me. I scooched closer to him and raked my hand through his thick hair. It was so soft.

He took a sharp intake of breath and gripped the steering wheel.

I let my hand fall and slid away from him before I caused an accident. "I can't make you want to be with me, Finn. But please don't put words into my mouth or feelings into my heart."

Once again, the four-door sedan was soundless aside from the podcast. I increased the volume, but it quickly became apparent the subject matter—relationships in the modern world—was more awkward than the silence, so I turned it off. I stole glances at Finn at regular intervals, trying to read his mind. A vein in his neck was twitching, and from the way he stared so intently at the road, you'd think he was driving in treacherous weather conditions, like the ones that had led to me sharing his room at the B&B, instead of dry and clear skies.

Suddenly, the doubts rushed in and heat suffused my body. I gripped the bottom of my seat with both hands. What was I thinking declaring my love for a guy I'd known less than two weeks? I didn't use *the words*, but he wouldn't need a translator to get the gist. Did I honestly believe Finn would trust me enough to change his entire attitude with respect to relationships and let me in?

My shoulders relaxed and I loosened my hold on the seat. It made no sense, but I hoped for it anyway. And I was proud of myself for communicating my true feelings in an adult romantic relationship, maybe for the first time ever. Score one for adulting.

Then I felt his hand squeeze mine.

# Chapter Forty

*I* stared down at our joined hands. Had what I said about not being scared off by his imperfect-on-paper family actually sunk in? I lifted my head and searched his face for answers. "Finn?" I hoped the one word communicated all the questions.

He raised my hand to his mouth and kissed it before turning back to the road.

When we arrived in Pleasant Hollow, he parked across the street from the B&B and said, "Wait there," before exiting the car. He came around to my side, opened the passenger-side door, and reached for my hand. After helping me out, he pushed me gently against the hood of the car and we stared at each other, unblinking and motionless. He stepped closer to me.

I sucked in a breath.

He inched forward again. The space between us was creeping toward nonexistent.

I watched his lips part before wetting my own, anticipating the inevitable kiss. I touched my hand to his heart, feeling it thump against my palm. I itched to pull him even further into my space but needed the first move to be his.

He lowered his head and softly—so softly I might have

imagined it—brushed his lips against mine. His restraint was masterful. Then he tugged my lower lip into his mouth and sucked.

My knees buckled and I moaned. Fuck restraint. I grabbed onto his shoulder with one hand and his ass with my other. There was no longer my space or his. There was only ours. We kissed long and deep.

While I still had it in me, I broke the kiss. "I haven't changed my mind about what I want." I was panting.

His ragged breathing matched mine. "That's good, because I have."

"Meaning?" My heart hammered against my chest.

He pressed his lips into a closed smile. "It means I'm tired of being so afraid to care. Because I care about you, Adi Gellar. I really do." He stroked the rim of my ear before tucking a strand of hair behind it. Then he leaned down and kissed the spot on my neck where I always dabbed perfume. "And I want you to care about me."

His words sent euphoric tingles up and down my spine. "I care. I really, really care. But are you sure you won't change your mind tomorrow? You were pretty adamant about not wanting a girlfriend. How can you change your mind just like that?" I snapped my fingers.

"It wasn't . . ." He mimicked my gesture. "Just like that."

"How was it then? Convince me." I softened my voice. "I'm on your side, Finn. I *want* to be with you," I said, rubbing his arms. "I just need to believe you've thought this through. I don't want to get hurt."

He licked his lips. "It's not about wanting a 'girlfriend.' I want *you*. More than as a hookup or a short-term 'we'll always have Pleasant Hollow' fling. But I wasn't exaggerating about how bad things get sometimes with my dad. That said, I can't make assumptions about what you can and cannot handle. I've laid it all out there, and if you're sure…"

"I'm so sure." I stood on my tippy-toes and pulled him to me so we could continue where we left off. "Let's go home." Hearing his chuckle, I giggled. "You know what I meant." I led him into the B&B, the common room empty as usual, and up the stairs. "Your room or mine?"

"Let's do yours this time. Switch things up."

I stopped climbing and turned to face him. With my lips pursed and arms folded across my chest, I said, "Are we already at the stage of our relationship where we need to spice things up?" Out of habit, I instinctively second-guessed my use of the word "relationship." But I didn't take it back. We were in a relationship, or at least on our way to one.

"Not even close, but I hope we get there someday." He winked. "Hashtag relationship goals."

My mouth broadened to a smile. "I've never been so turned on in my life." I grabbed his hand and we raced to my room at the end of the hallway.

Not bothering to turn on the lights, we undressed slowly. Our hands were everywhere as if we couldn't decide what to touch first. Kissing paused only to kick off a shoe, shrug off a pant leg, unclasp a bra. I placed my lips on a freckle on his now bare shoulder. "It's like strip poker without the poker."

He chuckled. "I'm wild for you, Adina Gellar." He pushed me gently onto the bed and knelt between my legs.

"I'm wild for you too, Finn Adams" is what I thought I said, though it was hard to be sure. He was now doing all sorts of exquisite things with his mouth and fingers. Speaking was tough, what with all the writhing and panting. When I was almost *there*, my legs shaking, I lifted my head slightly off the pillow. "Condom?"

He paused. "I desperately want to get you there this way."

"I . . . I can't." I fisted the sheets.

"I know, and it's been bothering me since the first time we were together. Let me try."

"What about you? Don't you want sweet relief?"

He brushed my inner thighs with a light touch. "Unless you plan to kick me out after you get off, there's plenty of time for that." His face turned serious. "Do you trust me enough to let go?"

This man, this beautiful man who was "wild for me" and had just put his faith in me to handle the toughest parts of his life, was desperate to make me come with his mouth. All *I* had to do was lie there and see what happened. My body trembled with the need to be touched. "I do."

He smiled. "Thank you."

"You're the one doing the work!" I closed my eyes. *Just let go.* His tongue was firm . . . he'd listened to what I said about needing hard pressure . . . using his teeth just enough to hurt so good.

*Give in to the bliss.*

The pleasure built and built. Rather than try to chase it, I let myself experience pure, unadulterated ecstasy in the moment, without worrying about whether it would lead to an explosion. At the point where it had always plateaued in the past—where I'd flip over and impale myself onto him—the rapture kept lifting, and soon I was writhing against him, completely losing control. *I'm coming!*

"I think I might..." I bit my lip, tasting metal, and gripped the headboard behind me. The vibrations started in my lower belly and moved south. It felt so different from coming from penetration. Not better, just...my eyes rolled back in my head. In those moments, I traveled to places I couldn't get to by plane, train, or automobile. And then: stillness.

Finn crawled to the top of the bed and pulled me against his chest. "Can the heroes in those small-town movies do *that*?"

I curled into him—my very own urban hero. "Maybe in *my* romantic story, I was supposed to fall for the city guy all along." I gasped and sat up.

Finn's eyebrows pinched together. "What's wrong?"

"Nothing. Abso-fucking-lutely nothing." I vaulted off the bed and jogged over to the dresser.

Finn patted the bed. "We're not done here."

Removing my notepad from my purse, I scribbled *Maybe in my romantic story, I was supposed to fall for the city guy all along.* I had no idea what it meant, only that it meant *something*. I'd figure it out in the morning but knew if I didn't jot it down right now, I risked losing it forever. *Not happening.*

I climbed back in bed with Finn and straddled him. Reaching between his legs, I smiled mischievously. "Now, where were we?"

# Chapter Forty-One

The next morning, I woke up with my arms around Finn's bare torso and my nose pressed against one of his vertebrae—the big spoon to his little—and I froze. Was I dreaming? Had our limbs accidentally collided again, only in reverse? I took a moment to place myself, and when I confirmed last night wasn't just a spectacular dream, a warm feeling of bliss showered my skin and the tension left my body.

Finn stirred. "Morning," he said sleepily before bolting up. "What time is it?"

"Um..." I grabbed my phone from the dresser. "Almost eight."

"Good." He fell back against the bed and stretched his arms over his head.

I hovered over him and planted kisses on his belly. "You thought it was later?"

"I was afraid we overslept." He flipped me over and pinned both my arms at my sides. "You make me forget not every day is a weekend."

I was trapped, and I liked it. "If you keep up the sweet talk, I'm never letting you out of this room."

"Oh, really?" His eyes twinkled. "Were you born this sexy?

Did Mensa reject you because you're too smart? Do you teach porn for a living, because damn, girl!"

"Too far!" I said, kicking him.

He laughed. "Is this too far?" He slipped a hand between my legs.

"Not far enough. Grab a condom." I slapped his butt as he climbed out of bed.

He waved the package dramatically. "Done and done," he said with an accompanying ripping noise that was almost drowned out by the sound of his phone ringing.

I joked, "Way to ruin the moment," until I saw Finn's face fall. "Oh."

His eyes flitted between me and his phone before he made his choice and climbed back into bed. "It can wait." When the ringing ceased, the kissing recommenced. I tried to revel in the morning delight, but despite the lushness of Finn's mouth and the heat of his skin on mine, I could feel he wasn't into it. And the overpowering thoughts in my head had taken over. We'd officially been together less than a day and I was already being selfish. I couldn't, *wouldn't* make Finn choose between me and his father. The phone rang again, and I felt Finn tense against me.

"Finn." I tugged on his ear with my teeth before pulling back. Running my hand through his messed-up, slept-in hair, I said, "Maybe you should see what he wants."

He gave a reluctant nod of agreement. "I'm sorry."

"No worries." I kissed his forehead and pushed him play-fully. "Go."

While Finn took his phone into my bathroom for a more private conversation, I hugged my legs to my chest. What reason could his father have for calling him so early in the morning? *Nothing serious, please!*

Now more than ever, I gave a silent thanks for my own healthy mother-child relationship. My mom instinctively knew when I needed extra attention and when I craved space, and she gave it to me. And while I hoped she knew I'd always have her back, there was never a question which of us was the parent. Not everyone was as fortunate, and Finn's devotion to his dad was admirable. I checked the time. Finn would need to shower for work soon, and the clock hadn't stopped ticking on my own deadline.

My mom was right. Just because getting this story published wouldn't keep us in our apartment didn't let me off the hook for writing it. This assignment and wherever it led could still bring me closer to the financial independence and career development I craved. Derek had granted me a rare opportunity to speak to the readers of *Tea*, and he hadn't snatched it away just because the story I'd pitched had fallen through. He'd given me carte blanche to write anything I wanted as long as it struck an emotional chord with his readers.

Despite conducting a handful of interviews with the people of Pleasant Hollow, nothing yet fit the bill. Grace and Laura's bookstore and nail salon success stories were lovely, but they lacked a common thread.

And then last night, something had clicked in my brain. I'd arrived in Pleasant Hollow with an abundance of expectations and preconceived notions about life in a small town, none of which panned out. I'd escaped the city, longing for the utopia of a Hallmark-town life, and found myself craving the comforts of home. I'd romanticized small-town men only to fall for a fellow city dweller.

What if I'd gone in search of other subjects for the story when it was me all along? What if *I* was the story? *Let's give it a go, shall we?* I booted up my laptop and started writing.

A few weeks ago, I was in a bad place. I'd been stood up, had another story pitch rejected, and learned I was in danger of losing my home. I blamed it all on New York City, where dating is as cutthroat as the job market, and housing costs are astronomically ridiculous.

My antidote: the Hallmark Channel, Lifetime, Netflix, or wherever I could get a comforting small-town romance.

Where better to escape my own career failures, romantic nonstarters, and economic strife than a small town where the nearest festival is a block away and the major conflict lasts about fifteen minutes before being resolved to everyone's satisfaction and sealed with a long-awaited, chaste kiss?

"I'm sorry that took so long."

I looked up as Finn stepped out of the bathroom, his face slack. "Is everything all right?"

I saved my document and closed my laptop.

He sat on the edge of the bed. "September is a particularly hard month for him. A clusterfuck of my mom's birthday, the day they got married, and the anniversary of her death. She'd have turned fifty-four this week."

"Oh, Finn." An abundant sadness swept over me. "There was

never anyone else? Besides your mother, I mean." I bit down on my lip, unsure how much he wanted to tell me.

"He had a steady girlfriend during what I call the sunshine years. She was nice." He cocked his head to the side, as if remembering. "It was like he went through a remission of sorts. He held a steady job. There were no incidents." He tugged at the comforter. "But she left him. I don't know why, and he never talked about it." He was silent for a moment. "There have been other women over the years, but..." Crinkling his forehead at me, he said, "You don't want to know."

I *did* want to know. I wanted to know everything. How could I support him if he left me in the dark? "What did he want this morning?"

"Just to vent. He was crying. It's been fifteen years, and it's like he's stuck in a time warp."

"Was he...was he drunk?" Finn said his dad was a functioning alcoholic, which was obviously horrible, but *functioning* suggested he could get through a day without calling his son crying. My concern was peppered with a pinch of annoyance, and I hated myself for it.

"He was coming down."

"What about AA?"

"What about it?"

"Has he joined?"

"You're a genius, Adi!" His exaggerated wide-eyed expression turned into a snarl. "I don't know why I never thought of that."

The air grew hot. "That was harsh."

Finn scraped a hand across his face. "I'm sorry. It's just... this is your first day, whereas I've been dealing with it for fifteen years."

I knew his defensive response wasn't personal, but it was hard not to internalize it. "I don't mean to be pushy. I just want to be there for you."

His expression softened. "I know, and I appreciate it. I'm not used to anyone else weighing in on how I deal with my dad. It's been just me for so long."

"That's what your partner"—I pointed at myself—"is there for. But I get it. I've been your girlfriend for a hot minute. It's a lot." I smiled, desperate to lighten the mood.

"Thank you." He smiled and kissed my nose. "I need to shower for work. Do you want to meet for lunch? I can take you to Lickety Splits."

I was grateful for the change of topic, even if it was only a temporary distraction. "Yes to lunch, but I'll pass on Lickety Splits for now. I got an idea for a story in between rounds of sex last night. Before I conduct more interviews, I want to see if I can turn the spark into a flame." I pointed to my computer. "I already wrote a paragraph!" I beamed with premature pride.

Finn's face lit up. "I'm glad my sexual prowess inspired your writing mojo."

"So am I." We made googly eyes at each other as if the drama of the morning had never happened. Only it had, and my gut said I'd need to get used to it.

# Chapter Forty-Two

When I learned about a remote town on the cusp of development by a real estate mogul from the city, it immediately brought to mind my favorite television movies. I jumped at the chance to write a story about a real-life small town where a familiar fictional plot was playing out in reality. Taking on this project would allow me to soak up the quiet life while jump-starting my journalism career, healing my financial problems, and escaping flaky local bachelors already onto the next best thing in one fell swoop. My best friend teased I might even fall in love with the town's hottest bachelor. I brushed her off while secretly hoping she was right.

"Come here often?"

I stopped typing and smiled up at Finn. "I love a guy in wool," I said, admiring his white Irish sweater, worn under his leather jacket, of course.

"And I love a woman in a purple hoodie, so we're even." He

bent to kiss me before sliding into the other side of our favorite booth at Pinkie's. "Were you waiting long?"

"Yes, but it was intentional." The bright sun coming through the window in the common room had given me FOMO, so I moved outside to the park. First I texted Kate with an update, using the bare minimum of specificity to protect Finn's privacy. She responded with a series of emojis expressing her delight, concluding with the eggplant and peach to demonstrate her immaturity. I'd planned to work on my story, but the weather was a bit nipplier than the blue skies suggested, which was why I arrived at the diner an hour before my scheduled lunch date with Finn.

He gestured to my laptop. "It's going well?"

"I think?"

"You don't sound so sure. Can I read what you have so far?" Without awaiting an answer, he reached for the computer.

"No!" I said, pulling it back toward me and slamming it shut. His mouth quirked into a smile. "Territorial much?"

"Sorry." I dropped my shoulders. "I'm not ready to share yet."

"Keeping secrets is a questionable way to start a relationship, but okay," he teased.

"It's not that. It's just…" I took a sip of my now-cold coffee and waved down the waitress—the one who wasn't Doreen. After we gave our orders, I turned back to Finn. "The story is about me."

His head swung back. "You?"

I sat up straighter. "It's a true fish-out-of-water story about a woman who left the city for a small town expecting one thing and found something else entirely."

Finn rested his thumb and index finger on his chin, saying nothing.

I held my breath. What if I was fooling myself to think the readers of *Tea* might relate to my unexpected experience in Pleasant Hollow?

Finally, he leaned in and opened his mouth. Except whatever he was going to say was interrupted by the ping of his phone. "One sec." His brows furrowed as he typed a response.

My legs bounced under the table as my impatience grew. "Dying here, Finn. *Dying!*"

He gave me the "hold on a second" gesture with one hand while continuing to type with the other.

Impatience switched to concern at the tight expression on his face. His dad?

Without looking up, he answered my unspoken question. "My dad."

When the waitress came over with our food, I thanked her and bit into my veggie burger. I chewed the dry patty unenthusiastically. Holy crap, I missed the food in Manhattan *bad*.

"Sorry about that," Finn said, flipping over his phone. "Where were we?"

I squirted a drop of mustard onto my sandwich. "My article."

His face brightened. "Right. I think it's brilliant."

"Yay!" My lips stretched into a grin and my shoulders relaxed. "I think so too."

"So why the doubt?"

I fidgeted in my seat. "I don't know." The beginning was easy—girl goes searching for a Hallmark town and finds the opposite—but I didn't have a clear ending in mind. Falling for the city guy after putting small-town men on a pedestal was an adorable twist, but was it enough? What about my housing situation? The next stage of my career? It seemed too premature to tie things up in a pink bow. What kind of ending would Derek want?

"I'm sure it'll be amazing." Finn squeezed my hand across the table but tugged it back as his phone pinged again. He sighed and typed something back. "He wants me to come around tonight with tacos. My mom loved tacos." He rubbed his eyes.

I studied him. "You look tired."

"Someone kept me up late last night." He smiled, but it seemed forced.

I fake-laughed. "Seriously, though. Do you always drop everything when he calls you?"

Finn froze with a french fry at his lips. "Who? My dad?" Answering his own question, he nodded. "I don't have a choice. He'll just keep calling."

"There's no one else to share the load?"

"Not really. Cheryl cut him off." He dropped the fry onto his plate. "He's not always this bad. It's just a rough month."

"I get it." *Let it go, Adi. Let. It. Go.* I couldn't let it go. "It's just…my mom lost her husband too. And she misses him. She misses him every single day. But she moved on, like he would have wanted. Your dad…fifteen years is a long time, Finn. Do you think maybe you're enabling him by jumping whenever he calls?" I bit down hard, knowing I'd gone too far by his flared nostrils.

"Bravo to your mom." Finn glanced around the diner, shaking his head as if wishing he could switch places with another patron. "If I don't keep up with my dad's rants, I risk him doing something stupid like emptying a bottle of vodka into his mouth." He studied me. "Are you sure you can handle this, Adi?"

My mouth went dry. "Yes! I'm sorry I said anything. I just worry about you."

I wasn't bothered so much by the interrupted meals and sex—not that I was a fan of those—but Finn was a grown-ass man who put his life on hold for his father. Didn't he deserve more?

I rubbed my chin. What did I know? Losing the love of her life and father of her child had crushed my mother, but it hadn't *broken* her. I should be grateful, and I was. But would I drop everything for her the way Finn did for his dad? I liked to think so, but the difference was she wouldn't ask me to. In any event, I wasn't going to say another word about it. Finn's girlfriend or not, it wasn't my place.

If he was okay with it, I would be too. "Let's change the subject. How was your day so far?"

His face brightened. "Andrew's tentatively scheduled me to transfer to his lower-income housing project in New Jersey next month. Except the crew here has threatened to sabotage the site to keep me longer. They don't want me to go."

I caught the blush in Finn's cheeks before his face was hidden by the massive turkey club sandwich he'd ordered. He was so adorable, I couldn't wait to devour him later.

"I have some news of my own," I said. "I claimed my spin classes and café shifts for this weekend, which means I need to head back to the city tomorrow." I'd debated staying in Pleasant Hollow a few more days but could no longer justify spending the money. I knew Finn would let me stay with him, but it would only prolong the inevitable.

"Okay," Finn said with a sad nod.

"I don't need to be here to finish the story. The only thing keeping me here is you, and we'll need to figure out this long-distance thing eventually anyway."

"I'll come to the city on weekends. We'll make it work." He

waved his hands around the room. "How are you going to say goodbye to your new friends?"

Even though he was joking, I got a little choked up. It was the end of an adventure. "I can come back here too. I'll need my fix of Brothers dark. Pleasant Hollow has absolutely ruined me for beer anywhere else. Maybe I'll even check out that ShortLine frequent-rider pass after all."

Finn's eyes sparkled. "We should do a farewell tour. Start with a pre-dinner beer, share a plate of garlic knots at the Oven, have our main course here, followed by ice cream at Lickety Splits, and return to Brothers for the grand finale."

"Sounds amazing, except the grand finale needs to be in one—or both—of our rooms for fireworks, if you know what I mean." I waggled my eyebrows.

"If I didn't adore you, Adina Gellar, I'd say never waggle your eyebrows again."

"Not sexy, huh?"

"You could probably make picking your nose sexy, but please don't try."

"It's a sacrifice I can live with," I said, grinning. "Tonight will be fun! Except..." I tapped my fingers to my lips. "What about your dad? The tacos."

Finn blinked. "I'll bring them to him tomorrow."

The momentary delay in his response left me unconvinced. I leaned in. "Are you sure?"

"Yeah. It'll be fine." He nodded assuredly.

"It's a date, then?" Excitement fluttered in my belly.

He reached over and rubbed the top of my hand. "It's a date."

# Chapter Forty-Three

Later that day, I nursed a pint of Brothers dark while waiting for Finn to join me. The place was empty. It was too bad they hadn't taken me up on my Oktoberfest idea, because it looked like they needed the business. Unless the cousins figured out a way to have more than one birthday each per year.

Greg approached. "The answer is still no."

I threw my hands up in the air. "I've been here several times since then and haven't mentioned it. Have I?" Left unspoken was: *Your loss.*

He smiled. "I suppose not. Where's your friend? The fancy guy from the city."

I choked on my beer. I'd never thought of Finn as "fancy." Fancy Finn. Maybe I'd call him that later…in the heat of the moment. "He's on his way."

Had I finally "arrived" here in Pleasant Hollow? Nothing said you were no longer the newbie like the bartender knowing who you hung out with. I glanced over my shoulder and waved at Jennifer and Monica. I had two "sort of" gal pals here too. Maybe I was becoming more of a small-town girl than I thought. Or maybe I'd just needed to give people a chance to know me before expecting to be best friends. A bell rang in my brain, and I pulled out my trusty notepad to jot down that gold nugget for my story.

I checked the time on my phone. Finn was a few minutes late. He must have gotten caught up at work. It was strange to think neither of us would be here in a month or two. Would Finn live in whatever town in New Jersey the lower-income site was located, or would he commute from Manhattan? I didn't like the idea of an Adi 2.0 staying in his next B&B and turning his head, but the possibility didn't stir real tension. I smiled into my glass. If this lack of insecurity was the norm when dating the right guy, I was a fan. I took a selfie with my beer and texted him.

> Hurry. Dark and I miss you!

When the dancing bubbles didn't appear right away, I flipped my phone over and took out my book. Kate had secretly repacked *Rescue Me* starring Finn McAllister in my purse. Now that I was solidly Team Finn again, I was happy she did. The hot K-9 handler would distract me until the real Finn—Fancy Finn to his friends—showed up.

I could get behind a sexy military hero with a German shepherd sidekick, but when I'd finished the first chapter with no response from *my* Finn, the hairs on the back of my head stood up. Had I gotten the time wrong? But wouldn't he have responded to my text to let me know if I had?

> Where are you? I'm getting worried.

I glanced from my left to my right and then over my shoulder before checking my phone again—nothing.

"I'll be right back," I said to Greg. I placed a napkin over my beer and walked over to Monica and Jennifer's table. They were in heated discussion about something.

"Hi there." When they looked up, I said, "I'm sorry to interrupt, but I'm going back to the city tomorrow and didn't want to leave without saying goodbye to you." I opened my arms for hugs, surprised by my sudden melancholy.

They responded with identical head-to-toe once-overs, followed by an overlapped "Good luck" and "See ya," and promptly resumed their conversation.

I let my arms fall to my sides. So maybe "gal pals" was an overstatement. "Okay, then. Well...bye."

I moped back to the bar and checked my phone, where there was still nothing from Finn. Where the hell was he? Had something come up at work? Was it his dad?

Having reached my limit of unanswered texts, I pressed call instead. Voicemail picked up. He'd probably never listen to it, but I left a message anyway: "It's me. I haven't heard from you, so I'm heading over to the construction site. Call me when you get this. I hope you're okay." I repeated the message in a text in case he was already halfway to the brewery and we were about to miss each other by two minutes like two tourists passing in the night.

I walked to the center of town with one hand pressed against the side of my hip to prevent my dress from flying over my ass in the breeze. The black-and-pink, cinched, pleated dress was one of my just-in-case outfits—just in case there's a blizzard, just in case there's a heat wave, just in case there's a black-tie event. I was for sure overdressed for the venues I'd be visiting, but my farewell tour was a solid enough occasion to gussy up. Besides, if anyone gossiped about the woman wearing a cocktail dress and three-inch heels to the diner later, I wouldn't be around to hear it. I hadn't considered all the walking involved in a bar/restaurant crawl or the increasingly windy nights as we crept further into autumn. My feet were killing me by the time I reached the construction site and my hair needed smoothing, but it would be worth it if Finn's eyes dilated in appreciation of my bare legs.

The site appeared to be closing down for the night. The crew were huddled together doing... I squinted... not much of anything actually.

Vick approached. "Adina. You're back again."

I felt a rush of affection. Vick was a lot like I'd imagined my dad would have been as an older man. "Good to see you! I'm looking for Finn." I glanced around but didn't see him. "Is he here?"

"He's in a meeting," Vick said, his smile strained.

"Oh. That would explain it. He was supposed to meet me at Brothers but didn't respond to my texts." I scraped a hand through my hair. Had I just outed Finn and me as a couple? Who cared? It didn't matter. Finn and I were consenting adults, and more importantly, Vick only *reminded* me of my dad. "I'll just wait here, then."

"It might be a while." He glanced toward the trailer, where I assumed the meeting was taking place.

"It isn't Andrew Hanes, is it?" Could it be? Even though the famous real estate powerhouse was no longer featured in my story, it would be fun to meet the original inspiration for it IRL. My toes lifted off the ground in excitement at the possibility.

"Not exactly." Vick removed his white hard hat and scratched his head.

Johnny and Emma joined us. "We're out," Emma said. Even wearing a hard hat over her chin-length jet-black hair and with safety goggles covering her dark blue eyes, she was sexy in black denim jeans and a bright red, white, and blue flannel shirt. A wrist tattoo peeked out from her sleeve. It was a good thing I wasn't the jealous type, because she was hot. Then I noticed the matching his-and-hers gold bands around Emma's and Johnny's ring fingers. They were married!

"You think he'll be okay?" Johnny asked, his blond eyebrows drawn together.

Vick returned his hat to his head. "He's a grown man. He'll be fine," he said, pacing from one foot to the other.

My skin prickled. "What are you guys talking about?"

The couple turned to me in surprise as if finally realizing I was standing there.

The pale skin of Johnny's freckled face turned red. "Nothing."

I opened my mouth to call bullshit as a loud crash sounded in the direction of the trailer.

"What the...?" I licked my dry lips. The heebie-jeebies took over like spiders crawling up my back. "Who's Finn meeting with, and why wouldn't he be okay?"

Three pairs of eyes refused to meet mine.

"I'll just have to see for myself." I stomped over to the trailer, ignoring the protests behind me, with every pulse in my body throbbing. The contrasting sounds of Finn's soothing voice with another, more agitated one coming from inside left me temporarily frozen, but concern for my boyfriend propelled me forward. I opened the door and stepped inside. Both men looked my way.

I'd pictured Mr. Adams like Crazy Earl, Wade Kinsella's drunk father in *Hart of Dixie*—old, with white, unruly hair and bad posture. Finn's dad, if this was in fact him, was the opposite: mid-fifties, tall and handsome, with thick, black curly hair peppered with gray. Only his bloodshot eyes gave him away.

"Who the hell are you?"

*Oh.* And he was mean.

# Chapter Forty-Four

Finn's father squinted at me. His eyes were narrowed to slits as if he lacked the coordination to open them all the way. "Who're you?" He swayed toward Finn. "Who's she?" He came at me.

I took a step back, stumbling on what felt like a shard of glass, but blessedly not losing my balance.

He hovered, waiting for an answer.

I shrank under his intense scrutiny and tried not to gag from the rancid odor of whiskey wafting from his skin and breath. My gut said he wouldn't cause me physical harm, but he was clearly in an aggressive state of mind. I looked pleadingly at Finn to step in.

Finn briefly closed his eyes. "She's my friend, Dad."

*Friend.* The snub cut like a knife, but I shook it off. The timing wasn't right to introduce his father to his *girl*friend, was all.

Finn kicked the glass to the side. "You shouldn't be here, Adina."

I whispered, "When you didn't respond to my texts, I got worried." I tried to communicate with my eyes. *What happened? Are you okay? Is* he *okay?* I hoped to God his dad hadn't driven from Middletown to Pleasant Hollow in this condition.

"I can *hear* you. Voices carry." Mr. Adams sang to himself, then yelled, "Hush hush!" before bursting into laughter.

At least someone was amused. I was legit freaked out, and Finn...well...I couldn't even pretend to have any idea where his head was. My gaze landed on more broken glass on the floor and the overturned chair in the corner. "Is there...is there anything I can do?"

"Did you bring tacos?" Mr. Adams said, his demeanor suddenly relaxed. His face shone with hope, and for a moment, he looked almost childlike.

"I...um...no. Sorry." My throat thickened. He'd asked Finn to bring him tacos—his late wife's favorite—and Finn had put him off for my farewell tour. *Shit.* "We could order takeout." Except none of the restaurants in Pleasant Hollow served tacos. I turned to Finn. "Or what about delivery? Or can I bring him water or coffee...or something else?"

Running errands was a small thing, but it was a thing just the same. For so long, Finn had been his dad's only caretaker—an odd word, considering the size and imposing presence of his father—but I was here now. I could help.

"Or...or...or...," Mr. Adams mimicked. "*Or*, you can get the hell out and let me celebrate my wife's birthday with my son." He sneered at me, no longer resembling a little boy in a grown man's body.

"Stop it, Dad. Please sit down." Finn picked up the chair.

I clamped my teeth shut to contain some harsh words that were dying to come out. He might be an obstinate, nasty man, but he was also Finn's father. I couldn't say Finn hadn't warned me.

Mr. Adams moved to sit and thought better of it. "What's with the pink hair?"

I reflexively touched my head. Yup. Still there.

He tilted toward me, his torso leaning forward and back while his feet remained on the ground, and pulled my hair. "Ugly."

I winced, my eyes stinging from the shock.

Finn stepped in front of me but said nothing.

"Is she your *girl*friend?" He burst out laughing like it couldn't possibly be true, then swayed back and forth.

I focused my gaze on Finn, willing him to answer his father truthfully. Or at least give me a secret look—an acknowledgment of our connection and my new place in his life—but he lowered his chin to his chest, my feelings seemingly the last thing on his mind.

Mr. Adams followed my line of vision, and his glazed eyes traveled between Finn and me. "You can do better than this pink-haired slut." Spit bubbles formed on the corner of his mouth.

My nose tickled and my body shook with the need to be hugged. *Don't cry, Adi. It's not personal. He doesn't know what he's saying. He's drunk.* I blinked away my tears and turned to Finn, who'd yet to stick up for me. Why? Yes, his dad was his main priority, but didn't I mean anything? Couldn't he utter a single word in my defense, if not for his dad's benefit, then for mine?

"I should go," I said.

*Tell me to stay, Finn.* His dad's insults meant nothing. He was a sick man. I knew this. *Let me help you, Finn. Just ask me to stay.*

He let out a low sigh. "You should go."

Tossing out a final olive branch, one more chance, I said, "To get food or coffee?"

His eyes locked on mine at last and he shook his head. "Just go."

Mr. Adams waved obnoxiously. "Don't call us. We'll call you."

Ignoring him, I searched Finn's face for a hidden message. I didn't even know what I wanted to see. Regret? Gratitude? Sadness?

He turned back to his dad before I could find what I was looking for, and so I did as told. I left.

# Chapter Forty-Five

*J*ust go.

I woke up the next morning with my cheek stuck to the dried tears on my pillowcase. My temples throbbed like it was New Year's Day, March 18, and the day after my twenty-first birthday party combined, even though I barely drank half a beer at Brothers. After being summarily dismissed from Finn's office trailer the night before, I'd returned to the B&B, where I crawled into bed still wearing my fancy dress and wept with the stamina of a colicky infant.

It was all so sad. A drunk middle-aged man driven to such belligerence over tacos, although of course I knew it went deeper than a weird food craving. Finn tiptoeing around him like he was made of eggshells. It was tragic, and my heart hurt for both of them.

Unfortunately, battling compassion and sympathy for my new boyfriend and his father was anger and resentment. It was one week into our relationship, perhaps premature for a live viewing of one of his dad's benders, much less my offer to help out like I was a member of the family. But would it have killed Finn to pull me to the side and communicate something… *anything?*

He could have spared one minute—thirty seconds—to say, "I need to deal with this on my own." Or "I appreciate the kindness, but it's better for you to go." Simply "I'll call you later" would have done the trick. Any of those sentences, spoken with the right tone and coupled with the appropriate facial expression, would have made all the difference.

Instead I got "Just go." He barely glanced my way, like I wasn't even in the room. Perhaps it was displaced shame on Finn's part, but it hurt like hell on mine. He'd shut me out. *Hard.* I was a willing ally treated like an enemy, and I was not okay with it.

And why hadn't he objected when his dad called me names? Sure, Mr. Adams was inebriated, but it didn't justify Finn's silence. I was his girlfriend. Shouldn't he have defended my honor? I kicked the comforter to the floor and grunted my aggression. Would it always be this way? And if so, could I live with that?

On the bright side, crying was exhausting. At some point, I wore myself out and slept through the night, only waking up now because of the sun shining through the blinds. In the bathroom, I brushed my teeth too hard and liked it. Despite my anger, I had texted Finn permission to come over no matter how late it was, but he hadn't even replied. For all I knew he was still in Middletown with his dad.

There was a knock on the door, followed by "It's me."

"One second," I yelled, hoping the words weren't too garbled by the toothpaste in my mouth. I spit it out and dried my face. I made a move to comb my hair and thought better of it. Bedhead was the least of our problems. Anxiety pooled in my gut, but there was nothing to do but let Finn in.

He looked terrible—as bad as someone as hot as Finn was capable of looking—purple half-moons under his eyes, pale complexion, wrinkled clothing, the works. Without a word, I drew him into my arms and squeezed, drinking in his scent. In my personal war of emotions, compassion was victorious over anger.

He squeezed back. Whatever else he was feeling, he needed this too.

I released him and stepped to the side. "Come in. Sit." I motioned between the bed and the desk chair, the only two seating options unless you counted the floor, the toilet, and the shower. Finn chose the chair. I sat on the edge of the bed. "How's your dad?"

He rubbed his forehead. "Better. He slept it off."

We stared at each other. I didn't know what to say. "How are *you*?"

"Exhausted. I stayed overnight." His shoulders slumped. "I'm sorry."

I clucked my tongue. "For what exactly?" Was he referring to his dad's behavior or his own?

"My dad can be a mean drunk. Sometimes he's a happy one. Other times he's morose. But mostly, like last night, he's mean." He grazed the fabric of the chair with his fingers.

"You warned me about your dad," I said, tapping my feet. "But I've gotta say, I didn't expect you to just stand there and let him insult me...yell at me." My voice shook.

"I don't think I could have stopped him," Finn said, scrubbing a hand over his face. "Sometimes it's easier to just ignore him than try to fight him on it. He wears himself out, like a baby crying himself to sleep."

Like I had the night before. "You didn't even try, though. You barely acknowledged me."

A flush crossed Finn's cheek.

I shrugged. "It seemed like you didn't even care."

Finn's eyes rounded. "Of course I cared! Watching my dad take his grief out on you gutted me." His faced twisted with anguish.

"How was I to know that when you didn't say anything…do anything?"

He blinked rapidly. "I was so caught off guard by your being there. I didn't know what to do."

"Anything beyond absolutely nothing would have been an improvement." I sighed. "Your dad's insults didn't hurt me, not fatally anyway, but your silence did. You said nothing in my defense. I know your dad wasn't in his right mind, but *I* was. Even if he woke up this morning with no memory of what happened last night, *I* remember all of it." My body pulsed with all my conflicting emotions. The idea of making this about me felt gross, but there was no denying what happened was relevant to us as romantic partners. "I keep reliving that moment when he said you could do better and you stood still as a mannequin. You couldn't even look at me and whisper an apology. Nothing." The memory sent a hot dagger through my heart. "Put yourself in my shoes…my very uncomfortable shoes."

"I never meant to hurt you, Adi. This is why—"

"I just wanted to help. Be there for you. You didn't have to accept what I was volunteering, but I hoped you'd at least acknowledge the attempt with a little more grace." I didn't know where I belonged in his life. *If* I belonged. Or whether I was even deserving of such knowledge after less than two weeks. But was the newness of our relationship a justifiable excuse for his behavior or a sign of what was to come?

He bowed his head. "It's a vicious cycle. He drinks and thinks about my mom. Or he thinks about my mom and drinks. Either way, he calls me, and when I don't jump, he goes off the deep end. Last night was the first time he tracked me down since I've been in the county. I'm just glad he had the sense to call a cab."

"Like I said, this isn't about your dad. It's about *you*."

Raising his head, Finn said, "But don't you see? My dad is part of the package. You can't have one without the other."

"I would never ask you to choose between your dad and me." I worked to keep my voice from shaking. "I just felt like an unwanted intruder, and you did nothing to reassure me otherwise."

"It didn't have to happen. If I'd just gone over there with tacos…but I put him off for your farewell tour." He stood, kicked one of my sneakers out of the way, and paced the floor. "I should have brought him the damn tacos."

I flinched. "Don't blame this on me." I got up, climbed over my open suitcase, and joined him in the middle of the room. "I asked about the tacos, and you said you'd bring them to him today instead."

"'Do you always answer the phone when he calls? Don't you think you're enabling him?'" he said, mimicking me.

I breathed in and out with purpose, choosing not to call him out on being a dick by parroting me. "It just kills me you have to bear so much responsibility on your own."

His expression softened. "Adi." He placed his hands on both of my forearms. "This is why I don't do relationships. I tell you I'm not boyfriend material, but none of you listen. You always promise you can handle it. You're 'dating me, not my father.' Famous first words. But then..." He dropped his arms and combed a hand through his hair until the ends stood up. "Here we are."

My posture went rigid. "Please don't lump me in with all your other girlfriends as if I don't have my own identity."

He huffed out a humorless laugh. "You're absolutely right. You're different. You and your romantic aspirations for im-promptu snowball fights and grand gestures are one of a kind."

I clenched my fists. "Don't throw my own words in my face! What do snowball fights and sleigh-riding have to do with any of this? I also mentioned strength and vulnerability. The way you treated me last night demonstrated neither."

He shook his head several times. "I can't be the hero of your dreams, Adi. You're always going to be disappointed with me, and I'm always going to feel like shit about it." His voice choked with emotion.

Guilt tugged at my chest. I *had* droned on and on *and on* at Lakeview House about my ideal man. Was I putting undue pressure on Finn to be the perfect boyfriend? I opened my mouth to apologize, when a vision of Leo popped into my head. So many times he'd blown me off when something else suddenly came up. When I called him on it, he would insist our plans had been tentative, then turn it around on me and call me needy or overly sensitive for being upset.

Finn was doing the same thing by claiming my frustration with him was a product of my own unrealistic expectations. The blood rushed to my head in the realization.

"I won't be gaslighted into thinking it's *my* problem, because it's not," I said. "So I've dabbled in fantasies of meeting the elusive unicorn guy and living happily ever after. It doesn't excuse *your* behavior. I don't need the fairy tale, but I don't want *this* either." My nails dug into my palms until it hurt. I *was* disappointed, and I wanted and deserved more from a relationship than simply *living with it*.

I'd dated Leo for almost a year, keeping my frustration to myself until I couldn't take it any longer, only to learn we'd never been on the same page anyway. Never again.

I wasn't going to give Finn the same opportunity to throw me crumbs. "If you're not boyfriend material, it's not because of your dad. That's a cop-out. It's because you're unwilling to let anyone be as important as him in your life. And worse, you're willing to throw people you claim to care about under the bus to placate him." I looked him straight in the eye. "Tell me I'm wrong."

The lines in his forehead creased. "I wish I could be the man you want, but a relationship with me comes with too much baggage I can't release."

I grunted. "I'm not asking you to abandon your father. I just don't want to be cast aside every time he needs you. I want to coexist with him. You said you wanted me to care about you. I do. Don't punish me for it now."

"I don't know what to say."

I didn't either. Finn kept his stare straight ahead at the wall while I locked mine on his profile. We remained motionless, awkwardness seeping into the silence until it was unbearable. Resigned, I released a deep exhale. "This isn't going to work out, is it? It's too hard. It shouldn't be this much work, should it?" I'd never felt this strongly for a man before, but the truth was we were practically strangers. My brain knew this. I just needed my heart to catch up.

He faced me and shook his head. "I wish I could snap my fingers and magically turn things around, because for the first time in a long while, I want this. I want *you*. But I can't promise there won't be more nights like last night. I can actually guarantee there *will* be."

I took his use of the phrase "nights like last night" to mean not only his dad going off the rails, but also him verbally attacking me while Finn did nothing to stop it. *No.* "And I'll never be okay with feeling as hurt and abandoned as I did last night."

He frowned. "I'm so sorry."

I hugged myself and forced a smile. "It was fun while it lasted though, right?"

His lips quirked. "We'll always have Pinkie's."

I nodded. "That's that, I guess," I said, touching a finger to my quivering chin. "I'd better pack and check out before Lorraine comes a-calling." I turned my back on him to avoid breaking down to his face. I opened my door, desperate for him to leave immediately and stay forever at the same time. "Good luck, Finn."

He stepped into the hallway and gave me one final sad smile. "I'll miss you, Adi Gellar." He studied my face so intently, like he was trying to memorize every freckle, then turned and walked away.

When he was gone, I sank against the door and whispered, "Farewell, Fancy Finn."

# Chapter Forty-Six

*W*hy did people do the exact opposite of what would make them feel better? For instance, why was I listening to the recording of my interview with Finn when hearing his teasing voice brought it all back? It was Saturday night, two days since I'd returned to the city from Pleasant Hollow, and after teaching a morning spin class and working an afternoon shift at the café, I was in for the night and draped across my couch. I played the interview from the beginning again. Even ten minutes in, a laugh would slip into Finn's answers—residual hilarity over my mistaking him for the token Pleasant Hollow single guy.

There were so many things to love about Finn—he was funny, sensitive, hardworking, gorgeous—and I did. Being the center of his attention, both in and out of bed, was everything, and I reveled in it.

I missed him something fierce, but walking away was the right move...the *only* move. He was never going to see things from my point of view, and by staying with him, I'd be accepting less than what I wanted or deserved from a partner. Finn had stood by and let his father spew insults at me and pull my hair because, in his words, it was easier than fighting him. I had no doubt he felt like shit about it, but not bad enough to promise it wouldn't happen again.

My next relationship would be with someone who cared enough about me to have my back, even if it was the harder choice. Besides, I wouldn't be happy in a relationship where I always came second to his dad, a man who might never welcome me into his life. I'd lost my own father and often wondered if I might get a second chance with my future father-in-law. Would it be so horrible to have someone to call "Dad" after all these years?

Bored with the pity party, I buried my phone under a throw pillow and scrolled through the TV guide until I got to the Hallmark Channel. When Lacey Chabert and Andrew Walker appeared on the screen, I shrieked and turned off the television. *Too soon, Adi. Too soon.*

I could drown my sorrows in wine. Except Kate was in lockdown studying for the bar. Drinking alone tended to exacerbate whatever mood I was already in, which meant I'd resume rehashing the premature end of my love affair with Finn.

*Ping.*

I pulled my phone out from under the pillow to see who'd texted me, hating myself a little for hoping it was Finn.

The clock is ticking.

I smothered a groan into the pillow. Thank you, DerDick, for the oh-so-subtle reminder. My article was written, aside from the ending. The reason I couldn't conclude the piece back in Pleasant Hollow was now clear. It was because I'd instinctively known the romantic angle wouldn't end on a happy note. From the start, there'd been too many knots in Finn's and my pink bow. But I had to write *something*. Just because my love life was in the shitter didn't mean I had to flush my career down the toilet too.

I opened my computer to a new document in Word and tapped the keys. An hour later, I read back what I'd written.

> Besides concluding that I was seriously naive in thinking the movies were anything like real life, and finding myself unable to write the story as proposed, I realized geography wasn't my problem and moving wasn't the solution. On any given weekend in New York City, there are dozens of local events—street fairs; arts and music festivals; food, beer, and wine tastings—to make up for what the small town lacked. For every connection I failed to make in the small town, I had a friend or family member missing me back at home. Those loved ones more than make up for the strangers who pass me on the street with zero acknowledgment or push me out of the way for a seat on the subway on a daily basis. I left the small town with a better appreciation for what was waiting for me in the expansive backyard of New York City: the pizza, the opportunities for growth and recreation, the people! There's no place like home. It took more than three clicks of my heels to get back, but it was worth the journey.

I rolled my neck. It wasn't bad, but it still felt unfinished.

"Too much or the perfect amount of cleavage?"

I looked up at my mother, dressed to kill in form-fitting black skinny jeans, a low-cut black tunic, and red kitten heels. "The fact that you *have* cleavage means you should guard your underwear drawer, because I might need to steal that bra." I smiled. "Which is to say, the perfect amount. Going out?"

"I'm meeting Terry at Vino at eight." She walked past me.

This news was a nice reprieve. I slid my computer a few inches away to seal the redirection of my attention to my mother. "This is a third date, right?" The light was now on in the kitchen, and I heard her emptying the dishwasher. "Don't. I'll empty it later. Third date?" I asked again over the sound of water running.

A moment later, she sat next to me on the end of the couch with a glass of water. "We were out of clean glasses. Yes. He has sex appeal, and I liked his shirt on the first two dates."

I was charmed by my mom's offbeat standards. She'd met Terry on Plenty of Fish. After their first date, the week before I left for Pleasant Hollow, she came home buzzed off two glasses of wine and had effused over Terry's colorful checkered shirt. On the second date, when he'd worn an equally appealing pink-and-green gingham button-down, she learned his brother owned a men's dress shirt company based out of South Africa. "Take a picture this time. Or bring him home so I can see for myself." I waited for her insistence it wasn't going to happen and was taken aback by the full-on blush on her cheeks. "Well then. I will retire to my room early just in case," I teased.

"I'm going with an open mind." She ducked her head. "But yes, if you could make Adi 'Scoop' Gellar scarce, I'd appreciate it," she said, referring to the time I'd peppered a date with twenty questions, prompting him to escape when she went to the bathroom.

I mock-pouted. "I was ten. And, by the way, any man worthy of your *assets*"—I started to waggle my eyebrows until I remembered Finn's discouragement of the gesture—"wouldn't be scared off by your precocious offspring. We're a package deal." Even though I was joking, my lungs constricted at the realization we'd be living separately in a few months and she'd no longer have to tell prospective boyfriends about her live-in fully grown daughter. It was a good thing. *Adulting*. Still.

"Enough about me. How are you holding up?"

I'd confessed everything that had happened with Finn from the time we'd walked out the door on Rosh Hashanah until I stepped back in with my suitcase in tow—a whole hell of a lot for a measly thirty-six hours—immediately upon my return. "Do you think I'll ever get it right?" I tapped my feet against her thigh.

She placed her glass on the table and pulled my legs onto her lap. "Get what right?"

"Romantic love." I blew a hair out of my eye. "Will I ever meet someone where everything comes together naturally without obstacles, like you and Dad?"

Her forehead wrinkled. "What makes you think your dad and I had no obstacles?"

"Obviously, you were deprived of your happy ending, but before that."

She let out a low sigh.

"What?" I bounced my legs.

"Things with your dad weren't as cut-and-dried as you think. We broke up at least three times before we were married."

My mouth dropped open. "You did? Why?"

"The last time was because he thought we were too young to get married. I said we'd been dating since we were sixteen and if he didn't know I was 'the one' after five years, I probably wasn't. I gave him an ultimatum and he didn't bite. I started dating someone else and he came back. As they do." She winked.

My legs stiffened in her lap. I was stunned speechless.

"I loved him. I loved him so much. But I do wonder sometimes what would have happened if he'd lived. Would we have grown together or apart? I like to think we'd still be together now, but we were so young."

Despite the shrinking feeling in my heart over what Mom had shared, I believed my parents would have weathered any storms and eventually celebrated their fiftieth anniversary. "Why are you telling me this now?"

She patted my knees. "Because you've always put our marriage on a romantic pedestal, and I didn't see any harm. I thought it was sweet. You had so little time with your father. Why not imagine the two of us as the perfect couple from day one? Now I worry the picture I painted gave you an unrealistic role model. Well, me and those movies you love so much."

"Are you saying you think my expectations with Finn were too starry-eyed?"

"I don't know. What did you expect?"

I sank my butt deeper into the couch cushions. "I thought he'd let me into *all* aspects of his life, not just the convenient ones. But when I walked into that trailer, he practically sided with his father, acting like I was an unwanted intruder, before kicking me out. It stung."

"Playing devil's advocate here, but maybe he was embarrassed.

What would you have done if Finn showed up here on Rosh Hashanah and I was three sheets to the wind? What if I threw noodle kugel at his head and called him an impotent loser?"

I gave her a side-eye. "I can assure you he's not impotent."

She side-eyed me back. "TMI, Squirt."

I giggled. "I would have apologized to Finn for my mother's atrocious behavior before locking you in your bedroom until you sobered up."

"Not everyone's as perfect as you."

I mock-glared at her.

"My point is Finn was in shock. He hadn't expected you to show up or for your first introduction to his dad to go down that way. It doesn't excuse his behavior, but it might *explain* it a little."

Finn *had* said he was caught off guard and didn't know what to do. But what about later? "What about the next morning? I just wanted him to acknowledge how shitty it was. He kept apologizing for not being the type of boyfriend I deserved, as if he had no choice in the matter."

"Maybe he thinks he doesn't."

I scrunched my face. "Meaning?"

Mom pressed her lips together in thought. "He's been single for a long time now, no?"

"We never discussed specifics, but it had been a while since he had a girlfriend. He was pretty set in his ways until I came along." I'd broken down his defenses somehow, which would have been flattering if I weren't 100 percent certain he regretted it now.

"Maybe he thinks he can't fit someone else into his life or balance his girlfriend's needs with those of his father because he's never tried. He was ashamed to even *tell* you about his dad, only to have you witness him at his worst, up close and personal, less than a week into your relationship. He came to you first thing in the morning expecting cuddles and was criticized instead. In his mind, all his fears about what would happen if he got seriously involved with someone came true."

I sat up, feeling my blood pressure rise. "You think I was too hard on him? What was I supposed to do? Say nothing?"

Mom smoothed her hands along my legs in a calming manner and softened her voice. "Of course not. Why set a precedent for bad behavior? By saying nothing, you'd be acquiescing to the status quo. You would have gotten resentful over time. I think the talk you had was inevitable."

I lay back down. "That's what I keep telling myself." This one time, I was glad she had an answer for everything, since it matched my own. "Where are you going with this, then?"

She gritted her teeth as if anticipating her next words wouldn't go over well. "Could you have expressed how hurt you were with a little more empathy and understanding? And maybe waited at least a day before confronting him?"

I stilled. I probably could have.

"You need to accept that even great relationships can be complicated. And maybe Finn needs to learn how to be a good son and a good boyfriend simultaneously, but that takes time."

"I could give him time!"

"Did you tell *him* that?"

We hadn't gotten that far. "You still think Finn and I could have a great relationship? Despite everything?"

"I know he cares about you. The stars in his eyes when he looks at you don't lie." She removed my legs from her lap. "I also know relationships take work and sometimes a lot of back-and-forth and compromise before you get it right. Love isn't always easy, but hard doesn't necessarily equal bad. Take me and your dad, for example. If we ended things after our first breakup, you wouldn't be here." She gasped. "Terry! I need to go."

After she left, I thought about everything we'd said. Maybe Finn and I had given up too soon. My own dating disasters coupled with my idealistic views on what constituted romance had trained me to run at the first sign of scummy behavior. Finn wasn't a scumbag, not on purpose anyway, but I'd experienced the incident through the lens of my past experiences. It was unrealistic to think he'd handle things beautifully the first time out of the gate. How Finn treated me was wrong, but it wasn't unforgivable, especially given how amazing he was every day before then. I could promise to exercise more patience moving forward if he'd agree to learn how to be there for his father without alienating or hurting me in the process.

But could he? And more importantly, *would* he?

I wasn't ready to talk to him directly yet—my feelings were too raw. At least when I bounced things around with my mom, I knew she wouldn't hang up on me. Finn might not be open to compromising or even trying to see things through my eyes. If it was his way or the highway, it wouldn't work. I clucked my tongue, and then it came to me: the ending for my story.

From day one, I looked out for the single, attractive, and eligible bachelor. While I did engage in a face-to-face with someone who met that description, unlike in the movies, there was no love connection. But I'd be lying if I said there was no romance. I didn't spark with the sexy town doctor (or handyman), but there was someone. In an unexpected twist, I fell for the enemy—the city guy, or rather one of his people. This man welcomed, listened to, encouraged, entertained, and accepted me more than any stranger ever had before. Believe it or not, I fell in love! I'm sad to report, we quickly hit a roadblock we couldn't get past, and our story ended before it really got started.

But what I realize now is this: Romances always work on television and in books because when conflict arises, there is a set page count or time limit by which it must be resolved so the couple can live happily ever after. Not many real-world relationships could survive if all their problems needed to be solved within two hours or 300 pages. Thankfully, we have the benefit of open-ended deadlines when it comes to love.

In the days since I've been back home, I've concluded I'm not ready to close the book on Adi and Finn just yet. The right one doesn't always come prepackaged and fitting like adjacent pieces in a puzzle. Sometimes both parties need to adjust their attitudes and behaviors until they harmonize together. Love doesn't always look like what we see on TV, but the relationships that take more work are no less special.

Finn: I could have been better—more sensitive and patient—and I'm sorry for that. If by any chance you, too, have given our ending thought and have your own regrets, maybe we should talk.

A tingling surge spread through my body as I read the piece from the beginning. It was finished, and it was fantastic! And maybe my story with Finn still had some life in it after all.

I opened a new email to Derek with the subject line "As Seen on TV," attached the story, and pressed Send.

# Chapter Forty-Seven

From my kitchen table, I glanced at the bottom right corner of my computer screen—11:57. It had only been two minutes since the last time I checked, which meant three to five more to go before *Tea*'s newsletter subscribers, of which I was one, would receive our weekly email with links to their newly published stories.

A week and two days had passed since I'd first sent mine to Derek. He accepted it with minor edits within twenty-four hours, and it was to go live today.

"Don't forget to breathe, Squirt."

"I'm breathing! You can bet your ass if I suffocate, it's happening *after* I see my story in print."

"No one can say my girl doesn't have her priorities straight."

It was only 11:58, and there'd been no sound to notify me of an incoming message, and yet . . . *refresh*. It was as if I had no control over my fingers—my still perfectly manicured fingers, thanks to Laura and her magic skills.

"You still there, Kate?" I chomped nervously on a Bavarian pretzel—brunch of champions. I heard paper shuffling, but she'd disappeared from sight. "Kate?"

My mother and best friend were at their individual offices working, while I had the afternoon off from both of my jobs. We were on a three-way FaceTime so we could read the story in sync when the newsletter landed in our respective mailboxes sometime between 12:00 and 12:04.

The paper shuffling stopped, and Kate's face once again appeared on the screen. "I'm here! Sorry. I'm buried in document review. Trying to multitask."

"One-minute countdown begins now!"

"Shall I bring out the noisemakers?" Mom joked.

"I got mine!" Kate shrilled.

"Me too!"

I gawked at my computer. Where was *my* newsletter?

*Refresh. Refresh.*

"Am I allowed to open it, or are we doing a synchronized thing here?"

Before I could respond to Mom's question, I gasped at the arrival of a bolded new message from *Tea*. "Guys." I pointed to the message, never mind that they had no view of my computer through their phones. "GUYS!" I repeated.

"What?" they asked in harmony.

"The subject line! 'As Seen on TV' is the title of my story! Every week, Derek selects one story to highlight in the newsletter header as a way to grab the readers' attention. This week he chose *mine*." My body tingled in a mixture of excitement and disbelief.

"Of course he did. No brainer, Squirt."

Kate clapped her hands. "This is the coolest thing ever. My bestie's got some serious clout!"

"Shh. Time to read." My limbs felt light with joy.

It was silent for a minute until Mom said, "Oh, Adi. This is wonderful." Her eyes shimmered with tears.

"It is," Kate agreed, her voice soft.

I read the story again, almost in a dream state. No matter how many times I saw my work in double-spaced, twelve-point Times New Roman font in a Word document, there was something about seeing it professionally printed in Garamond typeface in a magazine (digital or not) that made it feel like it was the first time, like it was someone else's piece, like it was *real*. I sighed happily. All the struggles that had come before—every rejection from Derek and others—had been worth it to reach this moment.

If my life were a movie, this scene would involve a dance montage for sure.

"I wonder if Finn will read it." Kate breathed sharply and slapped her hand against her red-painted mouth.

"It's fine. The thought has crossed my mind too." *An understatement.* The only way he'd see the story was if he sub-scribed to *Tea*. Or if the article went viral, but I wasn't even confident it would reach the twenty thousand unique visitors Derek had thrown out as the condition for the full-time staff position.

At least once a day since talking things through with my mom, I drafted a text to Finn: Can we talk? How are you? I'm sorry, but only if you're sorry too. Then I deleted the text without sending it. The story was my way of opening the door, hoping Finn would walk through it.

Was it cowardly? Perhaps.

But a text could go both ways. If Finn was on the same page, it would be instant gratification. We'd kiss and make up.

Hooray! But on the flip side, if he blew me off, I'd also have my quick and dirty answer: No.

Since I wasn't ready to have my heart smashed into a million pieces yet, I chose purgatory.

Communicating indirectly through my story prolonged the hopeful, if not uncertain, stage. It kept the dream alive a little longer, while also giving me time to process the possibility he'd moved on. With any luck, by the time I accepted it was over— if it came to that—it wouldn't hurt as much.

It also made for a much better story.

"You were brave, and I'm so proud of you. That said, I hate to read, gush, and run, but the waiting room is full of patients here on their lunch hours."

"Same. Except in my case, I need to bill some time to clients before I go home and study. What does the famous essayist have planned for the rest of the day?"

I was glad for the subject change. "The famous essayist," I said in a fancy voice, "is going to start researching her next story." Of course, I'd be doing this in between reading the comments. Writers were urged to step away from the comments because readers could be cruel, but... well, *that* wasn't happening.

We ended the call, and I read the article for the third time. I was still in shock it made the headline. Alone in the room, I said, "This is a big deal." Derek's confidence in the story put a lot of pressure on me to deliver. I gulped. If the response was overly critical or completely lacking, it could seal my fate as a forever out-of-work freelance journalist.

To place boundaries on my comment-stalking, I set a timer for an hour, during which I researched my next pitch. A journalist was only as good as her last article. The material Grace from

Books on Main had shared, about her fathers meeting and falling in love while competing for the lease on the store, had inspired a new story about business partners turned lovers. Over the next hour, and with the help of Instagram, I found a true story about old friends who reunited at their high school reunion, discovered a common dream of opening a bakery, and pooled their savings to do just that. Two years later, their Hoboken pastry shop was flourishing, and the former classmates were now engaged.

When the timer went off, I set my phone to the side and refreshed the page on my published story. With my teeth threatening to dig a hole in my lip, I scrolled through the text, past the random embedded advertisements for The Company Store and Weill Cornell Medical Center, to the bottom. Next to the links to share on Facebook, on Twitter, and via email, a thin, blue, two-and-a-half-inch-long block prompted me to read the fifty-seven comments. I sucked the breath I was holding further into my mouth and clicked the blue line.

**Tara Stein**
**New York, New York**

OMG, I loved this story and how Adina rediscovered her passion for our fine city. Go, Adina!

I released my breath. So far, so good.

**William Witherspoon**
**Jersey City, New Jersey**

Adina: You're a twit. Everyone knows Hallmark is fake.

I rolled my eyes. *Clearly not everyone, Bill.* I paused to gauge my reaction to the name-calling. It didn't sting as much as I'd feared. Moving on.

**Paula Rund**
**New York, New York**

I enjoyed the vulnerability. But I want more on Finn!

I chewed on a nail, manicure be damned.

**Patrice Vasquez**
**New York, New York**

I'm with Paula. More details about Finn and the real-life romantic comedy, please!

I bit off the nail and spit it into my hand before tucking it into a napkin with some pretzel crumbs.

**Laura Olsen**
**Warwick, New York**

Puleeze. My small town is just like the movies: cozy, warm, and perfect. Adina is another snobby Manhattanite bragging about how fabulous the city is. Go home, Carrie Bradshaw. *Sex and the City* was canceled a long time ago.

*Oh, go fuck yourself, Laura Olsen.*

### Kate Park
### New York, New York

This was one of the best essays I've ever read in *Tea*. The author is so open and honest about her journey, and while I'm personally devastated to learn not all small towns are picture-perfect, I admire the author for taking the time to find out and for putting herself out there. That Finn fellow would be a dumbass not to call her PRONTO. Please publish more of Adina Gellar's stories, as she's a writer to watch!

I blew a kiss at the screen. *I love you too, Kate.*

By the time I got to the bottom, three more comments had popped up. It was an almost equal mix of insulting ("how pathetic"), mushy ("how sweet"), and nosy ("how about a sequel?") remarks. I wasn't about to put a crown on my head and proclaim myself queen of the personal essay, but I had no desire to jump out of our four-story apartment to end it all either.

I minimized the story, set the timer for another sixty minutes, and refocused on my pitch. By the end of the hour, I'd found one more colleagues-to-lovers couple and felt confident I had enough material to put something together to send to Derek, or, if he canceled me, another editor.

I refreshed my story again and blinked. The number of comments had more than doubled in the last hour to 117. I allowed myself to imagine one of them was from Finn saying he also wanted to talk. Logically, I knew the chances of him reading the story, much less leaving a comment, were slim, but as the feedback grew in quantity, so did the strength of my wishful thinking.

**Candace Fink**
**New York, New York**

Now that you've ruined the fantasy of small towns for the rest of us, I hope you feel better.

*So much better, Candace. Thank you!*

**Red Sox fan**
**Boston, Massachusetts**

Was this a story or a poorly disguised advertisement for New York City? Is "Finn" the code name for your useless mayor?

Ouch.

**Kate Park**
**New York, New York**

The commenters above can bite me. I'm sure the author has way better taste in men.

I chuckled while fighting the urge to text Kate to focus on her job so she could go home and study as planned. My selfish need for her ferocious loyalty was all-encompassing.

**Brad Cowen**
**Glen Cove, New York**

I really enjoyed this piece, but I agree with
the others that it ended too abruptly. Have you
heard from Finn, Adina?

I chewed my lip. The negative feedback didn't bother me
nearly as much as the pleas for further details about Finn, since
I didn't have any.

My phone rang. "Hi." For the first time ever, I answered
Derek's call without fear attached to me like a third arm. The
mere volume of feedback, good or bad, meant the story had
been read. This could only be a positive. For every person who
left a comment, there were probably twenty more who hadn't.
The nerves in my tummy shimmied and shook knowing Finn
might fall into the latter category.

"Congratulations, Gellar. I told you to find a story, and
you did."

"Thank you!" I put the phone on speaker.

"Finn."

"What about him?" The fear was back. What if Finn had
called *Tea*'s offices to complain about his name being used?
Could he do that? Nothing I said would be considered defama-
tion of character. I hadn't even used his last name! I was being
paranoid.

"Have you spoken to him?"

"No." My hand shook as I scrolled through more comments.
None of them were from Finn.

"Track him down. Open a dialogue about whatever

happened between you. Write a part two. Share it with our readers."

I froze with my elbows on the table. The idea left me cold. I hoped this story would lead to another (and another, and so on), because...well...*duh*! But I wasn't comfortable using Finn to secure another publishing credit for my résumé. Also, I aspired to write feel-good stories, and I didn't know if this one would have a happy ending. "How about I think about it?"

"Fair enough." He paused. "About the full-time staff position. You want it?"

Did dogs like having their bellies rubbed? Did Rory Gilmore like coffee? *Slow your roll, Adi. Ask about starting salary, health insurance, and retirement planning.* I smoothed down my hair. "Yes!"

"Love the enthusiasm. It's yours. But not until after Christmas. Jo is leaving the city to move with her boyfriend to Arkansas." He scoffed. "What is it about small towns?"

"I have no idea." I conjured an imaginary selfie taken with my temporary Pleasant Hollow neighbors—Doreen with a pencil behind her ear, Aaron and Greg holding up half-washed pilsner glasses, Lorraine pursing her lips in annoyance—and smiled. "None at all."

"Right? Anyway, she writes our love and romance column. I think you'd be a good fit."

"I'm thrilled for the opportunity!" My whole body vibrated with joy.

A month ago, I'd left for Pleasant Hollow determined to write my career-making story, and I'd succeeded. Much remained unknown, like where I'd live in four months and if I'd ever see Finn again, but I would be a full-time journalist very soon. Whatever else happened, it was a great day.

# Chapter Forty-Eight

**W**e'll get started in a few minutes. Does anyone need assistance setting up their bike?" I gave this spiel before all my classes. The majority of the people who took my Tuesday evening class were regulars, but I never ruled out newcomers or beginners who had no idea what they were doing but were too bashful to ask for help.

When no one answered, I double-checked that today's playlist, a mix of popular and more eclectic music spanning five decades, was ready to go, and hopped on my bike. "Is anyone new to spinning?" I did a quick sweep of the studio and smiled at the mostly familiar faces. No one spoke up. Last question. "Is there anyone here who's never taken one of my classes before?"

"I haven't."

I couldn't see the source of the deep voice that came from the back row of the full studio. I stood up with one leg on either side of the bike. "Can whoever said that please wave your hand?" My eyes followed the line of the raised muscular arm down a few inches to his face. I gasped.

It was Finn.

My body trembled, and I dropped back into my seat and

white-knuckled the handlebars for support. How had I not seen him come in?

"Welcome to my class. I hope you won't regret it!" I looked down at my shaking thighs and joined in on the room's laughter, although mine was less "ha ha, I'm so funny" and more of the nervous variety.

It had been two weeks and one day since my story went live. When I didn't hear from Finn, I decided it was either because he'd read it but was already over me, or because he *hadn't* read it but had come to no similar epiphany on his own about giving us another shot.

At least I'd opened the door. Rather than force things, I'd accepted it was over. The story was over. Pleasant Hollow was over. *We* were over. In time, I'd recall Finn as just another guy who wasn't the one.

Except now he was here, and I had to wait at least forty-five minutes to find out what he wanted.

We hadn't even warmed up yet and sweat was already dripping down my back. I started pedaling and in my peppiest spin instructor voice said, "This is a forty-five-minute interval ride. There are two rolling hills, a bunch of sprints, some jumps, and one Tabata interval, which I'll explain in more detail when we get there. Trust me. You'll know when we get there." My evil laugh morphed into choking. I grabbed desperately at my water bottle, managing to spill at least two mouthfuls onto my lap. If I couldn't even drink water in the guy's presence, how the hell was I going to get through this ride without losing my shit—like literally shit my gray-with-pink-swirl-designs exercise pants? I swallowed hard. The ride must go on. *Inhale love. Exhale stress.*

It helped that he chose a bike in the back row. Even when we stood up and jogged in second position, he was blocked by Lenny, my new favorite regular by virtue of his broad torso and super long legs, which enabled me to pretend Finn wasn't right there behind him. My playlist also served as a sort of meditation to get me through the first half of the ride. I focused on the rhythm of the music to turn off my brain as best as I could.

And then we reached the halfway mark. This was where I usually jumped off the bike and walked around the room to subtly correct form and shout out kudos to my hardest workers. But what if my legs gave out when I approached Finn's bike? Or I had a sweat mark on my crotch? Or I had a wicked case of BO? I discreetly brought my nose to my armpit as we climbed to "If You Really Love Me" by Stevie Wonder. *So far, so good.*

I couldn't walk around and conveniently avoid his area. Only Finn would notice, but he was the only one who mattered. No. Hiding wouldn't do. I had to behave like he was no different from any other student in my class. Except he wasn't remotely like anyone else. He was special, to me anyway.

The song ended, followed by the beginning notes of "Paris" by the Chainsmokers. I purposely chose it for sprints on a hill. It was the perfect spot in the ride to get up and encourage my class to turn up the resistance dial, push outside their comfort zones, and go, go, go! I should have been up already, but my body felt glued to the seat. I gave myself five seconds to make it happen. I glanced down at my legs...still in the seat. My inner voice screamed for me to stop being a wimp and get the hell up. This time I listened.

I walked to the right side of the room and down the front row of bikes. I risked a glance in Finn's direction. As if sensing me, he turned his head and stared back with a grimace caused by either physical or emotional distress, but I couldn't tell which. I pretended my legs were made of sticks so they wouldn't wobble and looked away.

"Can you guys go a little faster?" I challenged.

I stopped in front of my current favorite person. "That's it, Lenny. You've got this!" I kept walking and clapped my hands. "You guys are killing it."

I continued to provide encouragement as I completed a lap of the front row and reached the back. Finn was now in clear view. I watched his strong calves work the pedals. His face glistened with sweat from exertion, and I was reminded of how hard he'd exerted himself pleasuring me. I snapped my legs straight—sticks—so they wouldn't give out from sheer and painful want.

"Can you add a little more resistance, New Boy?" Finn's head snapped up at my goading. I was just as surprised. "I dare you," I said, shooting a wicked grin before jutting my chin at his resistance dial. *This isn't so bad after all.*

He smirked and gave it a full turn.

"Nice." I took a step forward, then thought better of it and stood still. "How about going a little faster?" The source of my bravado was anonymous yet appreciated.

Finn growled, but did as told.

I chuckled. "You can do anything for ten seconds, New Boy. Work harder. Push faster."

Finn slowly raised his head and pinned his dark eyes on me. "Work *harder*." He grunted. "Push *faster*."

A surge of heat infused my body. Was this a spin class or soft porn? I snapped out of it and hurried back to my bike, hoping like hell no one else felt the sexual tension in the room.

When the class finally ended and the studio emptied out, I busied myself changing my sneakers, wiping down my bike, and shutting down my laptop to avoid watching Finn's every move and waiting for him to approach me.

"Adi."

With my back to him, I closed my eyes for a beat and tried to calm down my heart. It was beating wildly. Then I slowly turned around. "Hi." He looked *good*—perfectly sweaty.

"Great class. You're tough." His strained smile was so different from his easy grins in Pleasant Hollow.

"Thank you. I hope I didn't work you too hard." I squirmed.

He blinked. "You worked me the perfect amount of hard."

"Thanks, Adina!"

"Great job today!" I said to the departing cycler before turning back to Finn. "You're the last person I expected to see in my class. Are you back in the city or just visiting for the day?" I cringed inwardly. Did I sound as awkward as I felt?

He scrubbed a hand through his matted hair. "Is this a bad time? Can we talk?"

"Here?"

"I was thinking we could get coffee or a drink."

"Pinkie's or Brothers?" A nervous chuckle bubbled out of me. "Kidding. Docks is next door, but we're a little too sweaty, I think. The Black Sheep is a few blocks away. It's a dive."

"Sounds good."

"I just need a few minutes to…um…" I was desperate to do something with my hair and put on some lip gloss, but I couldn't tell him that. "Pee."

"Take your time. I'll be out here regaining my strength after your class." The playful expression on his face captured a glimpse of the "old" Finn and the way he used to look at me.

I couldn't *not* smile at that. "'Kay."

In the crowded locker room, I scrounged for an open spot where I could recapture my wits in peace. Finn was here. But it didn't mean we were on the same page. It was too soon to get excited or get my hopes up. He might have interpreted the ending of my story as a one-sided apology where I conceded to being exclusively in the wrong.

I walked over to the mirror. My exercise clothes would have to do, since I'd planned on going straight home after class and hadn't brought a change of clothes to shower here. I removed my hair from the rubber band and flipped it up and down before brushing it straight. It had more lumps than homemade mashed potatoes. I brushed it back into a long, tight ponytail, dabbed some lip balm from my tube of Kiehl's, and frowned at my reflection in the mirror. I'd have answers to all my questions and more in just a few minutes, and how I looked wouldn't change any of them.

# Chapter Forty-Nine

The Black Sheep was crowded and smelled like buffalo sauce. Over the din of the football game playing out on the numerous television sets over the bar, I said, "A far cry from Brothers Brewery, huh?"

"You referring to the patrons?" Finn gestured at the twenty-somethings still dressed up in "work" clothes. "Or the fact that there's more than two beers on tap?"

"Both." I found an opening at the bar and made eye contact with the bartender. I smiled in acknowledgment of her "one second" gesture. "I can't imagine Greg and Aaron wasting all these pennies either," I said, motioning to the copper coins that lined the entire length of the bar.

"The cousins miss you."

I touched a hand to my heart. "They do?"

He nodded rapidly. "Everyone does. In fact, the town held a special leaf-jumping contest in your honor last weekend."

I slouched in disappointment. "You suck."

His eyes twinkled with mischief. "You're so easy, I couldn't resist."

Work *harder*. Push *faster*. My cheeks flamed, and I was

grateful for the bartender's attention. We ordered drinks, and I quickly slipped her my credit card, rejecting Finn's protests. Still hustling my two jobs for now, I couldn't exactly afford to treat myself, much less anyone else, to drinks, but (a) at least it was happy hour, (b) I'd received payment for my story, and (c) my pride wouldn't let me accept drinks from Finn, at least until I knew where this meeting was headed.

"Should we sit?" Standing hip to hip at the bar was fine for friends out for drinks or a couple on a date. I wasn't sure what Finn was to me at this point, but it was neither of those.

He agreed and we made our way to the back, where we draped our belongings across our chairs and under the table. Then we stared at each other awkwardly, presumably waiting for the other to say something first. He'd crashed *my* class, which meant he should initiate the conversation. It was only fair. He knew I wanted to reconcile, but I knew nothing. I felt exposed like I was stripped down to my underwear.

"I take it you read my story?" I shook my head at my own pathetic-ness. So much for waiting for him to go first.

Finn did a double take. "It was published?" His eyes lit up. "When?"

*Wut?* "You didn't know?" Then what was he doing here? "It went live two weeks ago." My phone vibrated with a FaceTime call from Kate. I ignored her in favor of taking a huge gulp of my Blue Moon.

"Congratulations!" Finn beamed as if thrilled for me.

I tucked a hair behind my ear. "Thanks. Derek hired me full-time too, but I don't start until after the New Year, when the position opens." I bit down a smile. My body buzzed with happiness each time I shared the news. It didn't matter with whom: my mom, Kate, the Uber Eats delivery guy... *Finn.*

"It must have been one hell of a story." His smile reached his eyes.

I mumbled, "You can say that," and the staring recommenced. I wanted to tell him what I wrote about us... okay, maybe *wanted* wasn't the right word. *Needed* was more accurate, but my mouth was stuck in the mute position. It would be better if he communicated what he wanted first, since, seeing that he hadn't read my story, I had no idea what that was. Kate called again. I dismissed it... again. "You said you wanted to talk to me?"

He rubbed at the condensation on the edge of his glass of Stella. "Have you... uh... been active on your dating apps recently?"

My eyes locked on his fingers stroking the glass. Then his question registered. Dating was the last thing on my mind since leaving Pleasant Hollow. My pain was too raw— yellowtail-sushi-roll raw. But answering "no" would be akin to confessing I still had feelings for him. Then again, my story already had.

*Wait.* I sat up straight. Did this mean *he* was dating again? Already? Hookups didn't require open hearts or emotional availability, but there was no need to rub it in my face.

"Adi?"

"Huh?" My glass shook in my hand and I carefully placed it on the table as my phone pinged a text message.

911. Call me NOW. Use FaceTime.

I froze. Kate didn't resort to 911 lightly. I jumped off my seat and pointed in the direction we'd come. "Be right back. I need to make an urgent call." I weaved through the patrons until I reached the exit. Outside, I paced in front of the entrance and called Kate back. The first thing I noticed was her super rosy complexion. "Have you been drinking?"

She pressed a hand to her cheek. "No! It's excitement, and some irritation."

I tensed. "Did you have an allergic reaction to something? Did you eat shrimp by accident? Where's your EpiPen?"

She glowered at me. "Irritation at *you*, Adi. I'm irritated at you for ignoring my calls!"

I whispered, "I'm with Finn," and glanced over my shoulder to make sure he hadn't followed me outside.

She squealed. "You saw it and didn't tell me?"

Before my eyes, her blush advanced from a subtle pinkish-reddish hue to a deep cranberry color. "Saw what?"

"I was on Hinge and—"

I groaned. "Not this again."

Her shoulders slumped and her eyes turned glassy. "I'm tired. So very, very tired from studying."

"So you thought you'd troll the dating apps?"

She pouted. "I was checking up on Finn. Which brings me to my call. Call*s*," she repeated, enunciating the *s*. "His updated dating profile is a love letter." She paused dramatically. "To you."

My mouth dropped open. "It's a *what* to *who*?"

Kate grinned. "I'm texting you screen shots now. Don't call me back. You've kept your man waiting long enough." She ended the call.

A series of texts came flurrying in right after, and I enlarged the various screenshots of Finn's Hinge profile as the phrase "your man" whirled around my brain.

**You should leave a comment if:**

You are Adina Gellar and you are interested in a long-term, monogamous relationship with a new and improved version of me.

I gasped.

**The dorkiest thing about me:**

I have recently become addicted to romantic comedies on TV, especially the ones with a woman trying to save her small town from development by an outsider.

I pressed a finger against my silly grin.

**Don't hate me if:**

I allowed my stubbornness to let the best thing that ever happened to me slip away. It won't happen again. I'm sorry.

My knees wobbled, and I leaned against the exterior of the bar. The next screenshots were from OkCupid.

**Looking for:** Adi Gellar for a serious relationship.

**I know the best spot in town for:** Pie

**My self-summary:**

I am the sensitive and vulnerable romantic hero
you want and deserve. Or I can be him with a
little patience. I throw a damn good snowball
and know how to make a toboggan out of the
lid of a trash can. I'm not boyfriend material
yet, but I can be if you give me a chance.
Please give me another chance.

I consciously slowed my breathing. If my heart thumped any
harder, it would explode from my chest and crash into some
poor, innocent pedestrian walking along Third Avenue.

This was huge. But how had Finn expected me to see his
profile if he hadn't messaged me? *Unless.* I closed out of my texts
and opened my OkCupid app. My skin tingled. There it was: a
message from Finn Adams.

I see from your profile you're a fan of Hallmark movies! Me too. I particularly like the
friendly people, the beer festivals, and the pie
(obviously).

I've made some changes to my profile. I hope you like them. I'd prefer to take it down completely and walk off into the sunset with you but thought this could be categorized as a grand gesture. How did I do?

The smile that broke out on my face couldn't be contained. It was the grandest of grand gestures. *I* wanted to try again, and *he* wanted to try again. We were on the same page! The best part: His message was sent the same day I delivered my story to Derek, which meant our epiphanies had been simultaneous. If I hadn't heeded OkCupid's warning about my profile becoming inactive, Finn never would have found me on there.

I rushed toward the entrance and SMACK into the chest of the burly and very tall bouncer. I craned my neck up...up...up at him. "Sorry!"

He peered down at me from what felt like four floors above. "ID?"

"My wallet's inside the bar." So was Finn.

The bouncer crossed his arms over his enormous torso. "No ID, no entrance."

"But I already showed it on the way in. I just came out to take a call. Didn't you see me? It's only been..." I had no idea how long it had been. I rocked in place. Finn must be freaking out. What if he thought I pulled a runner?

The bouncer yawned. "I just started my shift," he said, turning away to inspect the ID of two more people. He let them in while still blocking me out.

"Please, sir."

He curled his lip.

Politeness counted for nothing with this guy. "My boyfriend is in there," I said, pointing inside as my pulse raced. "And the problem is, he doesn't know he's my boyfriend because we broke up. But now I know he wants to try again, but I'm not sure *he* knows *I* want to try again too. Relationships aren't easy. Even the great ones can be complicated. We're one of the great ones, or we can be, if you just let me inside!" I stopped to take a breath and wiped the perspiration from my forehead.

"Why don't you just call him?" the bouncer said, pointing at my phone.

"Oh." I hadn't thought of that.

"That won't be necessary."

Two heads, mine and the bouncer's, turned toward the entrance, where Finn stood with my gym bag and a silly grin on his gorgeous face.

The bouncer snorted.

Finn led me to the sidewalk. "I just read your story."

I scratched my head. "And decided to leave?"

"I was afraid you'd been kidnapped."

I dipped my chin. "I'm sorry I was gone so long. Kate found your dating profile."

"Again?" He bit back a smile.

"Was that what you wanted to talk to me about?" I pressed my hands to his chest, needing to touch him, but thanks to a hurried pedestrian bumping me from the side, we ended up in a hug. It was a position I had no desire to abandon, but Finn let go and motioned to the less populated strip of grass between the sidewalk and the street.

"You didn't respond to my message."

"I didn't see it, on account of taking a break from dating." I gazed at him from underneath my lashes. "I'm still not over the last guy."

He stroked my cheek. "I'm so sorry, Adi. It took me a few days to realize how wrong I had it. My dad *is* a problem, but he's not the reason I'm not boyfriend material. He didn't force me at gunpoint to check out on you while he called you names. I should have had your back and handed him his ass on a plate for speaking to you that way. I'll never forgive myself for that."

I was a puddle. "What if I forgive you for both of us?"

He leaned in. "You can do that?"

I nodded. "One unfortunate event doesn't have to mean it's over. All I needed was for you to recognize that your dad doesn't control your behavior, only you do."

"I get that now." A smile stretched across his cheeks. "You are one of a kind in all the best ways."

My heart plumped. Then I thought of something. "How many fake Adina Gellars responded to your updated dating profile?"

He blushed. "There were quite a few impostors, in fact."

I gently poked his flat belly over his sweaty T-shirt. "You could have avoided the posers by calling me."

"*Pfft*," he said, with the matching face. "What kind of grand gesture would that be? I had to live up to hero standards."

A twinge of guilt stole my bliss. "About that. I loved my grand gesture...so much. But I'm sorry I made you feel like you had an impossible standard to live up to." I touched a finger to his lips. "My ideal man is you, and I would absolutely give you the final rose on *The Bachelorette*. Who your father is changes nothing."

Finn frowned against my finger. "We fought."

I dropped my hand. "You and your dad?"

"It wasn't only my behavior that was unacceptable that night. He can't treat the people I care about like shit. And he needs to stop using my mother's death to justify his actions. That excuse expired a decade ago."

"You didn't..." My skin felt itchy with guilt. "I don't expect or want you to desert your dad because of me. He's your family. Family is important." I studied him with unease. "How'd you leave things?"

"He promised to be better. Said he'd go back to meetings and get clean."

I clapped. "That's amazing!"

Finn smiled tightly. "I'd hold my applause if I were you. He's made these promises before. But I'm cautiously optimistic this time will be different, because *I'm* different."

"I'll support you every step of the way if you'll let me." I reached for his hand.

He raised it to his lips. "Yes. Unequivocally, yes. You, Adina Gellar, bring me joy. I want more of it...more of you. More of the girl who mistook me for a small-town boy, will stop at nothing to get her story, even singlehandedly trying to cozy up a cold-as-winter town, steals bacon off my plate, calls me out on my bullshit, and kicks my ass in the game of the same name." His voice grew quiet. "You light me up from within, Adi. Please never give up on me." He studied me pleadingly, as if there was even a possibility I was going anywhere without him.

My heart swelled large enough to house a small child. It was the most romantic monologue I'd ever heard, and it was for me. Finn was talking about *me. I* brought him joy. *I* lit him up from within. And I could say all the same things about him. We'd hit our first round of conflict and emerged to kiss and make up. The story wasn't over, but we were both prepared to fight another day.

Speaking of kisses. "Now that we've made up, can we get to the kissing part?"

"You read my mind." He stepped closer.

I drank in the fondness on his face, although this time it looked more like love. Then I closed my eyes as he cupped my face. My lips parted in anticipation until I felt the heat of his mouth on mine. I grabbed onto his shoulders and deepened the kiss. It was glorious. How had I gone so long without it? It was over too soon, thanks to the wolf whistles and clapping, but we'd asked for it by face-smashing on a crowded city street. I buried my head in Finn's chest.

"One more thing," he whispered into my hair. "I'm going to keep my phone on silent more often. My father has cockblocked me for the last time."

I pulled away and smiled wickedly. "In that case, have you ever had post-spinning make-up sex?"

Said no one in a wholesome TV movie ever.

# Chapter Fifty

At a window table at Bubby's overlooking North Moore Street in Tribeca, a young couple shared two slices of pie—Michigan Sour Cherry and Meyer Lemon Meringue.

"She looks just like you, down to the pink tips in her hair," Finn said from where we stood watching them about forty feet away.

"He's got the same facial hair as you, but you're hotter."

"I thought it went without saying you were more attractive."

"Next time, how about you say it?" I teased.

A man approached. He looked somewhere between twenty-five and forty, and wore black jeans, a T-shirt, New Balance Sneakers, and a Yankees cap. "You're the writer, Adina Gellar, right?"

"I am. And this is Finn."

He shook both of our hands. "What do you think so far? I'm the director, but no need to hold back the critique."

It took everything I had to keep my feet solidly on the ground. The day Daniel Jones called to say my submission was accepted to the *New York Times*' Modern Love column was the highlight of my writing career—until Finn's and my love story also got chosen for the spin-off television series.

Pleasant Hollow seemed like a lifetime ago, yet it had been the catalyst for so many changes in our lives. After a few ups and downs and false starts, Finn's father had now been sober for six months. While I didn't foresee calling him "Dad" anytime soon, his relationship with Finn was the healthiest it had been since before his mother died.

After our lease expired, my mom moved into a one-bedroom apartment a block away from our old one. The close community she'd found and nurtured over the last two decades was proof you didn't need to leave the big city for a slice of small-town life. She was still dating Terry, who, it turned out, had much more going for him than his nice taste in shirts.

Kate passed the bar on her second try, which came as no surprise to anyone.

As for Finn and me, in the months after our simultaneous grand gestures, our feelings grew stronger and deeper. Eventually, he asked me to move into his apartment on the Upper West Side, and I happily accepted. Because he lived on location at one of Andrew Hanes's low-income properties several months out of the year, I enjoyed solo living and my permanent position writing for *Tea* while also eagerly awaiting his returns. Absence not only made the heart grow fonder but also rendered Adina and Finn hornier, leading to delectably spicy reunions.

Which brought us to right now—the filming of *our* episode of *Modern Love*.

Turning back to the director, I said, "Thanks for letting us watch today. It's so exciting!"

"Our pleasure. I hope we do your essay justice."

"I'm sure you will!"

"I'd better get back to it." He joined his camera crew. A series of commands by various members of the crew followed.

We returned our attention to the couple. Her eyes went wide as he pulled a small velvet box out of his hand before kneeling before her. "Adi Gellar, I promise to never take you anywhere without homemade pie if you will agree to be my wife. Marry me?"

She agreed, palm against her heart, tears in her eyes, head bobbing enthusiastically. Then she joined him on the floor, where they sealed it with a kiss.

I squeezed Finn's hand as the diamond ring on my left ring finger twinkled. It was a perfect retelling of Finn's proposal, but nothing beat the real thing.

# Acknowledgments

If you've gotten this far, it means you've read my book. Oh. My. God.

I wrote most of *As Seen on TV* during the pandemic. I had nothing else to do when the world shut down, but I truly adored every moment spent with these characters. It was the best escape from a troublesome reality that I could have hoped for. That said, you wouldn't be reading this if not for the support of so many others acknowledged below.

Thank you to my agent, Melissa Edwards, for so many things, but mostly for green-lighting this project instead of the other three ideas I pitched with it! You have such great instincts, you're my steady legs when I'm flailing about (or dancing on the ceiling), and I am so very grateful to you.

Leah Hultenschmidt. You were my dream editor before we ever worked together, and the reality proved even better. I'm still pinching myself that you loved Adi and Finn and wanted to spend more time with them and me. Thank you for providing such fabulous insights and challenging me to dig deeper.

Thank you to my copy editor, Lauren O'Neal, for catching *so many* inconsistencies.

My utmost appreciation goes to the entire team at Forever,

including Sabrina Flemming, Estelle Hallick, Jodi Rosoff, Dana Cuadrado, Luria Rittenberg, and so many others behind the scenes for everything you do.

Thank you, Libby VanderPloeg, for creating my gorgeous cover. It perfectly captures the essence of the book, and I spend an inappropriate amount of time looking at it.

Samantha M. Bailey, thank you for being the best friend and critique partner in the world. I'm not sure I could write a book without you, and thank God I don't have to! Thank you for pulling no punches with your feedback and for your brutal honesty. Most of all, thank you for being a loyal friend, a patient ear to vent to (oh, how patient you've been), and a constant cheerleader. Time and time again, you assured me that my dreams were within reach. You said, "Trust me. I'm right." You were. I love you so much.

So much love goes out to my fellow Beach Babes, the aforementioned Samantha M. Bailey, Josie Brown, Eileen Goudge, Francine LaSala, Jen Tucker, and Julie Valerie. I hate that we missed our 2021 retreat. Hopefully, by the time you've read this, we'll have been together in California, where we made up for all the hugs we missed and enjoyed a week of eating, drinking, laughing, writing, talking shop, and simply reveling in our special friendship. Our lives have all changed so much since that first trip, and our bond continues to grow stronger with time. It's everything to me.

Thank you to fellow authors Hilary Grossman and Stacey Wiedower. I love you both!

Shout-outs to Tracie Banister, Tracey Livesay, and Nancy Scrofano for our long-standing Hallmark-movie chat on Facebook. Hopefully, you'll appreciate what I've done here!

I am so thankful for the support and enthusiasm of book influencers, bloggers, and avid readers, some of whom have supported me since way back when, including Andrea Peskind Katz (Great Thoughts' Great Readers), Suzanne Weinstein Leopold (Suzy Approved Book Reviews), Jamie Rosenblit (Beauty and the Book), Jennifer Gans Blankfein (Book Nation By Jen), Kate Rock (Kate Rock Book Tours), Tamara Welch (Traveling With T), Danyelle Drexler, Melissa Amster (Chick Lit Central), Sarah Slusher (Really Into This), Lauren Margolin (Good Book Fairy), Kathy Lewison, Suzanne Fine, Ashley Williams, Kelly Perotti, Bethany Clarke, Amanda Lerryn (Chocolate Pages), Chrissy (The Every Free Chance Reader), Kathleen Higgins-Anderson (Jersey Girl Book Reviews), Emily (Mrs. Mommy Booknerd's Book Reviews), Gina Reba (Satisfaction for Insatiable Readers), Kaley Stewart (Books Etc.), Samantha March, Mary Smith, Regina Dowling, Brenda Gray, Susan Schleicher (The Book Bag), Charlotte Lynn (A Soccer Mom's Book Blog), Linda Levack Zagon, Lindsay Lorimore, and Rebecca Moore.

Thank you to #TeamMelissa for the laughs, constant exchange of information, and sibbie dance parties.

To both of my '22 debut groups, my gratitude for the collaboration and support in the months (year) leading up to my release day. Congratulations to all of you on the publication of your own brilliant books!

To Mom, Dad, Melissa, Marjorie, and Jim: Thank you for the unconditional love, for not disowning me after too many broken plates and stained shirts, for spoiling me rotten as a kid and sometimes as an adult (although not as much as I'd like), and for bringing my fabulous nieces and nephews into this world (and not only for the convenient access to the Gen Z/ young Millennial perspective in my writing).

Ronni Candlen, Shanna Eisenberg, Deirdre Noonan, Jenny Kabalen, Megan Coombes, Deborah Shapiro, Elke Marks, Phyllis Porter, Lily Barrish, Amy Ehrnsperger, and the "Spinettes": Thank you for being a friend.

Finally, to Alan Blum. I wish you were alive to see this. Can you believe it? Of course you can. You always knew.

# About the Author

A born-and-bred New Yorker and lifelong daydreamer, Meredith Schorr fueled her passion for writing everything from restaurant reviews, original birthday cards, and even work-related emails into a career penning romantic comedies. When she's not writing books filled with grand gestures and hard-earned happily-ever-afters or working as a trademark paralegal, she's most often reading, running, or watching TV…for research, of course.

To learn more, visit her at:
MeredithSchorr.com
Twitter @MeredithSchorr
Instagram @MeredithSchorr
Facebook.com/MeredithSchorrAuthor